R.A.T.S: REVOLUTIONARY ARMY OF TEENS

WE ARE ONE

Claudia Daher

R.A.T.S: REVOLUTIONARY ARMY OF TEENS

WE ARE ONE

Vanguard Press

A CIP catalogue record for this title is available from the British
Library.

ISBN 978-1-83794-375-3

This is a work of fiction. Names, characters, businesses, places, events
and incidents are either the products of the author's imagination or
used in a fictitious manner. Any resemblance to actual persons, living
or dead, or actual events is purely coincidental.

Vanguard Press is an imprint of
Pegasus Elliot Mackenzie Publishers Ltd.
www.pegasuspublishers.com

First Published in 2025

Vanguard Press
Sheraton House Castle Park
Cambridge England

Printed & Bound in Great Britain

Dedication

I dedicate this book with gratitude to G-d, the wellspring of inspiration and guidance in my life. To my beloved husband, Kenneth, whose unwavering support has been my rock. To my precious children; Mila, Keith and Brian—your love kindles my creativity. To my dear mother Virginia, your endless encouragement uplifts me. A special tribute to my grandparents, Elias and Antonia, who raised me with love and care, and who have now completed their earthly journey. To my father José Antonio and grandparents Fabio and Julieta, my eternal love. Your legacy of kindness and strength continues to shape me. As these pages unfold, may they echo the warmth and fortitude you've instilled in my path. With profound appreciation for all who have touched my life.

Acknowledgments

Writing is often seen as a journey taken alone, but it's surrounded by a world of inspiration. Before one word hits the page, there's a universe of ideas, and after, there's the magic of refining it into something beautiful. I would like to express my heartfelt gratitude to the profound teachings of the Torah, the enlightening insights from the *Zohar (Book of Splendor)*, and the *Wisdom of Kohelet*. These sources have greatly enriched my journey in writing this book. I am also immensely thankful for the unwavering support of my dear Rabbi Ahron Blasberg and his beloved wife Chaya Blasberg. Their prayers to the Divine on my behalf have been a source of strength and inspiration throughout this endeavor.

Grateful acknowledgments extend to Kevin Anderson and Amanda Ayers Barnett, whose skillful translation and editing has profoundly shaped my writing.

Illustrations created by me Claudia Daher with my friend Luis Par.

With heartfelt thanks and deep appreciation, Claudia Daher.

Chapter 1

In the Beginning—San Francisco, 2012

The silver jet began its slow, steady descent through the cloudless blue sky, floating over the snow-capped Sierras until suddenly the city popped into view like a surprise treat sprung from a birthday cake. Rachel looked out the window next to her seat.

"Look, Bri, there it is."

Her best friend, Briella, barely stirred in the seat next to her.

"You'll miss it, wake up," Rachel said, poking her friend in the ribs.

"Ouch, cut it out. I'm sleeping." Bri turned away and pulled her blanket over her head.

"Look how red it is. The Golden Gate Bridge is so red!" Rachel was practically jumping out of her seat with excitement.

"Okay, so, it's red. Now leave me alone."

Rachel stared out the window. The azure waters of San Francisco Bay rippled below the bridge into the Pacific Ocean, which was dotted with sailboats and motorboats and cargo ships like the ones she'd seen in the Rio de Janeiro harbor on a school trip two summers ago. Across the rust-red bridge, scores of automobiles moved in both directions. From this height, the cars looked like the miniature ones her brothers played with on the cool, marble floor of her family's Sao Paolo living room. Rachel missed Brazil and her family already, though she would never admit that to Bri; she barely admitted it to herself, as determined as she was to make this trip special, both for her friend's sake as well as her own.

Although Rachel had traveled all over South America and Europe, this would be her first time in California. She was eager to share it with her friend but was also a little worried. In the days leading up to the trip, all Bri could talk about was the fancy Prada shoes and the Burberry coat, and the Tiffany bracelets she was going to buy at the Westfield Shopping Center on Market Street.

"Imagine, Rach, all those fancy stores in one building! I get goosebumps just thinking about it. I bet I'll even find Gucci and Prada at Bloomingdale's!" Bri said.

"We'll certainly have time to shop, but there's so much more to do. We can drive up the coast to see the giant trees, put our feet in the Pacific Ocean, and maybe even visit Alcatraz. I read about the Indians who took over the prison in the 1970s to protest the loss of their aboriginal lands and the decimation of—"

"C'mon, Rach, this is our time for fun, fun, and fun. Besides, we read all about that stuff in school and we're done with school now. It's time to party."

Rachel sighed. It was one thing to read about the giant sequoias or the hundreds of sea lions inhabiting the coastal rocks along the Pacific or the fog layering San Francisco in a thick mist on a summer evening or the cable cars that clambered noisily up the hilly city or the protesters occupying a prison for nearly two years. It was another thing altogether to put your hand on the trunk of a redwood tree or hear the barking symphony of those whiskered ocean creatures or feel your heart rush and your skin tingle as the cable car screeched to a stop at the bottom of a hill on a moist San Francisco night or walk the halls of a prison where the ghosts of generations still haunted the cells. Rachel had studied the world's sacred wisdom. It taught her that the Earth and everything in it is a gift to be cherished and cared for. To her, that meant always being willing to throw herself into experiencing everything on Earth fully, feeling it with her body, letting it wash over her soul. So, when Bri had asked to come with her on this trip, she saw it as an opportunity to show her friend something different; it was time to take a leap.

Rachel watched light dance across the bay and remembered a weird dream she'd had the night before they'd left Brazil. In the dream, she was wandering the halls of the concrete and glass, saucer-shaped Contemporary Art Museum in Niterói – Rio de Janeiro with her classmates. Someone called her to come to the window. In the waters of the reflecting pool below the circular building, she saw something glimmer. It grew brighter and brighter until it was so brilliant, she had to look away. When she did, she discovered she was alone in the building, alone with the light, but, oddly, not lonely.

"It's okay to go," she whispered to herself. "It's okay to go."

The plane suddenly banked left, jarring Rachel out of her memory. Her stomach did a somersault as the city appeared below her, an expanse of land narrowing to a point where a dense jumble of tall buildings clustered tightly together at the tip. A second longer bridge connected the city to another spit of land further east.

So much water, thought Rachel, "*so much life.*

She tried to remember what states the pilot has said they'd flown over miles east of California. Was it Arizona and Nevada? Whatever, it didn't matter. She was certain she'd never have any reason to find out.

The plane flew over the bay, away from the city, and then banked and turned back again, descending closer and closer toward the water. Now all Rachel could see was water.

"Bri, wake up, wake up. Look, how beautiful!"

Her friend moaned, pulled the blanket down from her face, and leaned across Rachel to look out the window.

"Yikes! Are we going to crash in the water? I can't see the runway," Bri said, the panic rising in her voice.

"Don't worry; we'll be on the ground in a few seconds," she said, like a seasoned traveler. Which, of course, she was. Every summer, Rachel traveled with her cousins and friends to various parts of the world. One memorable trip took them soaring over the majestic Andes, exploring the breathtaking landscape of Argentina and Bolivia. Another year, Rachel flew from Brazil to Lima, caught a smaller plane to Cuzco, and journeyed by train and a rickety bus to the base of Machu Pichu. Their travels took them to dozens of destinations, each filled with its own unique charm and sense of adventure.

"Just because you've flown a million times doesn't mean something can't go wrong now," Bri said, grabbing Rachel's hand and squeezing it.

"You worry too much, Bri. Calm yourself; say a prayer or something."

"You know I don't pray."

Still, without letting go of Rachel's hand, Briella closed her eyes and whispered to herself. When she opened them again, she could just make out the edge of the runway. Fifteen seconds later, the plane touched down on the tarmac.

"See," Rachel said, "I told you. Perfect landing!"

Rachel's cousin, Rafael, met them outside the terminal near baggage claim. He was tall, tanned, and muscular, with short silk chestnut hair, an olive complexion, captivating green eyes, and a lively personality to match his handsome looks. Bri swooned on the spot.

"Stop it, he's too old for you," Rachel whispered.

"Not according to the beat of my heart," Bri said.

"Hop in the car, girls," Rafael said after loading their luggage in the trunk of his cherry red Ferrari convertible. "We'll be in the Sunset in no time."

"Sunset?" Rachel looked at the sky. The sun was still shining as golden as an egg yolk.

Rafael laughed. "Sunset. It's what they call the neighborhood where we live in San Francisco. And believe me, when we get there, you'll understand how it got its name." He winked at Bri.

"He likes me, no?" Bri said, poking Rachel in the ribs before getting into the back seat.

Leave it to Bri to start the trip out with flirtation, Rachel thought and tried to ignore her.

The traffic was worse than anything she'd ever seen, even in Rio. The only difference was the air didn't seem as filled with smog. The road snaked along toward downtown San Francisco. When the traffic came to a standstill, Rafael took a shortcut through the city streets. Below the freeway, Rachel saw homeless people, sometimes whole families, living in tents or shacks made of rags and cardboard. There were baby carriages and shopping carts and bicycles parked next to the makeshift structures. Litter overflowed garbage receptacles. Loud music blasted into the afternoon air, amplified by the concrete pilings that supported the freeway above. Rachel thought about the cars rushing onward above them, oblivious to what they were driving over. It was hard to look, but Rachel forced herself to take it all in. It reminded her of the *favelas* in Brazil. But here, in the United States, she never expected to see such desolation. Before they'd reached the end of two blocks, Rachel had counted at least seventy people.

They stopped at a traffic light. An old woman who looked like she was wearing everything she owned wore a sign around her neck that read, "Will work for food." Rachel dug into her purse for some money and handed it to her through the open window.

"Bless you, my child," the woman said. "Have a nice day!"

"You shouldn't do that, you know," Bri said as they pulled away. "She'll probably only use it for drugs."

Rachel shook her head, too tired to argue with her. *When you give, you receive*, she thought to herself and said nothing more for the rest of the drive.

"What a cute place!" Bri said, admiring the two-story, chalky white stucco building with a red-tiled roof in front of them. There were bright fuchsia flowers growing in planters outside the windows and climbing up a trellis on the outside wall. Rachel recognized them immediately.

"Bougainvillea!" Rachel shouted with a smile.

"From Brazil." Rafael took their bags out of the trunk. "Mama snuck some cuttings into her suitcase on a return trip from Brazil about fifteen years ago. Good thing she did it then because she'd never get it past that beast of a beagle sniffing everyone's luggage in the baggage claim area for botanical contraband."

"I know," Bri shrieked with laughter—*A little too loudly*, Rachel thought. "That dog came up to me. I'd forgotten I'd put a mandarin orange in my carry-on. Made me feel like a smuggler when they took it away."

Rafael carried their bags into the house and up the stairs to the guest room. "Make yourself comfortable, *minhas gatas*. Mama is preparing a special meal of *moqueca* to celebrate your arrival, and you know what that means. We probably won't eat until midnight," he laughed.

"You forgot something," Bri said, batting her eyes, trying to look coy.

"You left something in the car? I'll get it." Rafael turned toward the stairs.

Bri caught him by the shirt. "No, guess again," she said.

He raised his hands in a gesture of concession.

"The Sunset. You said you'd tell us why this neighborhood got that name."

"Ah! Well, does it look very sunny here now?" Bri shook her head in response. "There's your answer. In another two hours, the sun will color all the windows on our street golden. This is the side of the city last kissed by the setting sun."

"*Muito romântico*," Bri said.

Rafael nodded and quickly left the room.

"I have an idea," Bri said after the door closed behind him. "How about we take a ride over the Golden Gate Bridge?"

"If this is your way of trying to get Rafael to drive us all around the city so you can keep flirting, forget about it," Rachel said.

"No, *I* want to drive," Bri said, pulling a small card out of her pocket with the sly look of a magician pulling a rabbit out of a hat. "I got my driver's license before we left Brazil. And I want *you* to ask Rafael to lend us his car."

"Are you kidding? The convertible?" Rachel's eyes widened in disbelief. "He loves that car like a baby."

"Of course, the convertible. When in California, act like a Californian, no?"

Rachel had to admit she was tempted. But to be driven on those freeways by a seventeen-year-old hotheaded Brazilian seemed borderline crazy. "Let's wait until tomorrow."

"We must go tonight. There's a full moon. We'll see the city and the Bay and the hills of Marin County on the other side shine in the moonlight, please, please," Bri pleaded.

The full moon! Now that was an invitation from heaven Rachel couldn't ignore. Besides, she thought, it couldn't hurt to ask. If Rafael said no, that would be that. "Okay. But you better be extra cautious driving."

Bri crossed her heart with her fingers, jumping up and down with excitement, and gave Rachel a big hug.

"He hasn't said yes, yet."

"*Voce está com a faca e o queijo na mão*; it all depends on you, Rach. Like it always does."

They took turns showering. Miraculously, Rafael handed Rachel the keys. As they pulled out of the driveway after sunset and headed north, she found she hadn't quite calmed the tiny quivers of anxious anticipation coursing up and down her spine. It couldn't be the drive that made her uneasy, she thought. It had to be something else tickling her brain. It felt as if something big was about to happen, but she couldn't remember what.

Half an hour later, they were snaking their way across the western parts of the city, already sparkling with lights, through Presidio Park, heading for the Golden Gate Bridge.

"How do you turn on the radio?" Bri asked, fiddling with the buttons below the car's GPS screen.

"You pay attention to the road; I'll figure it out." Rachel pushed a button and the radio screamed to life with the news of the day.

Two weeks ago, the first outbreak of a novel respiratory virus was reported in the Middle East. Scientists remain uncertain of its pattern of transmission, warning travelers about journeying to the region.

In other news, the Chinese spacecraft, Shenzhou 9, *carrying three astronauts, including the first Chinese female, successfully docked with a module orbiting Earth...*

"I don't want to hear about viruses and spaceships," Bri said. "Let's listen to some music." Without wanting for Bri's reply, Rachel reached over and twisted the dial, her fingers moving with a rebellious urgency. The static hissed for a moment, and then, as if summoned from another world, the opening notes of California Dreamin' burst through the speakers, filling the car with the haunting melody of the past.

"The Mamas & the Papas, yes!" Bri raised her fist in the air and turned the music louder. "My mom used to listen to this all the time."

Just as they crossed onto the bridge, Rachel drifted off into a reverie. She was entranced by the light swirling in the night sky, the sounds of the ocean pounding the bridge below them, the lingering fragrance of pine and eucalyptus, the warm air caressing her whole body. She leaned her head back and let out a sigh.

"Bri, what would you be if you could change your nature?"

"California dreeeemin', on such a winter's—what? Did you say something, Rachel?"

"I asked what you would be if you could change into something else, something not human."

"Whoa, that's heavy," Bri said. "I don't know where you come up with this stuff sometimes, Rach. Let me think." A seagull swooped over the car. "A bird! I'd be a bird so I could fly thousands of miles across the land, from one continent to another, thousands of feet above earth. I'd be invisible, like a spy in the sky. What about you, what would you be?"

They'd reached the middle of the bridge and the evening traffic had slowed to a crawl. Rachel stretched both arms toward the sky, which had become a color of purple that seemed to swallow the last traces of light.

"Maybe a wave in the ocean," Rachel said. "Or maybe a tiny branch on the tree of life."

"Figures you'd pick something inanimate," Bri said with the slightest trace of jealousy in her voice.

"Trees are alive," Rachel said. "And so is the ocean. We share the same atoms as the sea."

"In a manner of speaking, I suppose," Bri said.

They drove on slowly in silence. The stars shimmered brighter than Rachel ever imagined they could shine.

"That's weird," Rachel said. "I thought the city lights and the moon would dull the stars. But they're dazzling."

Bri looked up for a second. "They don't look so dazzling to me," she said.

"Well, they're brighter than I've ever seen them, anyway." Rachel sighed again. She loved her friend. They'd known each other all their lives. They had so much in common—music, dancing, horseback riding, sailing, giggling about boys. The one thing that separated them was the sense of mystery Rachel felt more and more every day. Despite Bri and Rachel having vastly different characters and personalities, they deeply respected and supported each other. Their friendship, with roots that ran deep, was unshakable by any storm.

"Not far to the other side now," Bri said.

Rachel was too lost in her own thoughts to hear anything.

Suddenly, a bright, silvery light bolted across the sky. She blinked several times to clear her vision. But when she opened her eyes and looked up again, the light had only got brighter and wider, so wide it looked like an illuminated river cascading across the sky, reaching from one end of the horizon to the other. Her body began to feel light as if she were floating out of the car, away from the bridge, out of the Earth's gravitational pull, and merging with the light itself.

In fact, she *was* floating. Something was carrying her up, up, up into the night, into the heavens, toward the stars themselves. The strange thing was, she wasn't afraid. Instead, she felt calm, like in the seconds before sleep quiets the mind and the body releases its grip on the day. She had the sensation of being filled with some ethereal substance, as if she were becoming both more and less than herself, as if she were the receptacle of an unbounded force. She opened her arms to embrace the stars. Then her body began to shake, and a voice called her name.

Rachel, Rachel.

She opened her mouth to answer but the only sound that came out was the hushed sound of her breath.

The voice again.

Rachel, listen to the spheres. One day, you will hear their sounds again. Then you will know it is time. You will become the harbor of a new beginning. Keep this symbol as a reminder of your destiny.

A gold ring with a clear stone appeared on the fourth finger of her right hand. It began to pulse and glow with a heavenly light. Etched on the stone was a tiny branch sprouting one leaf.

Another voice shouted her name now and broke the spell. "Rachel, Rachel, wake up!"

She opened her eyes to see Bri's startled face hovering over her. "You gave me a real fright! You fainted. You must have been more exhausted than I realized. I shouldn't have made you—"

"—I didn't faint."

"What are you saying? I watched you pass out. I had to lay on the horn to get the other cars out of the way so we could get off the road and into the rest area."

Rachel looked around her. It was true. They were on the other side of the bridge now. She looked back at Bri. "Didn't you see that light? It was amazing."

"What light?" Bri crossed her arms and gave Rachel an exasperated look.

"That silver river of light that reached across the whole sky. It was beautiful, I—"

Rachel.

"What?" Rachel said.

Bri shook her head. "I didn't say anything."

When the time comes.

Rachel looked down and saw a ring pulsing on her finger. A strange feeling overcame her, the sensation of a force at once distant and near. *Keep this symbol as a reminder of your destiny.* She covered the ring with her left hand. "You're right, I think I just need to sleep. Let's go back."

Chapter 2

Family secrets have a strange way of oozing out of the places where they've been hidden at exactly the moment you need to discover them. Maybe it's only by chance that you find an old letter or faded document telling you something you didn't know about the past. Or maybe something else drives you to pull out a file you've never seen before, urges you to open it, and helps you locate the key to the future. Is it fate or is simply destiny masquerading as serendipity?

***

A few days after his father's funeral in 2000, HB was sitting in his old bedroom in his parents' house, high in the Berkeley hills, watching the sun setting over the Golden Gate Bridge. He'd been away for four years at college back east, but his room looked as if he'd just left.

In one corner was a shelf lined with his favorite books—*Bullfinch's Mythology*, *The Iliad*, *The Odyssey*, along with other Greek classics, as well as scores of books about archaeology, geography, comparative religion, and computer technology. On another set of shelves sat his collection of old video games and cartridges, including a copy of the Atari classic, *Space Invaders*. Laughing at the sight of it, he remembered the day he'd traded with a high school friend to get that relic of a game.

What an idiot he was to exchange a brand-new stereo for that ridiculous piece of plastic, he thought and put the Atari console and the game into a box to save his mother the trouble of sorting through all his old junk. She'd already told HB she was moving as soon as she could find an apartment. In the week he had left before he needed to return to his job as a computer programmer in Washington D.C., cleaning out his things was the least he could do to help her prepare for the move.

"It's too hard to stay in this big house by myself, surrounded by so many memories," his mom had said the night before, after dinner. "Your father designed everything in it. I can't touch the beautiful wooden banister leading down the circular stairs to his study without thinking of him; I can't stand it. It hurts so much. To think, he'd just retired and now he's gone."

"I know, Mom," HB said, comforting her.

He sealed the box, remembering how much he and his father had enjoyed those games, when his mother came into his room and stood next to him, not saying a word at first. Then she turned to face him and looked up at him. He was over six feet tall and towered over her. He had the same hazel eyes and dirty blond hair as his father. Except for the scar on his chin, he was the spitting image of her beloved husband. She touched the scar. "I remember you got this falling down the stairs. Your teeth cut through your bottom lip and your father rushed you to the hospital. I wanted to stay with you while you got the stitches, but you insisted on your father being there instead. You were only four and already so stubborn." She smiled.

He hugged her.

"Oh, I almost forgot!" She broke out of the embrace. "Your father wanted me to give you something. Wait a minute." She left the room and returned with two large manila envelopes. "I got these out of the safety deposit box yesterday," she said, handing them to HB.

HB looked at them with intense curiosity. "What are these?" he asked, taking them from her.

"I don't really know. Your father was very secretive about the contents of his deposit box. I found all sorts of strange items in there—some shells, a piece of what looked like lava, a ginkgo leaf preserved in a glass mount, these envelopes, and an old hat."

"A hat?"

"Yes, it was pretty beaten up. I don't know why he kept that old thing in the safety deposit box."

"Can I see it?" HB asked, trying to stay calm.

"I threw it in the donation pile with some of his old clothes."

HB darted from his room down the hall to his parents' bedroom.

"I don't know why you care so much about that old rag," his mother called after him. "I should have made him throw it out years ago."

He found the hat at the bottom of a pile of socks. It was wide-brimmed, sable in color, with a faded gray ribbon wrapped around what once must have been a tall crown. He pulled the hat close to his face and inhaled his father's scent—*Brylcreem*. He'd never forget that smell or the jingle his father always sang while he pomaded his hair:

Brylcreem—a little dab will do ya! Use more only if you dare; but watch out! The gals will all pursue ya! They'll love to run their fingers through your hair!

What a character his father had been! He remembered the day his father bought that hat.

He was eleven and had begged his father to take him to see *Indiana Jones and the Last Crusade*. His mother wasn't keen on the idea; she worried HB would have nightmares about Nazis. But his father assured her there was much more to the story than fascist dictators and booby traps.

"It's about perseverance, about protecting the sacred from the profane," he'd said, and bought tickets for them to a matinee performance in San Francisco. After the movie, they walked past a shop featuring fedoras exactly like the one Indiana Jones wore in the movie.

"I think I ought to have one of those. What do you think, HB?"

"You mean you want to look like Indiana Jones, Dad?"

"Well, I am an archaeologist, after all; I may as well look the part."

His father wore the hat everywhere. He said it was to keep his students' attention during lectures, but HB suspected it had some other, deeper meaning for him, something even more important than a memento of a fun day spent at the movies with his son.

He ran back to his room. His mother had gone down to the kitchen to make lunch. Alone in the room now, he picked up the top envelope and ripped it open. Inside, attached to a file of papers, was a letter addressed to him.

Dear son,

I want you to keep these papers in a very safe place. Hiram Bingham's son, whom I met in the 1950s when I worked for the State Department, gave them to me decades ago.

Wait a minute. The State Department? His father was a professor of archaeology at UC Berkeley; he studied ancient civilizations of the Americas. Since when did he work for the government? HB kept reading.

I am sure it will come as a shock to discover your father was an undercover government agent. Well, not a spy, exactly. I worked on a secret project Hiram's son and I developed, based on Bingham's Machu Picchu research archives.

As you know, Bingham thought he'd discovered the lost ancient city of Vilcabamba, the last refuge of the last Inca King, who fought against the Spanish conquest. What he'd found buried in the vines was something much more spectacular.

He'd stumbled upon the ritual site of the last remaining Intihuatana—the stone tied to the sun, which the ancient Incas used to predict astronomical events.

Bingham recorded little about the ritual. He wasn't a very spiritual man. I visited Machu Picchu many times over the years, always during the winter solstice in June, when the Inti Raymi or "Festival of the Sun" is celebrated in Sacsayhuaman Fortress, near Cuzco in Peru. I'd expected to discover the secrets of the sun ritual. But I failed. Perhaps I, like Bingham, wasn't spiritual enough.

Bingham's son kept the papers in these files separate from the rest of his father's papers, which were donated to Yale. I bequeath them to you now. Study them carefully. Perhaps you'll find a clue that I missed.

I believe that something mysterious and wonderful in Machu Picchu may yet reveal itself to the right person on the right day.

I only wish I could be there the day you finally unlock the mystery. It must have eluded humans for many centuries for a reason I've been unable to fathom.

Your loving father

HB continued to stare at the note before him in disbelief, as all the words washed together before his eyes.

There was so much he wanted to ask his father. What project did the State Department have in Machu Picchu? Why had his father never talked about this project before? He never would be able to ask him now. But maybe that was the point. The legacy his father had left him was an invitation to discover these things for himself and share what he found with the world. But how was a computer programmer supposed to solve an archaeological puzzle that had defied people for centuries?

He rifled through the pages that were attached to the letter and then set them aside to read more carefully later. Then he reached for the second envelope and opened it. Its contents were even stranger than what he'd found in the first. Inside were photographs of his father in some kind of uniform he didn't recognize. In a few photos, he was standing with a group of a dozen or so similarly uniformed men, scattered around a large table littered with maps. Around the room were blackboards filled with mathematical equations and drawings of what looked like a design for a spaceship. Other photos were of his father hiking what he recognized as the Inca trail to Machu Picchu. But the most interesting photo of all was one where his father was standing on the highest plateau of the ancient city next to a huge boulder carved like a three-tiered altar. He had an expression of wonder on his face as he gestured toward the sky, as if he'd just seen something uncanny or startling.

I must find out what section of the State Department my father worked for, HB thought as he went downstairs to the kitchen.

"Mom, did you know dad worked for the government?"

His mother was setting the table and almost dropped a plate. "The government? Your father never worked for the government."

"He left a letter for me in the envelope you gave me. It said he worked for the State Department."

"Oh, that." She laughed. "He had a grant from the State Department for his Inca research. They gave him a State Department ID. He used to tease his lefty colleagues by flashing it at parties, saying they better watch out or he'd turn them into HUAC." She laughed at the memory. It was good to see her laugh.

"HUAC?"

"The House Un-American Activities Committee. During the 1950s, you know, Joseph McCarthy and the Red Scare? Didn't they teach you any history at that college you went to?"

HB shook his head. "Not about that."

"Anyway, the State Department thing was a joke. Your father simply received a government research grant."

It became clear to HB that his mother was unaware of the scope of his father's research. Better not press her on the subject anymore. It would just upset her to learn her husband had kept secrets even from her.

"I didn't think he'd be some kind of agent," he said. But, of course, the first thing he knew he'd do now, once he got back to Washington, was to try to find out the truth.

"The only kind of agent your father could be was an agent of happiness. Now, let's eat."

HB had planned to start graduate work in computer engineering at George Washington University the following year, but the mystery of his father began to lead him in another direction. When he returned to Washington a few days later, he went to the State Department and requested files on his father.

"Sorry, sir. Those files are classified."

"So, they do exist. And if they exist, why can't I see them? He's my father. Don't I have a right to that information?"

"No, sir. Not if you don't have security clearance."

"How do I get security clearance?" HB set his jaw and leaned across the counter in what he hoped was an intimidating gesture.

"Well, sir, you could join the military," the clerk said, sitting back in his chair with a smirk on his face.

"What a great idea!" HB said, not wanting to be upstaged in sarcasm, and left the building.

When he got back to his apartment, he looked again through the photos in the second envelope. Suddenly, he noticed something in the corner of one of them. In the photo of his uniformed father with a group of people gazing at maps on a table, he saw a sign on the wall of the room. It read, "Air Force: Project Blue Book." A simple computer search led HB to discover that this was the code name for the U.S. government's investigations of unidentified flying objects and that the project records were on microfilm in the National Archives. The summary findings on the website also told him the conclusions the project had reached: no UFOs the government had studied were considered national security threats, no unidentified sightings represented technologies beyond present-day science, and none could be categorized as extraterrestrial.

So why was his father working on UFOs and what did that have to do with Machu Picchu? Was there some secret Air Force unit that didn't even make it into the official record? HB had to find out. Even if it meant joining the Air Force.

He spent the next two months conducting research in the National Archives until he reached a dead end and decided there was only one thing left to do. A month later, he went to the Air Force recruiting office and signed up.

***

As it turned out, joining the military wasn't such a strange move for an intelligent person interested in computers and cosmology, especially one with determination and a commitment to service. Five years after he'd joined, the Air Force sent HB to graduate school in computer engineering. His expertise in computer design prepared him for a special expedition to Machu Picchu just like the one his father had led decades earlier.

In 2012, Major HB walked into the briefing room, carrying a small parcel. In the room was the team he'd been asked to assemble. Major Sarah Esther Hoffmann, an astrophysicist with a Ph.D. from MIT, and a special interest in research on extraterrestrial communication; Captain John Singer, an Air Force jet pilot in command of their flight to Peru; and several other officers responsible for supplies and records. Lt. Colonel James Patterson called the meeting to order.

"Ladies and Gentlemen, I am sure you are aware of the seriousness of this mission and the necessary secrecy surrounding it. For years, we've been monitoring astronomical events in the area of Machu Picchu. In the last year, there has been an increase in activity, whether due to changes in the Earth's atmosphere, or the increased heat of the sun, or other unidentified factors, we remain uncertain. As a result, we have tasked Major HB Williams to lead another expedition; he's studied the region for more than a decade. I leave this mission in his capable hands; he will explain your responsibilities and the timeline to you now. Major," he said, and gestured for HB to take over the briefing.

HB walked to the front of the room and placed the parcel he'd been carrying on the table in front of him.

"At four a.m. tomorrow morning, we will leave for Peru. In a mere eight hours, Captain John 'Jetson' Singer here will whisk us to Lima and from there to Cuzco. We'll leave behind our supersonic chariot-of-the-skies, and after observing the Sun Festival, we'll board a train and then a bus to Aguas Calientes at the foothills of Machu Picchu. There, we'll meet a local guide—"

"—and sample the local brew," John added. The room erupted in laughter.

"You can sample the brew, John. I'm going to sample those volcanic pools I've read so much about. I hear they have special healing powers," Sarah said.

"If they'll heal your sense of humor, I say give it a go, Jokester," John teased, using Sarah's nickname. "Maybe I won't have to hear any more of your knock-knock jokes after that."

Sarah scrunched her face into a grimace and pretended to be hurt by the comment. But HB knew it was all an act. The truth was the guys teased her because they respected her. She was smarter than all of them put together; he trusted her insights the most. She had such an inquisitive mind. Like him, she was always searching for a deeper answer to the questions the universe kept tossing in their direction. He was always careful to treat her as an equal, which of course she deserved, given her rank and accomplishments.

HB finished the briefing without further interruption. "You know what we're looking for, now let's get out there and find it." Then he reached into the parcel on the table, pulled out an old hat, and put it on his head. Everyone in the room whooped and cheered.

"Who's in da house? Indi's in da house!"

That night, questions rumbled around in HB's head as he prepared for the journey to Peru, making sleep difficult. What forces had really propelled him along the long road he'd traveled from the discovery of his father's secret past until now? What powers were behind the strange urge he felt to retrace his father's steps to Machu Picchu? What else could he possibly find among those ancient Inca ruins that all the other explorers before and after Hiram Bingham had not yet uncovered?

The flight's departure went smoothly and the next morning, the team found themselves in Cuzco, surrounded by thousands of tourists gathering for the Festival of the Sun. The streets were also filled with people dressed in the traditional, colorful costumes of celebrants heading toward the Qorikancha Temple, where the festivities would begin.

HB overheard John talking to Sarah and moved closer to them.

"You realize those people dressed as Incas are actors, don't you?" John said. Sarah nodded.

"You don't always have to be so cynical, you know," Sarah said. "I think it's still a pretty mesmerizing sight to see a rainbow of color spilling into the streets of Cuzco, to hear the people speaking their native language, and to think, actors or not, that people have been walking along these stone-covered streets on the same day of the winter solstice for thousands of years."

"As I'm sure you know, Jokester, it's not exactly the real winter solstice. I read the conquerors forced the Incas to change the date to June 24," John said, with a self-satisfied cross of his arms.

"Of course, I know. As well as I know the concept of time is an illusion. We're here now, for a reason. And that reason is to observe and absorb," Sarah replied in a tone that told HB she'd had enough of John's teasing for the moment. It sometimes surprised HB that an astrophysicist like Sarah could be such a softy about ritual. But then, he thought, science was its own kind of ritual, its own attempt to comprehend mystery through the repetition of tasks.

After all, wasn't experiment a kind of prayer to the universe?

After the festival ended at the Saqsaywaman fields, the group traveled on to Aguas Calientes, where they checked into the inn. Before they went to their rooms, John suggested a dip in the volcanic pools after dinner.

"Sounds like a great idea," Sarah said, already past any annoyance she may have felt with him before.

"I think I'll pass," HB said, heading toward the courtyard around which their rooms were arrayed.

"Oh, come on, HB; it'll be fun," Sarah said.

"I'm a little tired and I need to be ready for tomorrow's hike. Let me walk you to your room and I'll say goodnight."

The truth was, he was beginning to feel a little strange. On the flight, he'd reread the notes his father had made about Bingham's trips to Machu Picchu. One part had caught his attention.

I began to have the sense that the old guy was beginning to have his doubts about exactly what he'd found at the site. In his diaries of subsequent trips, I found more and more mentions of sensations he felt of the Earth breathing, of some incredible power emanating from the volcanic springs at Aguas Calientes. He wrote that he could find no other name to describe these sensations and reluctantly called them holy. Imagine, the great Hiram Bingham used the word holy in the same sentence that announced the significance of his discovery!

His father had dismissed those descriptions of Bingham's as signs of anxiety. But, outside in the courtyard, as HB breathed in the air, felt the welcoming earth beneath his feet, and looked up at the brilliant, star-laden sky, he wasn't so sure.

"Sarah, I know we've been working on this project for a long time, and have found nothing more than we already knew. But what's your gut tell you? I'm the one who crunches the numbers of what your fine-tuned instruments record. You're the one with more direct contact with those stars. Do you think it's really possible we're the only ones here in the entire universe?"

Sarah hesitated, kicking a rock with her toe. "I don't know, HB. All I can say is sometimes, what I want more than anything, is to discover that we're not alone."

They said good night and HB crossed the courtyard to his room. He really was feeling tired. He kicked off his shoes and sat down on the couch. *I should take a shower. I'm sure it'll make me feel better*, he thought and got undressed.

The water was refreshing. He reached for a bar of soap and noticed a few drops of blood fall into the bottom of the shower. Then a few more drops fell at his feet, until he was standing in a small puddle of bloody water. He pulled aside the curtain and saw his face in the mirror opposite the shower. His nose was bleeding. He began to feel a little light-headed, turned off the shower, and got out, drying himself with a towel and taking another towel to stanch the flow of blood from his nose.

He wasn't really worried; he figured the bleeding was just a response to the high altitude and walked to the other side of the room near the fireplace, which was lit. He didn't remember lighting it. Thinking it must be one of those gas fireplaces, he ran his hand across the wall searching for the switch. No switch. The fire went out and then back on. He reached for the phone to call the front desk when he heard water suddenly gushing in the bathroom. *I know I turned the faucet off*, he said to himself. *How can it be on?*

He went into the bathroom. The water had filled the washbasin and was spilling across the floor, heading for his feet. It was flowing so fast he had to move out of the way not to get wet. *I'm a scientist; there must be a rational explanation for this.*

That was the last thought HB had before he passed out.

When he opened his eyes, HB was surrounded by darkness. He could feel cool air caressing his body. Little by little, his eyes adjusted until he saw where he was and cried out in shock. He was sitting high atop Machu Picchu. *Impossible*, he thought, still feeling dizzy. The last thing he remembered was being in his room at the inn.

He struggled to his feet and turned slowly, scanning his surroundings. Everything around him on the dusty plateau began to be illuminated by an eerie light. He looked up at the night sky and saw seven bright stars pop out one at a time, ringing around the full moon. They swirled and swirled like dancing dervishes, growing brighter and brighter, until the moon and the stars seemed to fill the whole sky. The image was so powerful, he held himself tightly and looked away. Then a beam of silvery light emerged from the center of the celestial display and engulfed him. Oddly enough, despite the cool color of the light, he felt as if he were being wrapped in a warm down blanket. He looked up again and saw a platform with seven stairs cascading down from the heavens. Four tall, shimmering figures, some kind of otherworldly beings, floated down the stairs toward him. They had torsos and limbs and heads, making them resemble a human form, but they were translucent and much taller than any human— elongated beings of pure, radiant light. He should have been afraid, but he felt nothing but peace and contentment, as if all the worries and cares and concerns he'd ever had about the world had disappeared in an instant and all that was left was this magnificent light.

The pulsating shapes of light spoke to him now. He heard their foreign tongue, yet somehow understood every word they said.

"We will take you with us for a while. We have chosen you to bring a message to your people. You will know what to do with what you will learn."

They placed a gold ring with a clear stone on his finger. Etched on the stone was a tiny branch bearing two leaves. He felt something pulled from his body now, as if he were being made weightless, as if he were being transformed into air. No, not air. Ether. He left his body behind and was remade into stillness itself.

Weeks later, some indigenous people found HB wandering the streets of Ollantaytambo in the Sacred

Valley, not far from the ruins of Machu Picchu. They found his military ID in his pocket and notified the authorities. He'd hidden the ring so no one would find it; he'd reveal its powers when the time came. Until then, he knew what he'd been chosen to do.

Chapter 3

The Legend of the Daktaryons
Atlantis, 9000 B.C.E.

"Burn it, burn everything! Leave nothing behind. Not a sheaf of papyrus, not a stone of inscription, not a fragment of our presence in this place." Such is the arrogance of the conqueror—to wreak havoc on their conquest, hide the evidence of their greed, and escape to another place far, far away to begin the same process of destruction all over again.

Such was the Daktaryon's plan so many moons ago.

Many millennia before Darwin declared that mere chance variations—both good and bad—determined who would survive one of ten thousand trials in the grand narrative of natural history, this society of giants, who lived first in the place we now call the Far East and who possessed technology far advanced beyond anything yet seen, threw a wrench in Darwin's ever-spinning machine of natural selection by declaring themselves the best of all species and then systematically shaping the world in their own image.

It must be admitted that they were a scientific people. They studied the stars and the moon and felt the pull of an immense force on the Earth's rotation, on the ocean tides, on the seasons of their own bodies. They recorded these things and developed elaborate systems to determine the best time to seed crops, the best time to seed themselves, and appointed a group of elders to create laws to prevent any variations or intermixing, whether of plant or of animal. In time, their society grew and prospered. They had more than enough to survive. *But what is enough, if we can always have more?* Such questions as these the Daktaryon youth began to murmur. They had grown tired of the old ways and knew no other values than acquisition. So, they pushed the elders to discover even more techniques to extract more and more from the Earth.

These new Daktaryons conducted experiments and invented advanced technologies to enhance the soil with special materials from grinding rocks. They bent the flow of water to increase the growth of crops and to power elaborate machines to dig into the Earth's crust, searching for new sources of energy. In this way, they altered the patterns of plants and animals, inventing new species. They even expanded the strength of their own bodies and enhanced the scope of their minds, though they failed to open their hearts even an inch to let love or mercy flow through their veins.

Instead, with all their instruments of extraction and transformation, they began to imagine that everything was possible, that there were no limits to what they could take from the Earth's bounty, and that if only they had more space, they might even annex the entire world, expanding their empire to the edges of the visible horizon and beyond, and remake it to fit the Daktaryon way.

The Daktaryons marched into adjacent territories, where they met the Shalticons, a peaceable people who lived in a different relation to the Earth and the sun and the moon. They were content taking from the Earth's bounty only what they could replenish. They, too, were inventive, yet more cautious than the Daktaryons. The Shalticons prayed in gratitude to the Earth and G-d for what they received. They meditated on his wisdom, listened to the sounds of the universe, and attuned themselves to its rhythms. They prided themselves on how well they stewarded the land.

The Shalticons were gracious, trusting people. When the Daktaryons arrived at their borders, they greeted them as they would have greeted any stranger. They hosted a traditional ceremony, welcoming the Daktaryons as guests. They served their finest dishes of roasted vegetables and fresh fruits, beautifully decorated with the best that nature had to offer. As night fell, they shared ancestral stories, telling how they came to this land of plenty and how they were chosen to guard it against damage.

"Our ancestors warned us about a miraculous, yet dangerous, substance found deep underground, nearer the Earth's womb; a substance so magical it could produce fire that burned brighter and longer than wood; a force so powerful it could not be contained. It would alter the air itself. To disturb the Earth's lifeblood slumber would be our ruin. So, we honor this force of life and give thanks for the harmony we have," Shalti, the Shalticon's leader, said.

The Daktaryons were stunned by these stories. They'd never imagined such an extraordinary substance could exist. Imagine what they could do with such power! They longed to seize it for themselves.

That night, they convened the council of New Elders to discuss how to gain control of this substance. Their leader, Grutan the Magnificent, spoke first.

"The Shalticons are fearful of this substance only because they fear change. But we are unafraid of change. We have altered the course of rivers; we know we can take this new source energy. We must discover the portal to this power, then we will be able to grow and expand our empire faster and faster. We must convince the Shalticon elders to guide us to that place."

"Why bother trying to convince them at all; we have strong weapons. Let us kill them all," one of the elders cried out. The others in the room began to nod in approval until Grutan's son spoke out.

"I have a better plan, Father. We do not need to use force to persuade them of our superiority. We can convince them of our wisdom with elaborate speeches. We will dazzle them with honeyed words; we can even use their own sacred beliefs against them." The room erupted enthusiastically in approval.

The next morning, Grutan asked Shalti if he would assemble the elders of his tribe. He told him the Daktaryons had a proposal to make. "We believe if we share our resources, both our tribes will benefit equally."

At the mention of sharing, Shalti agreed and called the tribal elders together to hear the proposal. The Shalticons dressed in their finest white flowing robes to attend this sacred meeting. The Daktaryons wore bright black uniforms decorated with silver stripes and medals and insignia from past battles, though they told the Shalticons these emblems of victory were merely symbols of their dedication to peace and protection, hoping to mask their true intentions and history of conquest.

Grutan the Magnificent rose to address the assembly. "We listened with wonder and awe to your ancestral tales of a mysterious, powerful substance deep within the Earth. Then, last night, I had a dream. In the dream, Mother Earth called to me. She told me she'd summoned us to this land to join together with you, the Shalticons; she was now ready to release her liquid magic into the land so that we may all prosper in her bounty. She asked that we, Daktaryons, use our special digging devices to loosen the Earth's crust and let her blood flow."

A low murmur of worry spread among the Shalticons. Had they not taken a sacred oath to protect the Earth from such desecration? They remained hesitant to share the location of this wondrous substance.

"This force must be respected like a G-d at rest, it must be allowed to slumber for it has the power not only to create but also to destroy," Shalti said. "We cannot risk our lives nor yours by disturbing it."

Grutan was undeterred. He spoke in even more elaborate ways, appealing to the Shalticons' trusting nature. "Do you not believe that dreams carry messages from G-d? To ignore such a message would bring disaster upon both our people. Do not doubt our good intentions. We promise to share whatever resources we mine. We guarantee with our very souls to protect everyone from danger." Grutan struck his heart with his fist and bowed humbly to demonstrate his commitment.

When Shalti saw this gesture of solidarity, he rose and walked toward Grutan. "Since you have made such a promise, we will lead you tomorrow to the Sacred Temple, where the ancestors had locked the map of our territory."

That night, the Daktaryons celebrated with whoops and cries of conquest. Their leaders' clever language had done the trick. Tomorrow, the wealth of the ages would soon be theirs.

In the morning, as the sun reached its warm golden rays across the land, Shanti led the Daktaryons to a spot marked with the sign of the crescent moon. As soon as the spot was identified, Grutan ordered scores of Shalticons to dig with devices the Daktaryons distributed. When Shalti asked him why the Daktaryons were not lending their labor to the enterprise, Grutan replied, "We respect your knowledge of this area, which is so much greater than ours. We remain ready to help should any danger arise in the process."

The Shalticons dug in good faith from sunrise to sunset, day after day, until the full moon shimmered in the night sky, when a trickle of thick, brown liquid began to ooze from the Earth.

Grutan was so excited when he saw this that he selected one of the Shalticon laborers to conduct a test. "Strike two stones to see if the liquid will ignite."

When the poor man shook with fear, Shalti interrupted. "Why do you ask him to take such a risk? Why not one of your own people?"

"We want to honor you by choosing one of your own for a sacred task. He will be unharmed."

Shalti remained troubled by the harm that might befall the man, but the worker insisted on performing the task. Shalti nodded and watched the man gather two stones and begin to rub them together. No spark appeared, so Grutan instructed him to strike them again, closer to the brown liquid. Again, nothing. Grutan grew angry. "Have you tricked me? Is this not the place on the map?"

"We are honest people, Grutan," Shanti replied. "We have not led you astray. Then he whispered some words. "Abracadabra." Suddenly, an immense flame erupted into the sky, scattering the onlookers. As the smoke cleared, the worker lay lifeless on the ground. The Shalticons cried out in anguish. Grutan raised his hand to silence them.

"This man bravely gave his life so that you and your children's children may live in prosperity."

He pulled a sword from his belt and raised it high, ordering the other Daktaryons to do so as well. The light from the silver swords of the Daktaryon army blinded the Shalticon onlookers, who knelt, trembling at the sight. "We will bury him in a place of honor. His family, and any other Shalticon families willing to sacrifice for greater prosperity, will be rewarded with our generosity. Tomorrow, we continue our work."

With sorrow-filled eyes, the Shalticons returned to their homes, worrying everything they'd known and cherished would be destroyed. Shalti gathered them together in a circle. "Today, one of us died because of the greed the Daktaryons have in their hearts. They intend to enslave us and sacrifice us for their cause. We do not believe in such sacrifice, nor will we lend our bodies and minds to support such evil. True sages generate positive energy; we are not part of this darkness. Let us use the wisdom of our ancestors to practice peace. Tomorrow, we will return to a place of peace."

That cold night, the Shalticons burned all their sacred books. When the Daktaryons saw the bonfire, they thought it must be for the community to keep warm.

The next day, the Daktaryons assembled in the digging place. Not one Shalticon appeared. They searched the village and found nothing but the dying embers of the fire they'd seen in the night. They raced to the hole they'd made in the Earth.

"Say those words we heard Shalti whisper," Grutan ordered. But words alone would not ignite the flame. The Daktaryon's intention was malicious, and a prayer meant to create something with words must have kind intentions to work; if uttered for harmful reasons, it will only bring harm.

The Daktaryons abandoned the place. And so, it was for centuries in every place they and their descendants went. They came, they took, they destroyed, and they moved on until there was no place on Earth left to go.

How superior they'd seen themselves. They declared themselves to be men and women of superior intellect. And so they were, but only because the yardstick they themselves had invented to measure superiority was possessing the technology and unbridled will to turn every rock, every stream of water, every breeze, every animal—including humans themselves—into coveted resources to sustain The Great Daktaryon Nation for thousands of years.

Except nothing human can ever be that perfect. Not even the Daktaryon Empire. Around them were troubling signs. The liquid they had unleashed gurgled and bubbled in veins that ruptured all over the Earth. The land warmed to intolerable temperatures, the seas rose, and whole species of animals and plants disappeared as if overnight. In the four corners of the Earth, from the furthest reaches—North, South, East, and West—civilizations of peace perished in the monstrous tide of misery wrought by the Daktaryons. The evil they had unleashed had consequences everywhere.

The descendants of Grutan saw these disasters and began to worry for the first time. If the Earth were depleted, might they be lost, too? They resolved immediately not to be defeated. With their advanced technologies, they prepared to annex the stars themselves and escape the damaged planet. Who among them would be saved? The leaders would determine whom to select.

The Grand Council of Daktaryons convened a secret session and met in their splendid homes on the great expanse of land past the Pillars of Hercules—the island the ancient Greeks would later call Atlantis. There they had built a tremendous fortress housing ships that would sail not on the seas but through space.

"We have, at most, a few years left on this planet before the air becomes unbreathable and the seas overtake us. We must launch the final solution," the Great Leader announced.

A great hush came over the assembled Council.

"I have assembled our wise ones. Together, they have designed a plan for our escape. We have room for all of you and your families, no one else. No one must learn of our plan."

One of the Council members raised his hand. "What about our neighbors, our friends?"

"If you prefer to send your neighbors or friends, you are welcome to give them your seat." Some Council members snickered at that remark; the others remained quiet and the meeting continued without further dissent.

And so, after wreaking havoc on everything they'd once called home, the Daktaryons' elite abandoned Atlantis, leaving everything to the gnawing criticism of rodents and insects, who survived only for a while on the garbage pile that remained. Soon, the tremendous force of energy the Daktaryons had harnessed from all the volcanoes on Earth and used to launch their escape created even more harm in its wake, until Atlantis itself began to convulse and erupt and sink back into the sea. They need not have worried about burning their records, since their own actions left nothing recognizable behind.

Our words and thoughts attract whatever energies we speak and think. If we speak and think harm, harm will come.

Whether that was the last of the Daktaryons, no one knew.

Until now.

Chapter 4

One Happy Island
Aruba, 2040, Friday

The morning sun greeted the island of Aruba with the gift of another day. As the birds started to sing and the iguanas started to parade, this small, magical spot of happiness off the northwestern coast of South America in the Dutch Caribbean gently woke up. Golden rays illuminated the California Lighthouse on the northern point and reached across the dunes, making them sparkle. With each ray, the aquamarine Caribbean seas that gave life to the island glistened more brilliantly than any shade of blue or green on an artist's palette. Soon, tourists arrived on the island's white sandy beaches to launch jet skis, boats, and parasails, spreading out across the water in a kaleidoscope of colors. Like David's mother, Rachel, always said, it was as if G-d had saved the most magnificent colors and clearest water to create Aruba and purify it as a place to rest after the six days of creation.

David remembered how his mother had taught him from an early age to see water as sacred. Because Aruba lacked natural sources of fresh water, the island desalinated seawater to produce the precious resource. "So always remember, David," she'd told him, "without the sea, there would be no water. And without water, there could be no life. But remember too, without love and family, there would be nothing. We are happy as a family because we share in each other's joys and sadness; we are here for each other."

Fifteen-year-old David felt like a lucky guy to be living with such a loving family—his mother, Rachel; his father, Kenneth; and his older brother, Daniel—in an elegant, super-modern house at the end of a quiet cul-de-sac near the northern end of the island. From a central portico supported by six limestone columns, his home stretched its two long wings, full of rooms, like an open-armed gesture of welcome. Five tall windows opened onto a lavish courtyard, where plumeria blossomed, dropping their fragrant white petals like blessings along pathways meandering through palm trees and pomegranate shrubs. From the outside, the house looked as if it had borrowed from the Spanish colonial past. Inside, though, the place was so full of the most modern technology, it felt almost alive.

His mother had designed their home to gesture simultaneously backward and forward in time, honoring both her memories of the past and her hopes for the future. It had every technological device to regulate the interior temperature, control security, filter the air, and solar power the appliances. Even the windows and lights were equipped with solar sensors to automatically darken and lighten the living spaces according to the shifting angle of the sun and the mood of each member of the family. Unless, of course, someone altered the program, which seventeen-year-old Daniel occasionally did to David's room, just to tease his younger brother.

The kitchen was the hub of family life. Below a rectangular, floating tabletop where his mother, and occasionally his father, prepared food, self-regenerating vegetables, and herbs grew in special, hydroponic receptacles. At another, larger floating table, the family shared their meals. Refuse was separated in electric bins that crushed recyclable items, transferred the organic remains to underground bins, and transformed it into compost used to fertilize an even more bountiful garden located in a large area on the house's far side. There, in an enclosure protected from the increasingly hot sun by specially designed panels that filtered out damaging UV rays, the family produced food year-round, enough to feed themselves and still leave ample amounts to donate to charity. Sadly, as the world's environment became further degraded by climate change, the number of people seeking refuge in Aruba from cataclysmic fire or drought had multiplied nearly five-fold in the last year alone. The family held close to their hearts the importance of helping everyone they could, believing that to give is to receive.

David's room stood at one end of the house, next to his brother's and another room that used to be his sister's until Ariel moved away to study and become a doctor in Brazil. Now, from his parents' room at the other end of the house, he thought he heard the family-friendly AI household assistant, Sonic, greet his mother.

"Good morning, Rachel," Sonic said in a voice sounding remarkably like Morgan Freeman's. "Did you sleep well? The children are about to awaken and prepare for school. It's a beautiful day, already thirty degrees Celsius. I'll preheat your shower soon. Then I'll feed Max, the dog."

David looked at the holographic clock on the wall across from his bed. It was almost seven a.m. After the bad dream he'd had the night before, he'd hardly slept at all. He needed time to recover from the scare and get ready for school, so he sent Sonic a message through a private channel on his earphone that only he and Sonic shared.

Sonic, I'm not ready. Please help.

David had a special relationship with Sonic; they'd communicated this way since he was a very young boy. He liked that no one else in the household could do that and trusted Sonic to keep their secret.

I need to do a few things before Mom starts to nag me about school, David said.

I'll turn back her clock thirty minutes while she's in the shower, Sonic said. *I'll tell her she awoke extra early. That'll give you more time.*

Great idea, thanks, David said.

For long hours, every day since David was seven, he'd played an alternate reality game on a screen which he could project anywhere—in his room—while he traveled to school or while hanging out with friends. He'd touch his chip-finger to a game button on a computer hub and then touch it again to select R.A.T.S, and the game would appear on a screen with one puzzle or another to solve. Through the chip, the game could access a whole bunch of vital statistics—health records, passports, passwords, and other important stuff people once stored digitally in their computers but could now keep on a tiny microprocessor inserted directly into the second finger of one hand. More than a decade ago, it became common for people to be chipped at birth.

R.A.T.S stood for Revolutionary Army of Teens. Despite its militaristic-sounding name, it was unlike any other game in the world. Instead of only battling belligerent armies with no other point than to kill or maim as many people as possible, R.A.T.S' players engaged with enemies, both human and extraterrestrial, in real-life situations, ones where they had to solve troubling ecological problems. Of course, some kids thought it was boring. They'd gotten so used to blowing up buildings and blasting through walls and destroying everything in sight for no reason at all, they couldn't even imagine how R.A.T.S could be exciting. That a player could get an extra adrenaline rush by figuring out solutions to things grown-ups had already messed up seemed to them like a stupid idea. But David understood what the game was really for. Playing the game educated youth about every possible environmental disaster, whether caused by humans or forces unknown. It was actually fun to solve problems together, fix things adults had ruined, and make the Earth healthy again.

David's grandfather, HB, was a computer engineer and had designed the beta version two decades earlier. With David's suggestions, he upgraded the game, adding more challenging features every year. The latest upgrade included EE, or Embodied Empathy. It made players literally feel in their own bodies what their avatars saw and smelled and touched and heard and even tasted in a scene.

That's why, last night, when he stopped playing, David had gone to bed thinking about water.

The scenario he'd been trying to negotiate involved a water dispute in the Salton Sea of the Imperial Valley, an area of intense conflict near the border between Mexico and California. David was excited. He had only two levels to go before rings would appear on every part of his holographic avatar's body, making it glow in silvery glory to mark his transition to Commander. But he was also a little nervous. The problem he was supposed to solve was complicated. It had defied the best scientists for more than a century.

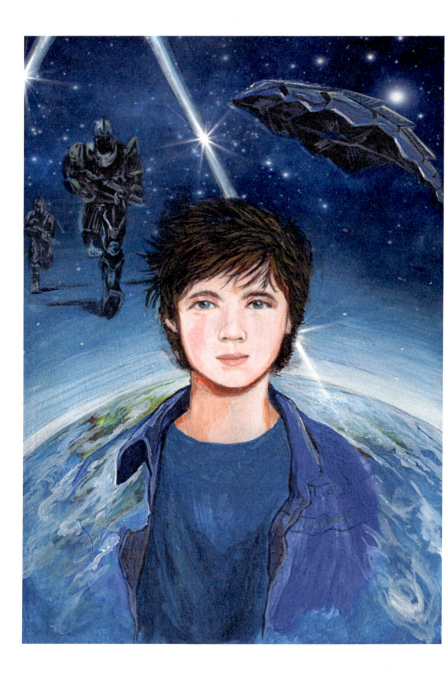

The Salton Sea was really a lake, formed by runoff from the Colorado River, which flowed through an irrigation canal that engineers had dug one hundred fifty years ago to provide water for the valley's farmers. For decades, toxic runoff from the farms and resort communities in the area had contaminated the water, spreading disease to humans and animals alike. Whole populations of birds had disappeared, and dead fish washed up onshore. To make matters worse, by the time the farmers finally figured out how to make less water flow into the lake, it had begun to evaporate, blowing dust west across the desert all the way to Los Angeles, where the air already was so polluted it was hard for anyone to breathe.

In the game the night before, as David watched the Salton Sea transform from lush to sickly in a rapid-motion video of destruction on the game's translucent screen, he walked his avatar across the lake's cracked surface. He felt his throat constrict, his eyes itch, and his heart race at the sight of a white pelican flying hopelessly in circles, searching for food in the desiccated lake. He could feel the bird's pain so sharply, it was as if he'd merged with the desperate creature, becoming one with its struggle.

The area is an environmental disaster, the game announced. *How will you R.A.T.S fix it?*

A heated meeting of a bunch of angry people appeared on the screen now. David listened as each group, from bird watcher to lettuce grower, battled for its side, dug into their respective foxholes, and waited for the other sides to blink.

How can this ever be resolved when everyone depends on water? David wondered.

"I don't believe how messed up this is!" another voice exclaimed.

David recognized who it was immediately. "Me neither, Becks," he said with a sigh.

Becky was a pretty girl with green eyes, long brown hair streaked with natural golden highlights, and a passionate temperament. She was the same age as David. He'd met her a few years ago, when she'd visited Aruba from Washington D.C. with her mother, Sarah, and her older sister, Sabrina. David's grandfather had worked with Sarah on some project he never talked about and invited Sarah and her daughters to the island for a vacation. They came for one week but ended up staying for three when his mother insisted it would be no trouble at all to put them up in the guesthouse.

David had liked Becky almost immediately. She wasn't silly, like the other girls he knew from school. Those girls liked to hear themselves talk, but they never talked much about anything important, and certainly never about R.A.T.S. Becky was more serious, especially about the game. Whenever her avatar appeared onscreen, David knew things would get interesting, really interesting, really fast. She'd squint her avatar's jade green eyes, which were the exact color of her own, and pull her hair into a ponytail and say, "Okay, let's figure this out." Who wouldn't fall for a girl like that? Well, maybe his older brother, Daniel, who liked sports and only dated girls who fell for jocks with fancy cars.

I shouldn't be so mean, David thought, pulling himself back to the present. *I love my brother. He'd do anything for me. And vice versa.*

"Hey, head-in-the-clouds boy." Becky's avatar poked him.

"Ouch…what?" David said.

"I asked if you thought it'd be a good idea to get Tutla's opinion. His tribe's been dealing with this kind of stuff for centuries who should control the water and all."

"Tutla told me he's busy with a special Pow Wow his tribe's called to deal with some land dispute he was all worried about. Something about artifacts that amateur archaeologists found. The guys were digging in sacred burial grounds."

"That's so wrong," Becky said. A ring of light on her avatar's suit began to glow. "Hey, look at that. I didn't know we could earn points just for saying something is wrong."

David laughed. "Grandpa and I thought up that feature a few weeks ago. I didn't realize he'd already programmed it in."

"What else have you guys cooked up that you haven't told us about yet?" Becky's avatar touched David's avatar's hand and he felt a tingle down his spine. He hoped Becky didn't feel his reaction. He hadn't admitted yet how much he liked her and didn't want his avatar to give him away.

"Anyway," he said, changing the subject, "we'll have to work on this water problem without him for now."

"Hold on, my mom's calling me." Becky disappeared for an instant. "I gotta go," she said. "Haven't done my homework and Mom's going ballistic. We can finish this tomorrow before school. I'll buzz your ear-phone when I'm ready."

"Okay, see you around," David said, and had signed off for the night. But he still hadn't been able to get the smell of that dust bowl out of his nose.

Hey, Sonic. David had called on their private channel.

Already on it, Sonic replied in his deep, comforting baritone of a voice. David's bed floated above the floor a few inches. The bed had been designed to be able to move effortlessly around the room to whatever position its occupant desired. Temperature-controlled pillows fluffed to the exact degree of pressure David liked, ready to cocoon his head in a cool, soothing cushion. When he lay down, he watched the heavens appear, full of shooting stars, on a translucent canopy curved over the bed. Hidden speakers and vents around the room released the refrains of an old song, "Calling Occupants of Interplanetary Craft," and the fragrant aromas of a field of wildflowers, helping David let go of those disturbing images he'd seen and felt moments before and imagine other worlds.

He signaled his thanks to Sonic, and in an instant, fell asleep.

Yet somehow, despite the calm of the room and the stillness of the house, tiny fragments of worry began to grow into ever bigger, more disturbing sensations that troubled David's sleep with a nightmare.

He was standing on the beach not far from his house, waiting for someone, when, all of a sudden, the sea began churning and churning with furious waves. But the most frightening thing was that the waves weren't crashing toward shore; they were moving in the opposite direction, toward something shaped like an immense funnel, as if the sea were being sucked away from the land by some otherworldly force. A dark parabola hanging in the sky like some U-shaped machine was pulling the sea toward itself until the water tumbled inside the funnel and disappeared. He wanted to warn his parents and his brother. He tried to run but couldn't move or speak, as if he were meant to witness this horrific event, but remain unable to do anything about it. Then a voice called out to him. 'This generation will certainly cry for the world.'

A bright, white light and a loud noise like a buzzer going off in his head startled him awake. He was back in his room, crying. He looked around; everything seemed the same, except for his ear-phone buzzing on his side table. He'd forgotten Becky said she'd call in the morning before school.

That's when Sonic told him his mother was about to shower and he realized he'd be in deep trouble if he didn't get ready for school soon.

Thanks to Sonic, he now had about fifteen minutes to play R.A.T.S with Becky. Maybe he should tell her about the dream, and ask if she ever got nightmares from playing the game. *Better not*, he said to himself.

Yeah, better not, Sonic said. *You might scare her away.*

Quit it, Sonic. What do you know about girls, anyway?

Just because I'm made out of computer chips and electrical signals doesn't mean I have no romantic feelings. And besides, I've been programmed with every love story known to humankind; I've learned to love everyone and everything.

Okay, okay. Now give me a break. I want to talk to Becky before Mom starts to nag me about school.

David inserted his ear-phone, tapped it, and accessed the game. Becky was already playing with a few other players around the world.

"Well, it's about time you showed up, David," Becky said.

"Sorry, I guess I overslept," he said. "How's it going?"

"Almost got it figured out," she said. "While you were busy sleeping, Deepak had a real brainstorm of an idea."

"Yeah, turns out we'd already had a problem like this in New Delhi with some cashew farms, where the runoff from irrigation had been polluting some streams," Deepak chimed in, eager to share his ideas. At nineteen, he was older than many of the other players. "A group of smaller farmers in the area formed a cooperative, and with some extra funding, they set up hydroponics facilities to grow their crops more efficiently and by using less water. They use drones to gather information about soil health and crop yield. Maybe we can try something like that in the Salton Sea."

"Cool," David said. "Let's get on it, R.A.T.S."

Each player began to send codes to the game. First, Becky calculated how many hydroponics farms could produce the same number of crops the farmers in the area already produced, while using less water and creating less waste. She fed the numbers into a computer program that instantaneously produced 3D blueprints Deepak used to generate a multi-sensory, multi-dimensional time-lapsed map of the area, complete with fast-forwarded images of crop growth and species repopulation. It was like being able to immediately calculate the impact of every decision before it was made. Then David maneuvered a drone over the simulated area. He deployed long-distance laser beams to extract soil samples and analyze them in a matter of seconds. With a special, super-high-resolution lens, the drone counted and recorded the rejuvenation of animal life. The whole process took less than a few minutes and gave them everything they needed to know about what should be done to solve the problem. When they'd finished the operation, the Salton Sea sparkled and dazzled like a lush paradise.

Great plan, R.A.T.S, the game said. *You've each earned enhancements on your uniforms.*

The three players' avatars glowed with an additional ring. David was now only two levels from Commander.

"I don't think I deserved to be rewarded," David said with embarrassment. "I didn't do much more than punch in a few codes. You two really figured out the solution."

"Of course, you helped," Becky said. "You'd already spent hours studying the problem before I joined last night."

"Besides," Deepak added, "the whole point of this game is to work as a team. We all contribute the best skills we have. I just happened to have special knowledge from my country and knew how to use it. After all, I am a Kshatriya."

"You're a what?" David asked, making his avatar look perplexed.

"A Kshatriya, a Hindu warrior, like this." Deepak changed his avatar's usual costume of jeans and a white T-shirt into a beautiful saffron-colored tunic belted in red and stood proudly next to a white stallion carrying a pointed spear. "This is what a traditional Hindu warrior looks like."

"Wow, cool outfit," David said.

"Love those pointy maroon slippers," Becky said. "I'd like to learn more about Hinduism."

"Another time," Deepak said. "It's nine and a half hours later here in India and I've got to prepare for a temple ceremony tomorrow."

"Okay, later, dude," David said.

Deepak's avatar jumped on the horse and was about to leave the game when David shouted.

"Hold on… The game just sent us a message."

Alert. Alert. Impending disaster. Utilize emergency powers now.

"What's happening?" Becky asked.

"It's a part of the game my grandfather told me about," David said. "Once you solve a problem, sometimes a bigger one gets put into play. The game keeps testing not only our technical skills, but also our ability to think in the moment, to anticipate every possible crisis so we can react to any situation, no matter how weird."

"OMG!" Becky yelled. "Look at that."

Some kind of meteor or supersonic alien force was headed right for the Salton Sea they'd just brought back to life.

"What do we do now, David?" Deepak asked.

"Suit up, R.A.T.S, and defend our project," he ordered, already changing his avatar into the white, silver, and gold suits R.A.T.S defenders wore whenever they were under attack. "Get to your stations now!"

The speeding object was within two minutes of destroying the Salton Sea and everything else within a thousand-mile radius of it.

"I've calculated what size defensive screen we need to repel the attack," Becky said, sending the data to Deepak.

"Got it," Deepak said. "The screen is now ready to deploy."

"Deploy screen," David ordered.

"Roger that," Deepak said. "Screen in place."

"I've got the object on my scanner," Becky said.

"What are the coordinates?" David asked.

"35.1361° N by 119.6756° W," Becky said. "Wait a minute, it's not heading for Salton. It's heading for the dead center of the San Andreas Fault. If it hits, it will trigger an earthquake that will send California into the ocean."

"Roger that," David said. "I'm positioning the defensive drones. Deepak, maintain screen location in case this is a decoy maneuver."

"Roger, screen maintained."

"Incoming in five, four, three, two… You've hit it, David," Becky said. "Target immobilized. Operation complete."

The three R.A.T.S avatars raced toward each other and embraced. "We did it, we did it!" Deepak exclaimed.

"That was a close call," David said.

"Thank goodness it's only a game because that really made my heart race," Becky said. "It was like I could feel the horror of the people on the ground watching that object hurtling toward them."

"Yeah, but it was fun," Deepak said. "Now I really have to go; see you guys later."

"Later," David said.

"Bye, Deepak, see you later," Becky said.

David heard Becky let out a long sigh. "Did that upset you, Becks?"

"You mean the game? No, it's not that. I don't know. Mom says I worry too much. It's just there's another hurricane warning; a big storm is headed toward the southeastern seaboard of the U.S. It's the fifth one this month. I don't think people are taking the news about what's happening to the climate seriously enough."

"It's pretty safe here in Aruba. The government put in all sorts of advanced precautions to deal with rising sea levels… Maybe you guys should come live here?"

"Very funny, David. I think my mom's job kinda makes that impossible."

"Well, we can do pretty much everything remotely today. Why not a remote presidency?" David laughed at his own joke, but Becky gave him a serious look. "I'm sorry, I didn't mean to tease. I understand the President of the United States has to stay in the White House and be seen by the people to reassure them and lead. Now tell me what's really bothering you?"

Becky sighed again. "My mom's been having a really hard time convincing Congress it needs to take action on this environmental bill she's proposed. Too many people here still don't believe in the science. I mean they just want to put their heads in the sand. No, what they want to do is build their houses on sand and then act all surprised when the ocean crashes down on them."

David didn't know exactly what to say. He'd never seen Becky so upset. "Your mom's smart. If anyone can convince people to stop being stupid, your mom can. Besides, she's got one of the best advisers in the world."

Becky looked at him quizzically.

"She's got you; you're a master at R.A.T.S. You'll help her figure it out," David said.

Becky's expression softened a little. She smiled. "No, David, we'll all help her. We're R.A.T.S!"

Just then, David heard Sonic's voice in his head. *You've got fifteen minutes to get dressed and eat breakfast.*

"Okay, Becky. Gotta go. Talk to you after school," David said.

He walked to his closet and pushed a button. The door to the closet displayed his clothes. From a rotating display of outfits, he selected a pair of jeans and a blue shirt with an emblem embroidered on the front. The emblem depicted a trio of interlocked arms forming a triangle. In each corner was a ring and in the middle were four letters—R.A.T.S. He finished dressing just before his mother knocked on his door.

"Breakfast is ready," she said. "Hurry up, or you'll be late."

David grabbed a small school bag, signaled Sonic to get his hoverboard ready, and followed his mother into the kitchen, where Daniel was already eating.

"Solve all the world's problems yet, brainiac?" his brother teased.

"I don't know how you can ever concentrate in school when you spend all your time on that game," Rachel said, with a worried look on her face.

"Rachel, don't worry," Daniel said to his mother; he'd always called her by her first name. "David is smart. He's never missed anything at school. By the way, where's Dad?"

"Here!" Kenneth said, walking into the kitchen and giving everyone a kiss. "Papa is *moe*, tired from so much work."

"Lucky today is Friday," Rachel said, giving her husband a hug. "We've both had a ton of work these past few days. I won't be here for lunch, but I'll be home after work, *Amor*, since Friday evening is for lovers."

David watched his parents' tenderness toward each other and felt his heart swell again with gratitude for his family, for his life, for everything on this One Happy Island. He kissed his mother goodbye, grabbed his hoverboard, tapped his earphone to music, *Here comes the sun, do, do, do. Here comes the sun, and I say, it's all right...* and followed his brother to school, the melody perfectly matching the bright morning of this new day.

Chapter 5

Mayday, Mayday
Various settings around the world. Saturday,
USA/Sunday, Others (one day later).
(Arizona, 9:00 PM, Tibet, 12:00PM+1, Israel,
2:00PM+1 Dubai, 3:30PM+1)

It was after nine o'clock on Saturday night when sixteen-year-old Tutla touched the family computer with his chip-finger and signed into R.A.T.S. The tribe was poor and few could afford computers but, as the son of the Chief, Tutla was lucky to have access.

He was still upset about what the elders had disclosed at the tribal meeting after the Pow Wow had ended. Several of the Havasupai tribe's oldest gravesites had been desecrated and sacred burial objects were stolen. The thieves weren't archaeologists after all, but treasure hunters searching for the precious blue-green travertine stone found near their tribal home in Havasu Canyon on the southwest corner of the Grand Canyon in Arizona. The robbers had disguised themselves as tourists and used phony names to get permits to camp in the area. They didn't intend to respect the land, as they'd promised to do, but wanted to dig for souvenirs. Souvenirs? His ancestors' bones and other sacred objects they'd taken weren't souvenirs. Tutla was outraged.

He wanted to talk with David about what had happened. David would understand the intense feelings he had and help him find some way to calm the rage boiling inside him. Even though Tutla knew it wasn't good to be consumed with such terrible feelings, he couldn't fight them off on his own, and he certainly wouldn't bother his father, the Chief, who had the worries of the whole tribe on his shoulders. But when he joined the game, his heart sank. It was after midnight in Aruba and David wasn't in the game; he was probably asleep.

Namkhai in Tibet, Chava in Israel, Omar in Dubai, Mariana and Juliana, two sisters in New York City, and a couple of other new kids Tutla didn't recognize were working on some complicated deforestation problem in the Amazon. When Tutla saw all the players' avatars staring at a denuded area of the forest as big as twenty football fields, he felt sick to his stomach.

I can't listen to people debating tribal rights, he thought, and made his avatar start to walk away. And then something strange happened. One of the illuminated rings on his avatar's suit began to flicker. He remembered a key rule of the game—listen to everyone's viewpoint before making any decisions. He shook his head, grumbling to himself. *So, what if I lose a few points; I'll earn them back later*. The ring stopped glowing and faded to dark. *Ugh, as if what happened to the tribe wasn't bad enough.* Then another ring on his suit flickered. *Okay, okay, I get it. Self-*

pity saps energy from the team. That ring brightened to its previous level, but the first one remained dim.

"Hey, Tutla," a voice called in the crackling register of a boy teetering on the edge of young manhood. Even before Tutla turned around, he knew the voice belonged to thirteen-year-old Namkhai. Dressed in the saffron robes of a novice Buddhist monk, Namkhai's avatar walked toward him. "I'm glad you're here. I've been trying to explain how indigenous knowledge helps keep lots of different animals and plants and the Earth itself alive. What do you call that again? Bio-something?"

"Biodiversity," Tutla said.

"Yeah, that's it. Biodiversity. Humans living while helping other creatures to live," Namkhai said. "In Buddhism, we call that *samma ajiva,* or right livelihood."

"What does that mean?" Tutla asked with an inquisitive expression on his face.

"It means to support yourself without harming others," Namkhai said.

"That's sure something I can relate to today," Tutla said, still hesitating about whether he should walk away.

"C'mon, my brother, join us," Namkhai said. "If we don't look after each other, who will look after us?"

"Okay, I'll stay for a little while," he said. Just then, the faded ring on his avatar's suit glowed back to life. Tutla shook his head, laughing. Even without David there, being in the game helped ease his worries.

"Hey, my man, Tutla," Omar said and raised his avatar's hand. "Give me five."

Tutla returned the gesture and then raised his hand again in the split-fingered R.A.T.S salute. Omar repeated the sign.

"In it, to win it," Omar said.

Tutla smiled widely. It always amused him that even though Omar was Muslim, he was comfortable using American slang.

"Not planning to leave me out, were you?" Chava asked.

"And certainly not us," Mariana and Juliana said, hands on hips, displaying their best uptown New York City swagger.

"No way. We definitely need girls with attitude on this team," Omar said, giving each of them the R.A.T.S' split-fingered salute.

"Are we going to get back to this game or what? Me and Butch haven't got all day," someone standing behind Tutla said.

Tutla turned his avatar toward the voice that had just spoken. "I don't think I've met you before," he said. "Where are you from?" he asked. As he raised his eyebrows at the strange outfit on the avatar standing close to him now, a second avatar appeared, wearing the same costume.

They were dressed in identical yellow and black checkered shirts tucked tightly into Wrangler jeans and belted at the waist with a shiny buckle bearing a strange cross-hatched symbol dotted with amber stones. On their feet were snakeskin boots with a snake's head at the pointy toes, and they wore wide-brimmed hats. Tutla knew they were cowboys and felt uncomfortable. Using every power he'd earned in the game, he kept his emotions under control.

"Name's Roy and this here's my cousin, Butch. Come all the way from Amarillo, Texas to play your little game. Not sure we got the hang of it yet, but don't mind us; we latch on quick as rattlesnakes. Don't we, Butch?" Roy poked Butch in the side.

"Sure do," Butch replied. "We're mighty interested in earning us some of them fancy, sparkly rings y'all are wearing. How do ya get them to stick?"

Namkhai, always eager to help strangers, become familiar with the game, explained the system of points and rewards.

"Earning the rings depends on a lot of things. Not only figuring out useful solutions to problems, but also how well we all work together. We get so many points for making good suggestions, and additional points for teamwork. We can also lose points for not following the game's rules or even for displaying a bad attitude."

"Bad attitude?" Roy repeated.

Tutla started to explain. "Yes, well, for instance, not listening to each other—"

"Kinda like throwing' in your hand and taking all your chips off the table before the dealers even finished dealing out all the cards," Butch said with a loud belly laugh.

"Yeah, something like that." Tutla felt himself getting annoyed. His ring began to flicker a little.

"Look there!" Roy pointed his finger at Tutla. "You're flashing again. Something wrong, mister? I didn't catch your name."

Tutla took a deep breath. With every bit of willpower and prayer he could summon, he maintained his dignity. "I'm Tutla. I'd be happy to answer any questions you might still have. But it's easiest to learn by watching us play and joining in when you have something to contribute." His dimmed ring brightened again.

"I think I get it now," Roy said, looking at the shining ring of light. "But, hey, thanks for the offer, partner. Let us get back to lassoing that their bull-in-a-rainforest."

Something weird about these two still bothered Tutla, but he couldn't put his finger on it and brushed it aside.

Namkhai clapped his hands and the eight players continued watching a rapid-motion film depicting the last fifty years of the Amazonian rainforest. By the end, more than half of its trees, and hundreds of thousands of plants, animals, and insect species had disappeared. As the forest on which they depended for food and shelter fell tree by tree, the native tribal population, along with its wisdom, nearly disappeared too. Where monkeys once swung from branch to branch in the high canopy of trees and colorful birds flew overhead, while iguanas and black caimans, wandered below, cattle now grazed alone on the cleared land.

"Sure, would like a few of them beauties on our ranch in Amarillo," Roy said.

"They belong in Amarillo, but not in the rainforest," Chava said with a tinge of impatience, though not enough to dim any of her rings.

"I was just teasing y'all," Roy said. "I get the point. I do. We got a saying in Texas. 'He's so low you couldn't put a rug under him.'"

"What does that mean?" Chava asked.

"Means some people are so low on the bad scale, there ain't nothing badder. And I think there ain't nothing badder than someone takin' something' without putting more back from where they took it."

"I must remember that saying of yours, Roy—too low for a carpet to fit under," Omar said, laughing. "It is so colorful and so very useful."

"You can say that again, Mr. Omar," Butch said and pointed to his cousin's avatar, where a silver ring had begun to shine around the ankle of Roy's right boot.

"Well, look here. I got myself a reward just for speaking my mind." Roy beamed and clapped Tutla on the shoulder.

These two may be a little strange, but maybe they're not so bad after all, Tutla thought. Then he looked over at Namkhai to find the young Buddhist deep in thought.

"What's the matter, Namkhai?" Tutla asked, seeing sadness wash over his friend's face.

"Watching that film made me think about what's happening to the nomadic tribes in my own country," Namkhai said, his voice catching in his throat with sorrow. "In Tibet, the ice caps have been melting more and more rapidly. The wandering shepherds and small farmers who live on the highlands have had their livelihood erased. The government turned all the nomads' land into parks and forbade them to graze animals there. Then they captured all the water flowing downhill so lowland farmers could grow more food and big city people could have more water."

"Now wait a darn minute. I thought you said clearing land and raising cattle was bad for the environment," Butch said, looking genuinely puzzled. "If folks need water, we should get water wherever we can." He slapped his thigh for emphasis. "Without water, no one survives. And why are we talking about Tibet anyway? I thought we were supposed to save the rainforest."

"It's all connected," Namkhai said. "The rainforest, the highlands of Tibet. Different places, similar problems. We know it's too late for the nomads to go back to their old ways; but that doesn't mean we should abandon them or ignore what knowledge they've gained over centuries of working the land."

Butch took off his cowboy hat and ran his fingers through his hair. "I gotta agree with you there. My grandpa knew a whole lot about farming, but those folks from the big company thought they knew better. They bought his land and thousands of acres more. Then they poured all of the poisons into the soil and, next thing you know, we got cancer spreading all over the country." A second later Butch's face lit up like the sun. "Say, you know what I think we should do about these problems we're discussing? I think we ought to call a big meeting of all the tribal elders, like a United Nations of First Nations. Get them talking. Then, we pool all their ideas and compare notes and figure this thing out together. Stop telling people what to do and ask them for their ideas instead! Maybe even figure out how to fix other places that people messed up."

Great plan, R.A.T.S, the game said. *You've each earned enhancements on your uniforms.*

Butch made his avatar jump ten feet into the air when he saw he'd earned a silver ring. The rest of the team each earned an additional medal. Everyone congratulated each other.

"Me and Butch gotta go now," Roy said, winking at Butch and shaking everyone's hand. "Us cowhands gotta get up at dawn and that's only a few hours away in Texas."

After Roy and Butch left, the remaining six players were about to leave, when the game flashed a message in bright orange on the screen.

Alert. Alert. Alert. Earth in jeopardy. Unidentified enemy attack.

The group froze, staring as the same screen transformed before them.

"It's Havasupai Falls!" Tutla shouted. "The most sacred space of our tribe. This can't be happening!"

The falls were stilled. The normally crystalline blue-green waters pooling below had turned an ashen gray. All of a sudden, the water began to churn and rise into waves, as if being pulled back into the falls themselves. The whole mass of water began to flow upward, as if sucked up by some invisible source in the darkened sky.

Mayday, mayday.

Tutla sprang into action. "Everyone, suit up and go to your defense stations. Chava and Omar, calculate the rate of water egress."

"Roger, calculating egress," Chava said.

"Fifty thousand gallons per second, Tutla. At this rate, the falls will disappear within thirty... no, make that twenty seconds," Omar said.

"Namkhai, activate the gravitational thrusters; aim them toward the falls, and wait for my command."

"On it," Namkhai said.

"Mariana, Juliana, scan the frequencies, find whatever channel this force is using and block it immediately."

"Already on it. Channel located and blocked," Mariana said.

"Thrusters activated," Namkhai reported.

"Hold steady, Namkhai. Five, four, three, two, HIT IT!" Tutla shouted.

Namkhai entered a pre-programmed code. The thrusters released a force nearly twice the strength of the Earth's gravitational pull. It shook the alternate reality setting so powerfully that each one of the players trembled.

Then, two seconds later, everything stilled, and the water once again spilled from the falls into the aquamarine pool below, as if nothing had happened.

Tutla was silent, awed not so much by what the R.A.T.S had accomplished as by the sacredness of the water itself. He became aware, more deeply than ever before, of the mission his tribe had been called to perform.

"The Havasupai are called the People of the Blue-Green Waters," he said. "We guard these sacred falls, not only for ourselves, but for all life on this Earth. From now on, whenever I look upon these falls, I will be reminded how miraculous it is that the Creator used the same four elements—earth, water, air, and fire—to make each one of us into beings so different and yet also so much the same."

He turned toward his five teammates.

"I will ask the Chief, my father, to list your names on the honor roll, as helpmates of our tribe for defending this precious resource from harm."

One by one, each avatar bowed in thanks, gave the R.A.T.S sign to the others, and left the game.

But the game had not left them.

Chapter 6

What's Happening?
Aruba, 2040, Sunday Morning

David awoke very early Sunday morning. His earphone message light was flashing. *Couldn't be Becky*, he thought. When they'd played R.A.T.S on Friday after school, she'd told him she was leaving that evening with her mom and some of her mom's key advisors for the presidential retreat at Camp David.

"What will you do while your mom is busy?" David had asked.

"Probably a lot of meditation…to clear my head so I can support Mom. She's going to rally her advisors to pressure Congress on climate issues," Becky explained.

"Actually, that sounds pretty cool. I do that all the time."

Becky giggled.

"What's so funny?" David asked.

"The idea of a kid from Aruba pressuring Congress."

"David laughed. "I meant meditation, not trying to influence Congress. I meditate all the time."

"Well, that's also hard to imagine. I didn't think you could go twenty minutes without thinking about R.A.T.S," she said.

"You should talk. Every time I'm in the game, so are you," David said.

"Yeah, anyway… I won't be in the game at all this weekend."

"Okay, guess I'll just have to keep the forces of evil away from this planet without you," David had said, knowing he'd miss Becky, even though she'd only be gone two days.

Wonder what she's doing now, David thought, as he inserted his earphone and tapped it twice to access the device's recorder and find out who'd left a message.

"Hey, buddy, can you meet me in the game tonight? I need some advice." It was Tutla, and by the agitation in his voice, he sounded pretty upset. He'd left the message around eleven p.m., Aruba time.

David accessed the game with his chip-finger and the GraphoScreen© in his room displayed R.A.T.S. He moved his avatar from one scenario to another, recognizing a few players. Tutla was nowhere among them.

He must have been playing late last night, when I was already asleep, David thought. *I'll catch up with him later.*

Just then, Sonic spoke on their private channel. *Your mom's got breakfast ready.*

I'll be right there, David said, and suspended the game, still wondering what could have been troubling Tutla as he walked into the kitchen.

"What's the matter, son?" Rachel asked. "Are you tired? Didn't you sleep well?" She took his face in one hand and touched his cheek twice with the other. David blinked back at her twice to relieve her concerns. They'd had this special way of communicating ever since he was a toddler.

"I slept fine, Mom," he reassured her. "I'm good."

"He was probably up all night playing that game he plays twenty-four-seven," Daniel said.

David sat down at the table next to his brother and gave him an annoyed look. "Actually, I didn't play at all last night. I fell asleep listening to music." Rachel put a plate of waffles on the table next to him. "Thanks, Mom. These look amazing."

"I'm just teasing," Daniel said. "I know you were listening to music; I'm the one who pumped it into your room last night to make sure you fell asleep. I didn't want any excuses from you today."

"Excuses about what?" David asked, looking confused.

"The beach tennis tournament this afternoon. I want my little bro there, cheering me on," Daniel said, shoving another big bite of waffle into his mouth.

"I don't know," David moaned. "I've got something else planned." He wanted to get back to his room to find out what had been bothering Tutla.

"Oh, c'mon, David. It'll be fun. Plenty of sunshine, tons of pretty girls, and the latest music—what could be better than that? We'll have a blast."

"Maybe next Sunday," David said, taking another waffle.

"There won't be any more games next Sunday. Today's the finals, David." Daniel crossed his arms and scowled. "And this is a real game, in the real world, not a bunch of electrical signals bouncing around in virtual space."

David sighed. It was no use explaining to his brother that even if he played R.A.T.S in a virtual world, he was still involved with real scenarios, with real stakes and real consequences. Anyway, he knew the problems he faced in the game could happen in the real world—they weren't just fiction. And the more he and the other players learned, the better equipped they'd be to guard the Earth one day.

His mother smiled at him then and nodded. Did she somehow know what he was thinking? *Impossible*, David thought. And what she said next seemed to confirm that impossibility.

"The sun is shining in a cloudless sky; how can you resist such a beautiful day, David? Besides, it will make your brother happy, and isn't that just as important as your game?"

David sighed again. His mother was right, as usual. Making other people happy always made David feel happy too. "Okay, I'll go. But if I get bored, or it gets too hot, I'm coming home," he said to his brother.

"Agreed," Daniel said. "Let's get ready. I want to go early to practice." He stood to leave the table. "And to show you how grateful I am for your company, I'll even let you use my hoverboard to get to the beach."

"Thanks," David said.

"Just remember," Rachel called after the boys as they headed down the hall to their rooms, "I want you both back here for lunch. Grandma V and Grandpa HB have returned from their Moon Station vacation and I'm preparing great-grandma's *picanha* recipe to celebrate."

David and Daniel came back to the kitchen to say goodbye a few minutes later. They were gathering their things when they heard a low, rumbling, like distant thunder. It almost sounded as if it was coming from somewhere deep within the Earth. They saw a few glasses rattle on a shelf.

"Earthquake?" David asked.

"What else could it be?" Daniel said. "Didn't feel strong, though. The epicenter must be farther away from here, probably Venezuela."

"Did you hear that?" Rachel said, running into the kitchen from an adjacent room. "Sonic, report, please."

Earthquake. 5.2 Richter. Epicenter: Ciudad Bolivar. No serious damage. River rose to overflow. No expected tsunami aftermath.

"Maybe you shouldn't go to the beach after all," Rachel said, clearly upset by the experience.

"Mom, you heard what Sonic said. No expected tsunami. We'll be fine. Anyway, I'm not missing the tournament," Daniel said. "Plus, Dad's there. If anything bad happens, we'll be with him."

"All right. I'll be watching the beach remotely. Come home right away if there's another quake."

The boys agreed and flew off on their hoverboards toward the beach.

David lasted three hours at the beach before he'd had enough of the heat. He'd watched his brother make it to the semi-finals. When Daniel took a break with a group of his friends to wait for the other teams to finish competing for the remaining semi-finals slot, David walked over to tell him he was leaving.

"Don't forget we promised Mom we'd be home for lunch," David said.

"I'll be there soon," Daniel said and turned back to laugh about something with his friends.

David hopped on his own hoverboard just as a huge flock of terns swarmed overhead, flying high and then far away from the beach. *That's strange*, David thought. A couple of minutes later, he walked into the kitchen, still thinking about the birds.

His grandparents had already arrived and were sitting at the floating table, recounting stories of their vacation on the Starlight Moon Station, while his mother set the table for lunch.

"I've traveled all over the world, stayed in the best hotels, but I've never experienced anything as spectacular as the accommodations we had there," HB said. "Our room had a panoramic view. Except for the wall behind the bed and the floor, it was like floating in an immense glass bubble in space. If the brilliance of the stars disturbed your sleep, you could say a command and the glass turned opaque. But I didn't want to do that."

"So, I had to sleep with my eye coverings on the whole time," V interjected.

"Anyway, I give it a five-Milky Way rating." HB laughed. "Five stars isn't enough to describe what a luminous experience it was to see the Earth floating like a beautiful blue-green beacon of pulsating life. I've never seen anything like that," he turned his attention toward his grandson. "David, come and give me a hug," he said, pulling him into an embrace and whispering in his ear. "How far have you gotten?"

"Only two levels left," David whispered back and then walked over to his grandmother to give her a kiss.

"You look a little distracted, David," V said.

"It's no wonder," Rachel said. "He plays that game day and night."

"Don't pick on the boy, Rachel," HB said. "He's playing with kids from all over the world. It helps develop cultural understanding, along with other skills, like creativity. And problem-solving. Right, David?"

David nodded. "And there's a problem I was in the middle of solving yesterday, Grandpa."

"Go on, then," HB said. "He who hesitates is lost."

"Of course, *you* think the game is great," David heard his mother say as he left the room. "You designed it after all." He lingered in the hall, listening to the conversation.

"There's nothing wrong with the inventor having a little pride in his invention, is there?"

"No, nothing wrong with that," V said sharply. "Unless the inventor becomes so busy meeting with other inventors, he forgets all about his wife, leaving her to wander the fabulous Moon Station all on her own."

"Meetings?" Rachel said. "I thought you were on vacation."

"So did I," his grandmother added. "He missed most of the shows. At least I got to see them all; I went with another couple whenever HB had meetings."

"Don't forget to tell her about the restaurant," HB said. "We ate there together every night."

"It was superb, Rachel. The son of Alain Ducasse is the chef. He already earned ten Michelin stars, the most recent one for Moonbeams. It's the best restaurant on the moon," V said. "I'd go back there just for the lemon confit!"

"And the spa," HB added, "where they treated you like a celebrity. So, you see, Rachel, even when I was busy, V was pampered in the most elegant style. I made sure of that, didn't I, my love?"

"It's true, I shouldn't complain." V gave a knowing nod to HB. "Now, about the game, Rachel," she said, shifting the subject. "I know you worry David spends too much time alone. But like I always said, better to be alone than with bad company. He has friends. He's a good boy…a very special boy."

When David heard what his grandmother said, he wanted to run back into the kitchen to kiss and thank both her and his grandfather. Instead, he went to his room. It was time to finally find out what had upset Tutla so much.

Using his chip finger to open the game, David began to swipe from one scene to another, searching for his friend. He finally found Tutla sitting by the side of the aquamarine waters below Havasupai Falls.

"Tutla!" David shouted. "I got your message. I've been worried about you. Are you okay?"

"Yes, I'm fine now. I was really upset about what happened to our ancestors' burial grounds."

"Becky told me about that. Some amateur archaeologists took some sacred things, right?"

"Not archaeologists. Thieves. They stole precious objects, and I became so angry I didn't know what to do. But last night, the game taught me something important, something I've heard you say before, but hadn't really understood until now."

"What do you mean?" David asked.

"Remember you told me your brother sometimes messes with your head? Like he changes the settings in your room, so the lights come on when you don't want them to, or music starts playing when you're trying to concentrate on the game?"

"Yeah," David laughed. "He did that to me last night. I think that's why I missed your message."

"But you're not mad at him now, are you?" Tutla asked.

"No, what would be the point of that, it only—"

"Would keep you stuck, right? See, that's what I learned from you, from the game, last night. I started out angry, but once I let that anger go, everything came together. It was like there were dark forces bubbling all around, trying to hurt us, trying to get us to hurt ourselves. But when we pulled together, those forces became weaker and weaker. We did it, David. We let our dreams guide us. We let in the light."

Before David could say anything, the game flashed orange across the whole GraphoScreen©. A loud buzzer sounded.

Advanced defenders, suit up! Prepare for an incoming attack!

Within seconds, David and Tutla exchanged their avatars' outfits for R.A.T.S officers' uniforms and transported themselves to an underground depot. At the end of a long tunnel, they entered a wide staging area, filled with screens monitoring the Earth from orbiting satellites in space. The setting was so realistic David had to remind himself that he was still in the game; what they were seeing was only a simulation.

Two circular beams of light shone onto the floor. Tutla stepped into one circle and David into the other.

"Defenders in place," David said, "awaiting orders."

Egress in four, three, two... The game counted down. Then, *Whooshhhhh!*

They were thrust into outer space. Below them, the Earth was ablaze. There were fires in the Amazon, and fires across the entire western United States. Volcanoes erupted in Hawaii, Iceland, on Reunion Island in the Indian Ocean. Even Mt. Fuji was spewing lava.

"I don't believe what I'm seeing! What do we do, David?" Tutla cried out. "It looks like we're too late to stop the destruction."

David heard a loud boom and then another.

"What was that?" Tutla asked.

"You felt it too?"

"Yeah, it felt like some kind of explosion," Tutla said.

"David, are you okay?" It was Becky.

"What are *you* doing here?" David asked her, both shocked and excited to see Becky's avatar appear.

"Mom told me to get back to D.C. right away. She wouldn't say why. I'm afraid something's actually happening, David. Something awful. Are you okay?"

"What do you mean, actually happening? This is just a game," David said.

This is not a test. This is not a test. This is not a test.

The warning echoed in David's ear. "Did either of you hear that? Tutla, Becky?"

"Hear what?" they both replied at once. "What's going on, David?"

"I'm not sure, I—"

Just then, Daniel rushed into David's room. "David, come quick. You won't believe what I saw on the beach! The water was receding, like some force was pulling it away. Huge waterspouts formed and ascended toward the sky. Hundreds of fish washed ashore. Hurry up, David! Mom and Dad are freaking out."

"What's happening, David?" Becky sounded more worried than ever.

I have to keep the team focused, David thought. He felt something poke him and looked down at his avatar's uniform. A pair of gold bars with gold wings glistened above the nameplate on his jacket.

"David!" Tutla shouted.

"I know," David said. "We've both been promoted. Alert the others; I'll be back in communication when I can."

"Roger that," Tutla replied calmly and signaled to Becky.

"Already on it," she answered. "I've ordered the other senior officers to stand by on high alert."

Then David disconnected from the game and ran down the hall after his brother, joining his parents and grandparents who were gathered around the GraphoScreen©. They watched in horror as oceans shrank, quakes erupted, and the Earth seemed about to crack open at the seams.

Rachel touched her earphone to call her daughter in Brazil, and Ariel appeared holographically in the room.

"Ariel, are you okay?"

"Yes, Mom. But there are fires everywhere; we're receiving patients by the hundreds."

"Come home, Ariel. I want us all to be together. Something awful is happening around the world; something we've never seen before," Rachel said, shaking. David had never seen his mother so upset. He felt relieved when his father put his arms around her to comfort her.

"I can't, Mom," Ariel said. "I have patients to care for. I must go now. Another ambulance just arrived. I love you, *Ciao!*"

David noticed the only one who seemed quiet in the midst of the storm was HB. He was watching the news with focused attention. Then, he turned toward David and uttered two words.

"It's time."

Moments later, HB's phone rang.

Chapter 7

Are You Ready, Sir?
Aruba, Same Day

HB stepped into the hallway to talk to the caller in private, deactivating the phone's holographic feature for extra security. David watched him leave and snuck out to follow him, hiding behind a large wooden sculpture in a corner. He was near enough to where his grandfather stood to hear what he said.

"General Williams here. Yes, hello, John, what's going on? Yes, I was watching those scenes with my family… All over the globe? How many fires? I see. The Iguazu Falls have frozen on the Brazil side? That's astonishing! My granddaughter's in Brazil; she said nothing about that… Oh, yes, John, I certainly understand… Yes, I agree. It's important to suppress that information until we know more, to keep people from panicking… Right, I'll be ready in one hour… And you'll have the military escort waiting at the airport to take me to D.C.? Good, good… No, no, I'm not shocked at all. In fact, I've expected something like this would happen. For decades it's been obvious to anyone with a brain what we've been doing to this planet. It was just a matter of time before the others found a way to take advantage of our weakness."

His grandfather returned to the kitchen and made some kind of announcement. A minute later, he heard his mother cry out. Then a loud conversation erupted.

"General Williams?" His father spoke in a sarcastic tone of voice David had never heard him use before. "I thought you were a computer programmer who designed strategic software and created videogames for teenagers as a hobby. When did you turn into a general? You're joking, right?"

"No, not at all. This is nothing to joke about, Kenneth, as you certainly ought to know. I'm needed elsewhere. V, get your things. We must leave immediately."

"You mean this is connected to the space engineering project I've been working on remotely for the last few years?" his father asked.

Since when has my father been working on a space engineering project? David couldn't hear his grandfather's reply, but his father's next words told him the answer must have been yes.

"Then why didn't you tell me?" Kenneth asked, sounding more disappointed than angry.

"Because you didn't need to know. Let's go, V; I'm on an extremely tight schedule."

"Can someone please explain to me what's happening?" His mother sounded frantic. "Mom, what's going on?"

"I need to go with HB," V said. "I'll explain everything when I get back. In the meantime, have the drones gather food, water, medicine—everything you might need. Lockdown the house. Wait for me to return."

"What are you saying, Mom? You're acting like—"

"The general's wife. And I'm telling you to prepare like we're being attacked. Because we are."

David ran back to his room, replaying his grandfather's words in his head. *It was just a matter of time before the others found a way to take advantage of our weakness.* The water around Aruba was disappearing, fires exploding, and earthquakes erupting all over the world. So much destruction; it had to mean something extraordinary was about to happen. He felt sure of it. But what exactly was happening and how would the world respond—with unity or with the kind of disorder that had allowed a virus to devastate millions of lives around the globe just a few years before he was born? And what part was he supposed to play in it all? How had he known he needed to keep his R.A.T.S' team focused as soon as he heard about the water receding? And why had those golden winged bars appeared on his uniform as soon as he'd decided to call the alert?

Suddenly, he remembered the dream he'd had two nights ago. Except now, he thought maybe it wasn't a dream but some kind of premonition, like a warning some other force had sent his brain. *Why me?* David wondered. Then, a strange blip of a memory flashed across his mind like a shadowy image beckoning him back through a tunnel of time.

"Sonic," David called out, "play my BioDoc in reverse display on the GraphoScreen©." He watched the recording play in reverse time, from the moment before, when he'd just returned to his room, backward through every moment of his life. When it reached the month of his birth, he stopped the recording and stared at the scene frozen before him. It depicted his mother leaning over his infant sleeping cot. She held something in her hand. He enlarged the image and saw that she was holding a small gold ring with a crystalline stone. The ring was the exact replica of the one his mother always wore on her left hand, next to her wedding ring.

"Play scene forward," David commanded. As the images moved forward slowly, he saw his mother touch the ring to his infant chest and heard her whisper some words like a prayer.

"My beloved son, I received a ring like this one a long time ago to remind me of my destiny. On the day you were born, a second ring appeared on my hand. Though I don't know how or why, I am certain it was intended for you. I will give you this ring when you reach the age of thirteen and cross the threshold to manhood."

David swiped the BioDoc on the GraphoScreen© to the day of his Bar Mitzvah. As the ceremony ended, he saw his mother take him aside and give him the ring. "Always treat others as you wish to be treated, David. Wear this ring tonight as a reminder of that sacred law," she said. He watched himself dancing and singing with friends at the fantastic party that his parents had thrown to celebrate him at a luxurious hotel on the island. Then, he saw something happen he hadn't remembered before. The ring began to change color and glow whenever he was alone, but it faded, becoming almost invisible, whenever anyone else was around. It was as if the ring had some message meant only for him.

He'd never worn the ring after that night. The weight of it felt too uncomfortable on his small hand. Until now.

It was just a matter of time before the others found a way to take advantage of our weakness.

The others! David nearly jumped out of his skin when he realized what his grandfather had meant with those words, what the game HB had invented had been training him and his friends around the world to do. Finally, with the tiniest bit of trepidation and a whole lot of humility, he realized what his role in this whole R.A.T.S enterprise was intended to be.

"Sonic, retrieve my special ring from the family safe. But don't let my mother see you."

"No problem, David. She's been occupied with securing provisions for the family during the lockdown and has gone to her room to rest before your grandmother returns."

Sonic delivered the ring. It began to glow as soon as David slipped it on his finger. A rush of warmth coursed through him as if every cell in his body was illuminated with light. His breathing eased. His heart calmed. His mind expanded, unburdened of worry, and for the first time, he understood the destiny that was his to fulfill.

If it's time, then it's time for me, too, he thought, and began to execute the plan.

Calling all R.A.T.S. Calling all R.A.T.S. Assemble at your command stations at 1400 for a briefing.

One by one, the senior officers of R.A.T.S began to appear on David's GraphoScreen©. First Tutla arrived, proudly displaying his Captain's bars on his uniform, followed by Becky, Mariana, Juliana, Namkhai, Chava, and Omar, each of whom had advanced to First Lieutenant. Around them, junior officers and other novice players assembled. Thousands and thousands of youths from every corner of the Earth arrived, forming a vast pyramid of strength, ready to carry out whatever orders they might receive. David knew they belonged to the game. Even though he didn't recognize all their faces, he was certain that every one of them had come because of a shared commitment to serve the future by saving the Earth.

He thought for a long time about what to say to his team. As soon as he began to speak, the words spilled out of him in such a great torrent that he surprised himself with his steadying eloquence as much as his friends.

"Today, we witnessed horrors. We've seen the heart and lungs of our planet being ripped apart. The Creator of all things gave us the gift of the Earth as a sacred trust. Long ago, our ancestors built this place into a home. Could any of us bear the thought that this gift we have received might be destroyed? That is why we, who are young and full of life, have been called to action. Through the game, we've learned how to think before we act, how not to shrink from danger, and how to make friends by giving, not by receiving favors.

"May G-d give each of us the strength and wisdom to see the difference between good and evil and find the courage to defend this Earth from all its enemies."

"Go home now, prepare yourselves and your families for the coming fight. Spread the word among other players in your regions. Encourage them to join us."

"I will instruct you further when the time comes."

A few of David's closest friends lingered after to congratulate him on the speech.

"Man," Omar said, "you really threw it down, brother. I expected a pep talk. Didn't think you'd go all Pericles on us. Like in that book about war by that Greek dude."

David beamed with a wide smile. "My grandfather gave me Thucydides' *History of the Peloponnesian War* when I was a kid. He said it was important to study ancient history. He told me he hadn't appreciated how much you could learn from the past until he was already an adult and didn't want me to make that same mistake. I loved that book so much, I read it a dozen times. Guess I must have absorbed more than I realized." David sighed. "But, to tell you the truth, I feel more like David about to fight Goliath. I trust G-d to help us win this battle for the Earth's life."

"Yeah, well, you sure got us all fired up. Now I gotta go deal with my father. He's not gonna be happy when I tell him I'm part of the R.A.T.S."

"Good luck!" David said as Omar's avatar disappeared.

Tutla came up to David next and touched his shoulder. "Thank you for honoring all of the peoples of the Earth in your speech," he said.

"Yeah, thanks for that, David," Juliana echoed. "Underneath our different skins, we're all brothers and sisters."

"*Estamos unidas*," Mariana said, grabbing her sister Juliana's hand. Then they both gave the R.A.T.S salute and left to prepare.

110

Besides David, Becky was the only one remaining. She walked up to him and smiled. "That was incredible, David," she said. "I don't think my mom's best speechwriters could have found more inspiring words."

"Thanks," David said. He wanted to hug her but held back, a little embarrassed by his own emotions. But before he knew what was happening, Becky leaned toward him and kissed his cheek. "That's for good luck," she said.

"I'm going to need it," David said, trying to still his rapidly beating heart. "Especially when my mom discovers where I've gone."

"We'll both need luck to handle our mothers," Becky said. "In fact, mine is calling me right now!"

David's avatar stood alone now on the empty field where the R.A.T.S had assembled at his command moments before. He took a deep breath, trying to absorb the enormity of everything that had happened in the last hour. He touched the ring glowing on his hand and prayed silently. Then he made the GraphoScreen© disappear and prepared to join his grandfather at the airport and head to D.C.

But, besides David, others had also anticipated his grandfather's plan. Not the others he'd heard HB mention, but even more sinister others—the others who'd hacked into the game, masquerading as friends but harboring in their hearts all the intentions of enemies.

"If it's time, it's time for us too," Roy said and laughed. "I don't give a rat's ass about all this *unidos estabambinos* or whatever they call it. It's time to take back what's rightfully ours. C'mon, Butch, let's us get ready for the real fight."

Chapter 8

Where Is David?
Aruba, Same Day

The commotion caused by HB's revelation of his secret identity and his rapid departure with Grandma V gave David the perfect opportunity to figure out how he could get to the airport undetected. He looked out the windows of his room and saw immense clouds darkening the sky. Every now and then, a zigzag of lightning would burst through, followed by the crackle and boom of thunder. Intermixed with loud sirens and the *whirr* and *buzz* of ambulances flying through the streets and overhead, the cacophony ruptured the island's tranquility.

The lights in his room flickered for a moment and then steadied again. David figured his father must have turned on the generator. It wouldn't be long before his mother would come looking for him in his room. He hurried to gather the few things he needed—a change of clothes, his extra Spher@, and solar battery pack—and then sent a message to his next-door neighbor, Tyler. The boy was the same age as David but unusual, and more withdrawn, as if he lived in another world. He didn't like to talk much, and preferred the company of his dog to most people, but had an uncanny ability to see patterns in the world and figure out problems, skills that also made him an accomplished R.A.T.S player. Even though the two boys had lived next door to each other most of their lives, it was the game that first introduced them to each other and made them fast friends.

"Tyler, are you there?" David waited a minute. No answer, so he sent another signal to his friend's Spher@. "Tyler, I need your help."

"Yes, I'm here. I've been trying to shut out all that awful noise outside; it's too much for me. But I heard your speech; it was awesome."

"I didn't see you at the assembly," David said.

"You know me, David. I don't like big groups. I was standing on the edge of the crowd, listening to every word. I'm ready—what do you need?"

"I need to get to the airport."

"You've got a super-fast hoverboard that can get you there in fifteen minutes."

"Yes, but I can't let anyone know I've left."

"Oh, I see. Let me think... I've got it! Come to the back gate of your property. I'll meet you there with my HoverMobile. We'll get to the airport in no time."

"Thanks, Tyler. But there's one more problem. I need to sneak past security. Can you draw me a map of all the airport passageways? You know, the ones only airport personnel can use?"

"I could, but I've got a better solution: Michael."

"Michael, your cousin?"

"Yes, he works at the airport."

David hesitated. It seemed risky to trust someone he'd never met.

"And, in case you're worried, Michael's one of us. He plays R.A.T.S. Guess it's impossible for you to know every player in the game, though."

"Yeah," David said, letting out a sigh of relief. "Our numbers have been growing so fast, it's hard to keep up."

"I have a surprise for you, David. I hacked into the game and created a database of every player—who they are, when they joined, and what rank they've achieved. Thought it would come in useful someday."

"You hacked in? But I thought the game's security was—"

"Impossible to hack? Yeah, to any ordinary player, it would be. But, for a guy like me, it was just one more puzzle to solve."

"Well, I'm glad it was you who figured that out, and not somebody trying to steal the game's codes."

"Nothing to worry about now; I also created a marker to detect anybody else who tries to hack in and mess with things. Even got promoted for doing that. So, you can call me Lieutenant Tyler from now on."

"Awesome work, Lieutenant. I'll meet you out by the gate in five minutes."

David grabbed his backpack and opened the door to his room. No one was in the hall. He was about to step out of his room, when he heard his grandmother calling from the front of the house. He closed his door and stood listening behind it.

"Rachel, Kenneth, boys. I'm back. Come quickly; I have news."

He heard the door to his brother's room open and close. A few seconds later, Daniel knocked loudly. "C'mon, David. Grandma V's back."

"I'll be there in a minute," David said. When he heard his parents greet his grandmother, peppering her with questions, he knew he only had a few moments left before his brother would be sent back to get him. Quickly, he recorded a message with his Spher@ and set it to delayed delivery.

Dear Mom and Dad,

I'm sorry I had to leave without saying goodbye. Don't worry; I'm safe with Grandpa HB. As soon as we get to D.C., I'll call you. Remember what you told me a long time ago? If we look back and find no way out, and then look ahead and still find no way out, we must start to look up. Well, I looked up tonight and saw this bright light. I am going toward it now. I feel certain it's what I was put on this Earth to do.

David found Tyler waiting for him in the HoverMobile by the gate. He climbed into the vehicle next to Tyler and buckled himself into the seat. Tyler activated the solar-powered engine and the sleek machine came to life, rising silently a dozen or so feet off the ground. When they reached the end of the cul-de-sac, he maneuvered the vehicle around the corner, heading south toward the airport, and then made it climb higher and higher into the night sky. The rain had stopped, and the air was eerily still. David turned around in his seat to catch a last glimpse of the shining beacon of Aruba's Lighthouse standing guard over the farthest northern point of the island. But there was nothing to see, nothing but the dark expanse of night.

They flew steadily on, past the tall buildings of the luxury hotels along Palm Beach, where tourists spilled out of them like ants escaping from a damaged hill. David stared at the beaches below him, where some strange, otherworldly force had pulled the waters back. Hundreds of fish lay dead on the shore. Then he thought he saw a strange shape in the distance.

"Look there," he shouted to Tyler. "Turn your high beam that way," he said, pointing toward a spot to the west. Tyler focused the light on the place David had indicated. "It's the Ghost Ship," David shouted, awed by the apparition. "You remember the story, don't you?" David asked. Tyler shook his head. "The SS *Antilla*. It was a German vessel from World War II, sunk by its own crew to prevent the allies from capturing it." The whole length of the sunken ship, once submerged more than fifty feet underwater, was exposed now on the waterless floor of the ocean, like the long-buried metallic skeleton of some ancient mariner, warning of yet unknown dangers that lay in the chaos ahead. David stared at it for a few seconds and then looked away.

The closer they got to the airport, the more frenzied the commotion in the crowded streets below them became. Hundreds of people scurried like startled animals toward the entrance, pushing and shoving each other out of the way. David gasped when he saw an elderly man trip and fall. A younger woman tried to pull him to safety, but the frantic, pummeling crowd stampeded over them both. Overcrowded buses and private vehicles clogged the airport entrance. People tumbled out of them, abandoning luggage as they ran inside. It was as if the entire island was emptying out at once.

David was about to say how lucky they were to be in the HoverMobile when he noticed the scores of other flying vehicles trying to land at the same time on the narrow approach to the airport.

"I'm going around to the back," Tyler said, and angled his aircraft left, flying over the terminal. "Michael, we're arriving near gate 15," he called with his Spher@. "Meet us there."

"Roger that," Michael replied.

"I'll have to do a touch and go," Tyler said. "They've got security vehicles all over the tarmac. Jump out and run toward that flashing light as fast as you can."

In the near distance, David saw the light Tyler meant. "Okay, thanks, Tyler."

"Michael will guide you through the airport to wherever you need to go. Good luck," Tyler said, giving David the split-fingered R.A.T.S salute. "I'll be waiting to hear from you when you land in D.C."

"How did you know where I was going?" David asked, looking stunned.

Tyler smiled and winked. "Your Sonic's good friends with our Serena. He told her to make sure I was ready to help whenever you needed it."

"I told you I had your back, David," Sonic said on their private channel as David ran toward Michael's light.

David just shook his head and smiled. "You sure did, Sonic, thanks."

Michael was standing near an entryway below the jetway with a large cart filled with cleaning supplies. By his crisply pressed khaki uniform and the knotted kerchief at his neck, David recognized him as one of the special needs kids the airport employed in different jobs on its Dignity Team. Some welcomed arriving passengers, others gave out water to people waiting for delayed flights, or worked behind the scenes keeping the airport spotlessly clean.

"Welcome, Major David," Michael said, greeting David with the title of his new rank. "Sorry to have to ask you to do this, sir, but would you climb into this cart, please? The only way to get past security is for me to sneak you through the halls in it. We have to get you to the other side of the airport, where your grandfather's escort plane is parked."

Without another word, David hid inside the cart. As they rumbled through the corridors, all he could see at first were scurrying feet, hundreds and hundreds of them running in every direction. The closer they got to the main departure hall, the louder the din of voices became until it reached such a raucous pitch. David felt as if the building would explode with the sound. People were shouting obscenities at each other and the airport staff. Every few seconds a taped announcement repeated over a loudspeaker. "Attention, attention. This is a security alert.

118

Stay calm. Keep your group together. We thank you for your patience."

"This is ridiculous," David heard a man say, "I must leave this island at once; I have a very important meeting to attend in Florida."

"My mother is very ill and all alone in New York. I demand a seat on the next flight to JFK," a woman shouted. "What do you mean there are no seats left! What's the matter with you people; don't you know how to deal with an emergency?"

People were camped out on the floor; whole families huddled together in corners. Children were crying, frightened as much by the sight of so many panicked adults, as by a situation they couldn't possibly comprehend. A powerful odor began to circulate in the air throughout the terminal. David covered his nose and mouth, trying not to inhale the smell of everyone's fear.

"Stay extra quiet now," Michael whispered. "We're almost there."

The hallway they were moving slowly through now held fewer people. David wasn't sure where they were, but he figured they must be near the immigration area.

"Follow me through here, General," he heard someone sounding very official say. "We're going directly through U.S immigration. We have a private room where you can wait until the jet is prepared."

General? That would mean his grandfather was nearby! David thought.

"Hold on a minute, sonny," another official-sounding voice said. "Where are you going?"

"To clean the lavatories in this wing, sir." Michael stopped his cart and replied without the slightest tremor in his voice.

"Okay but make it snappy. We've got a large group to clear, and I don't want any delays."

"Yes, sir," Michael replied, pushing the cart forward again. "Almost there, Major," he whispered to David, turning the cart into the men's washroom. "Okay, we're safe for a few minutes," he said, pulling back the curtain covering the cart and helping David out. "I've put a sign out in front saying the restroom is closed for cleaning. Quick, change into these." He handed David a uniform like his own, which was hidden inside a garbage receptacle. "Then follow me out and do everything I do."

After David dressed, they walked back into the hallway. Michael folded up the sign and David helped him pack it into the cart. Staring straight ahead, they moved slowly toward the rear door that led out to the jet waiting on the tarmac. Another security officer stopped them, but when he saw their uniforms, he smiled and let them pass. "Let me give you boys a hand," he said, entering the security code and opening the door for them. "Give that one out there an extra special cleaning," the officer said. "It's got a very important mission."

"Yes, sir," the boys answered in unison, staring straight ahead and heading for the door.

The supersonic jet was enormous. David had never seen anything so modern or so huge. It had a wide, squat fuselage with many windows that changed colors depending on the clouds and the sky. Its wings thrust out from either side of the plane's body and came to a tipped point at the end. The enormous thing looked like a gigantic stingray had emerged from the sea and was ready to take flight.

On either side of the stairs leading up to the plane stood two soldiers in full military regalia. "Where are you headed, boys?" one of them asked.

"They're okay, Lieutenant," the man who had helped them exit the terminal called out. "They've got a special pass."

"Okay, boys," the officer said with a smile. "But make it quick. We have to stay on schedule."

Michael nodded, grabbing a bucket and a broom from the cart and handing them to David. Then he took another container full of cleaning products and followed David up the stairs to the open door of the jet.

Inside the cabin, a girl in a different uniform was busy supplying the galley with food and drinks. When she saw the boys enter, she stopped what she'd been doing and came up to them. "Name's Manuella," she said in a low voice, turning toward David. "It's an honor to meet you, Major. Michael informed me about the plan." She was the same height and size as David, with the same wavy brown hair and blue eyes. In fact, David thought she looked so much like him they could have been twins. "I've got everything ready. Let me show you." While Michael kept watch by the doorway, Manuella led David to a corner of the cabin where two large gray leather armchairs faced into the center of the room. "You can hide behind here. No one will see you," she said.

David nodded, nervously scanning the room. Unlike other planes, he'd taken on trips with his parents, this one had no rows of seats. Instead, it was outfitted with large, comfortable couches and several tables. On one whole wall, an electronic map was covered in tiny, flashing lights pinpointing spots around the globe. In the cockpit, David caught a glimpse of the pilots, briefing for the flight. No one else was around.

"We have to exchange clothes, now," Manuella said. David looked at her quizzically.

"So, I can exit the plane disguised as you," she explained. "And in case you're wondering why they won't come looking for me, I've already programmed the robotic food truck to return to the canteen with a message that I'm taking my break. My sister, Giovanna, who also works here, will meet me with another uniform and no one will know we've exchanged clothes! Now, hurry." She ushered David toward a bathroom. "The General will board any minute."

David changed quickly into Manuella's service uniform and returned to the cabin. Manuella, now dressed as a boy, helped him hide.

"I'll await further orders, sir." She saluted David and then exited the plane with Michael.

A few minutes later, David heard people entering the plane, his grandfather among them.

"You'll find all the briefings necessary to prepare for your meeting with the president in the computer on board. Is there anything else you need, General?" David didn't recognize the voice, but from the accent and the officious tone, he guessed it was someone from the Aruban military who'd escorted his grandfather to the airport.

"I don't think so, Colonel Jansen," his grandfather said.

"Very good, sir. I'll leave you then. I hope you can rest on the flight. And good luck, sir."

"Thank you," his grandfather said and sat down at a table across from where David was hiding behind the chair.

"Please fasten your seat belt, General. It's going to be a rough ride in this storm, so I recommend you keep it fastened for the duration, sir," the co-pilot announced over the intercom.

David felt the engines roar as the plane began to speed down the runway. It lifted off and banked quickly to the left at such a sharp angle that David gasped.

"Who's there?" his grandfather exclaimed. David held his breath, preparing to reveal himself. But before he could stand, his grandfather was towering over him with a surprised look on his face. "David! How did you? Never mind, come out from behind there." HB led David to the chair next to him. "Buckle up. Now, tell me what you're doing here. Your mother will be terribly upset with both of us, as I'm sure you know."

"Sorry, Grandpa, I'm sorry. It's just, I overheard your conversation and, well, after seeing what's happening all over the Earth and knowing you were called to D.C. to help, I couldn't stay home and do nothing. Besides, you need me. In fact, we need each other. Don't forget, I helped you program the game... I know what's going on... Something big." David held up his hand. The stone on the gold ring glowed brightly. "And I understand now that my role is bigger than I ever imagined."

HB's expression softened into a smile. "We're very much alike, David," he said. He reached into his pocket and pulled out a ring. Except for a branch with two leaves on it, it looked exactly like David's.

"Where did you get that? Did you know Mom has one too?"

"I suspected as much, David. But now I must tell you a story, a rather remarkable story. Many years ago, when I was in the Air Force, the U.S. government sent me on a secret expedition to Peru. The government had been tracking strange events there in a mission called Project Blue Book."

"Why did they send you, Grandpa?"

"Because I had special information. My father had inherited papers from the son of Hiram Bingham, the man who had been the first non-native to discover Machu Picchu. When my father died, he left them to me and asked me to continue his research. I also had unique computer skills and helped the Air Force analyze the strange occurrences documented in the region. But what happened to me on that trip was so extraordinary, no computer program could have predicted it."

"You met the others, didn't you?" David sat up straight in his seat. "The ones you talked about back at my house. I overheard the conversation. The others are beings who are trying to hurt us; they're aliens from outer space, aren't they?"

"David, you're a very smart boy. Yes, I met extraterrestrial beings. But not the ones who are responsible for what's happening now."

"What do you mean? They took you prisoner, didn't they? How do you know they're not the ones doing these awful things to us now?"

"Because, David, the beings who abducted me were kind, peaceful beings of light. They didn't intend to do harm, but to instruct and to warn."

David settled back in his seat but looked confused. "What was it like to be with those beings?" he asked. "I mean, where did they take you? What did they look like? Weren't you afraid?"

"The last thing I remembered was standing on the plateau of Machu Picchu surrounded by the brightest light. I looked up and saw four shimmering figures coming toward me. As they came closer, I felt as if some pure, pulsating energy were engulfing me, comforting me. The next thing I knew I was in a spaceship with beautiful, peaceful music playing. I felt weightless and utterly calm and content, as if I were floating in the most incredible dream.

"The beings spoke to me. They told me they'd been with us earthlings since the beginning, observing us, trying to help humanity not to forget the difference between good and evil. But what they saw us do to ourselves led them to judge us harshly. We've been a menace to each other and to our planet, they said. All the evils in our history— slavery, poverty, injustice, pollution, violent wars—we've caused ourselves. As recordings of the millennia of human history unfolded before me, I realized I should not be afraid of them, but of us. We have betrayed this planet. Instead of sustaining peace and spreading love, we have killed and maimed and stolen to satisfy our most selfish interests. We have brought this apocalypse down on ourselves."

David was so overwhelmed by what HB described, he could hardly speak. Finally, he asked the question burning in his mind. "But, Grandpa, I don't understand. If the beings who took you away are so good, why are they allowing these others to attack us now and make things far worse?"

HB took David's hand in his and looked at him with a somber expression.

"Because, David, we are responsible even for these most recent events. We've made ourselves vulnerable to this attack. Only we can choose to restore harmony and order; it cannot be imposed on us. We are not robots or puppets. With our G-d-given free will, we must defend ourselves."

Tears of sorrow came to David's eyes, as he felt the full weight in his heart of the profound truth his grandfather had spoken. He stood up, gave HB the split-fingered R.A.T.S salute, and declared his willingness to defend the Earth from her enemies, both on Earth and beyond.

"Major David, reporting for duty, sir."

Chapter 9

What Is That Music?
Grand Canyon, Arizona

As the special military jet sped toward D.C., David sent Tutla a telepathic message, explaining where he was heading and why.

"You're my closest friend, Tutla. Although we come from different cultures, you're like a brother to me. I want you to mobilize all the other R.A.T.S for the mission I mentioned earlier; I've just learned more about it from my grandfather. It's something I believe we've been preparing for all along."

"You mean the game's been preparing us, don't you?" Tutla took a deep breath. "I've suspected as much."

"Yeah, it's been training us for something really huge—to be defenders of the Earth, and not only from drought and fires and earthquakes humans have caused but also from alien forces. They're trying to steal all of Earth's water! They've already pulled back the sea around Aruba."

Tutla remembered that scene he'd played a couple of days ago, where they'd protected Havasupai Falls from an extraterrestrial attack. *So, it wasn't some fantasy; it was a practice.*

"What was practice?" David asked.

"The night I sent you the message about wanting to talk, the game had us defend Havasupai Falls from being taken by aliens."

"Who was there?" David asked, sounding a little worried.

"Me, Omar, Namkhai, Chava, and the New York girls, Mariana and Juliana. A couple of other new guys showed up too, but they left before the attack on the water. I started to tell you about it right before—"

"—before the game sent us to that underground station and we got pulled into outer space. I see where we're heading now."

"You can see D.C. already?" Tutla grew excited at the idea of his friend visiting the White House.

"No, I mean where the R.A.T.S are headed. That station we were sent to in the game, Tutla—well, it really exists; it's where we're supposed to meet. My grandfather told me it's outside Las Vegas, in the desert. I don't have all the details yet, but I need you to call a meeting of the other lieutenants. Tell them to prepare to assemble for battle. They'll know they've been summoned when they hear this melody playing across the airwaves on our special channel."

What Tutla heard next was like nothing he'd ever imagined it could be possible to hear. It was as if every star in the galaxy was emitting a singular note in some celestial symphony, sounding a chorus of heavenly vibrations, intoning a plea for the Earth, summoning his generation to rise in defense of their home. "What is that music?" he asked.

"It's a recording my grandfather got from the beings who abducted him; he played it for me a little while ago. Amazing, isn't it?"

"Hold on, are you telling me your grandfather was abducted by aliens?"

"It's a long story. I'll explain everything later; we're about to land now. Get the troops ready. You're promoted to Captain."

"Roger that." Tutla felt dizzy with the news David had just given him. *So, the aliens were real, and the underground station, that was real, too.* He sat down in a chair next to a window in his family's trailer in Havasupai Valley and tried to steady himself. Everything was moving so fast. He looked out the window. The sky was a hazy shade of orange, discolored by smoke and soot from the fires burning all across the western United States, from the Pacific Coast up through the Rockies and into the Dakotas. It wouldn't be long before their whole valley became a raging inferno. And if those alien forces succeeded in taking the Earth's water, nothing would survive. There was no time for hesitation; he'd have to act quickly, decisively.

He could hear his father in the next room making frantic preparations to evacuate the tribe to higher ground. As distraught as the chief was about abandoning their sacred lands, Tutla knew he'd become enraged when he learned about the mission his son was about to undertake. As if facing the tasks ahead of him weren't weighty enough, having to confront his father doubled that burden.

He pushed aside that worry and began alerting the other officers, as David had ordered. One by one, they joined a special briefing room in the game that Tutla had created for them to discuss the plan.

The first avatar to enter had such a forlorn expression on his face that Tutla didn't recognize him at first. The flowing saffron robes told him it was Namkhai.

"Why do you look so sad, Namkhai?" Tutla asked.

Namkhai shook his head, unable to utter anything but a Buddhist chant. Over and over, he repeated the same words—*Ohm Mani Padme Um, Ohm Mani Padme Um.*

"What is it, Namkhai?" Tutla worried his friend had suffered such a grievous loss he'd gone into a deep trance.

"The disasters I've witnessed are worse than anything we imagined, Tutla. Whole villages washed away; massive earthquakes swallowed thousands of others. Everywhere, nothing but suffering." Namkhai raised his head and gave the R.A.T.S salute. "Though my heart is sick, I'm determined to defeat whatever evil has caused this destruction."

Tutla was relieved to hear the strength returned to Namkhai's voice. "I've heard from Major David. We're to organize our forces and standby on high alert."

"How will we know when it's time to assemble?" Namkhai asked.

"Wait a minute, dude. I missed the first part of this briefing," Omar said, arriving out of breath. "You wouldn't believe the sandstorms and wicked thunderstorms we've had. And the heat! No one can go outside."

131

"We've had floods here and terrible heat, too," Chava chimed in. "Where're the New York girls?"

"We're here," Mariana said.

"We came over to our cousin's apartment because her building has a generator," Juliana added. "The whole city could go dark at any minute. It's happened before. People are freaking out. There's already been looting in some parts of the city."

"We've all seen terrible things," Tutla said, thinking of the raging fires. "But we can't let our individual troubles distract us. We have a bigger mission to carry out." He called the meeting to order. "Major David said we'll receive a signal when it's time to travel."

"Travel? You mean, like for real? Together in the same place? I thought we were just going to, you know, work on our own problems," Omar said, sounding hesitant, which surprised Tutla.

"Dear brother Omar," Namkhai interrupted with an understanding response. "Our problems are each other's problems, no? But I think you're worried about something else; something I think we're all worried about."

Omar let out a deep sigh. "It's my dad, dude. He wants me to go with him tomorrow to the mosque to pray for order and peace on the planet. He thinks we can leave it to others to do the fighting for us. Besides, he's always hated when I played R.A.T.S, I don't know how to tell him I've been called up." Omar's avatar sat down, put his head in his hands, and began to sob. "And I can't go without his blessing."

Namkhai's avatar touched Omar's shoulder. "None of us can leave without our parents' support. But remember, Omar, our parents raised us with the values that bring us together, despite our different religions and beliefs, to defend this beautiful planet. We are not rebelling against their teachings; we are putting them into action. We will thank them and trust that they will understand."

Tutla noticed that Omar relaxed a little at those comforting words.

"And besides," Chava added, "we'll remind them that they were once young and idealistic. My parents were in a kibbutz, after all. I plan to use that fact—with deep respect—if they give me any trouble when I tell them where I'm heading."

"My father is a proud, yet stubborn man," Omar said, still unconvinced. "I'm afraid he'll use all his power and influence to prevent me from joining this mission."

"No more stubborn than my father," Tutla said. "Right now, he's organizing the tribe to leave our ancestral lands, while all the time yelling about our enemies, the ones we've been fighting off for centuries. Still, I believe I can convince him of the importance of our mission, once he learns of its scope."

"What do you mean by scope?" Juliana asked. "Oh, wait a minute, I get it," she slowly nodded her head in realization. "It's like that scene we played a couple of nights ago, that water theft thing. It's them, isn't it? Aliens. They're for real attacking us, aren't they?"

"You mean space aliens are coming after the Earth?" Mariana turned toward Juliana in shock. "*Dios mio!*"

Tutla nodded his avatar's head. "And we must defeat them."

"Wow, that's heavy, man," Omar said. "How will we know what to do?"

Tutla hesitated to say anything about what David had told him about his grandfather's abduction. He didn't even know the whole story. Besides, he figured it was David's story to tell.

"David will send a musical signal to summon us to the staging area just outside Las Vegas."

"Las Vegas! Cool! I've always wanted to see that place. And music will bring us together; I love it," Juliana said. "Music unites." She pulled Mariana into a dance, and soon the whole team was singing together, dancing their fears away.

The energy was electric, as their favorite track blared through the speakers, the bass thumbling in perfect sync with their racing hearts. The lyrics soared, fueling their resolve and igniting their spirits for the battle ahead. This was their anthem, their call to arms, and they embraced it fully, ready to face whatever came next.

They continued humming the tune as, one by one, they left the game to alert their parents and ready themselves for departure.

His spirit buoyed by the empowering sense of purpose he felt from dancing with everyone, Tutla went into the next room to talk with his father. He decided he'd appeal to his father's sense of the sacredness of the falls, the enormity of their meaning to the peoples of the blue-green waters, the tragedy that would befall them if this holy place disappeared.

The chief was hunched over his desk, organizing some kind of tribal records. He looked up for a second when Tutla entered and then turned back to his work.

"Have you finished the tasks I gave you?"

His father had told him to pack all their blankets and ceremonial robes and feathered headdresses into special containers. He'd nearly finished when David contacted him. "I have only two more boxes to pack."

"Well, hurry up. What are you waiting for? I've ordered the horses to be ready to take us all up to the canyon's edge. We will leave in less than an hour."

"Father, I need to talk to you." His voice quivered with nervousness.

"There's no time. And when you're done, go help your mother. I told her not to bother taking any of her crafts, but it seems to comfort her to have a few special things with her."

Tutla swallowed hard. "Father, I've been called away on a mission; I must leave now."

The chief swiveled in his chair so suddenly, the papers flew off his desk like a flock of scattered birds. "Leave? Have you forgotten your obligations to the tribe? You are the chief's son. Your duty is to remain with us."

Tutla bent over to help pick up the papers. "Let me help," he said.

His father pushed his hand away. "The only help I need from you is for you to fulfill your duty. Now get out; do as I told you."

Tutla stood up and walked toward the door. "Father, please understand. By leaving, I will be fulfilling my duty—to you, to the tribe, and to so much more. We are about to be attacked."

"Do you think I don't know that?" His father stood and shouted. "The oppressors have always attacked when we are at our weakest. The fires raging all around our lands will only be their latest excuse to claim every bit of this territory for themselves and deny us our ancestral home forever."

"But these attackers aren't the same ones as before and their goal isn't only to take from us, but to ruin the Earth for everyone."

"Foolish boy! Have you learned nothing from our history? As the ancestors warned, these greedy ones would ruin the Earth for everyone with their wicked, selfish ways."

Tutla had never seen his father so angry. How would he ever be able to explain his mission, much less get his father to bless his leaving? "Father, are we not the People of the Blue-Green Waters? Isn't it our obligation to protect the sacred springs which feed our lands?"

"Of course, it is, which is why I am so pained to leave here. And now you have added to that pain by refusing to fulfill your duties."

"But that's what I've been trying to explain. I am fulfilling them. I am Tutla, great warrior of the Blue-Green Waters and lieutenant in the R.A.T.S army formed to defend the Earth from alien attackers."

"R.A.T.S army? Aliens? What nonsense are you speaking now?" The chief's eyes widened in shock. "It's that game you play all the time, isn't it?"

"Yes, but it's much more than a game, it—"

"I forbid you to have anything more to do with it, or with any of those you've met through it. We have nothing to do with those people. They've only caused destruction and death in this world."

"I can't believe what you're saying, Father... It's not time to judge, but to help. You say you don't want anything to do with them. But we have computers and Spher@s...everything they make. You even gave me that game."

"I thought it was educational. I should have known it was just another trap set to distract us with mindless entertainment."

Tutla could think of nothing more to say. He needed to convince his father of the source and scope of the impending attack. Out of desperation, he called up a recording of the scenario they'd played the other night and the waters of Havasupai Falls began to recede again on the GraphoScreen© appearing before his father's eyes.

His father cried out in horror. "What is this? Some kind of computer trick?"

"No, it's what will happen to our sacred waters and all the oceans and streams and rivers of this planet if I don't join my friends to protect them from the aliens who intend to steal our most precious resources. I must meet them at the underground station prepared for us in the desert outside Las Vegas."

Tutla watched his father collapse back into his chair. "I understand now. It is the end of days. The time the ancestors prophesied when a *Supai Kachina*, a medicine man of our tribe, would leave the Canyon, taking many blessings with him, to warn the Earth of her doom. And the four races, the four sacred colors of red, white, yellow, and black, would once again unite from their separate regions." He looked at Tutla with a mixture of sorrow and worry. "You, my son, have been chosen for this task."

Tutla knelt before his father. "Would you honor me with your blessing now, Father?"

"The eldest among us will bless you, my son," his father said. "And your mother must be here too." He left the room to search for his own father.

Tutla's grandfather returned with a special eagle feather and handed it to him to begin the blessing ceremony. His parents stood on either side of him, their hands gently touching their son's shoulders. His grandfather began to pray.

"From the waters of this Canyon, we were born. From the sun, we received energy and warmth and from the Earth, we received the bounty that sustains us. We have made a sacred covenant with the Creator to honor and protect these things. Go now and continue to honor this covenant."

Tutla rose and embraced his parents.

"Take our best horse, my son," his father said. "I will meet you at the plateau as soon as I have made sure everyone has evacuated safely. We will reach Las Vegas in a few days."

"You would come with me?" Tutla exclaimed.

His father smiled. "Not only I, but many other tribes will join to escort you to the desert when they learn of your sacred calling."

"Trust in our love to return you to us safely," his mother added. "As we trust in you to protect our mother, the Earth, from more harm."

Tutla felt his heart overflow with love, stilling any remaining worries, then bowed to the four corners of the Earth and walked toward his waiting horse.

Chapter 10

The Moment of Truth
Aruba, Same Day

"HB's gone to Washington D.C.," V announced just as Daniel joined his parents in the living room.

"I don't understand. Why would he leave when we're in the middle of a crisis here on the island?" Rachel rubbed her temples, trying to ease the headache that had erupted in the chaos. She had been coordinating the drones to deliver a month's supply of food and medicines, as V had instructed her to do until she returned. Despite the pain relievers she'd taken to stop it, the pain persisted as if some long-buried memory was trying to push itself from the deepest recesses of her brain into her consciousness.

"I told you, Rachel. He's a General in the Air Force. The president needs him to help plan a response to the global emergency."

"And how could he even get a flight?" Kenneth asked, putting his arm around Rachel's shoulder to comfort her. "All the planes have been grounded."

V turned to answer Kenneth. "The White House sent a special jet to transport him."

"That's crazy. HB is a computer programmer, not a military officer." Rachel sat down on the couch and leaned her head back against the cushions, hoping to relieve the throbbing in her head.

V sat down next to her and took her hand. "Daniel, go rinse a cloth in cool water for your mother to ease her headache."

Before Daniel could leave the room, his mother stopped him. "I don't need a cloth," she said, pulling her hand away, annoyed her mother was taking charge. "What I need is an explanation." She looked sternly at her mother and then over at her husband, who had settled himself into the large white leather armchair adjacent to the couch. "And I need one from you, too, Kenneth. I heard you say something to HB before he left about a space-engineering project you've been working on for the last few years. That's news to me."

"All right, Rachel." V stood up and walked to look out the large picture window that faced the courtyard.

Seeing her mother's tiny frame outlined against the ten-feet-tall windows – with the palm trees surrounding their home's circular drive swaying and bending behind her as if they were dancing in the growing storm – made Rachel feel more overwhelmed and oddly calmed at the same time by the enormity of everything that had happened in the last hour. For a split second, she had the weird sensation that whatever V was about to recount was something she somehow already knew.

V turned away from the window, walked toward the chair next to Kenneth and sat down. "Do you remember when you were a little girl and I'd just met HB? He'd come to Aruba to visit a friend who'd just opened an aquatic company. He was an excellent sailor and planned to help operate boat tours for tourists. He had such an air of mystery about him; I became intrigued the minute I met him. As he fell in love with the island's beauty, I fell in love with him."

"Mom, I already know all that," Rachel said with an impatient wave of her hand. "Now, please, tell me something I don't know." *Or you think I don't know.* She touched the ring on her left hand. Without looking at it, she knew it had begun to glow.

"Soon after we began dating, HB told me he was a government official and wrote special reports for the government. At first, he wouldn't say anything else about his work, but over time, as he began to trust me, he explained more about his job in the U.S. Air Force, especially their research in Peru." V paused for a moment. "HB's father worked as an undercover agent for the U.S. State Department. He and Hiram Bingham's son—"

"—Hiram Bingham was the guy who discovered Machu Picchu," Daniel interjected. "We read about him in school this year."

"That's right, Daniel," V said. "Bingham's son worked with HB to develop a research project based on the Machu Picchu archives Bingham left behind, including unpublished manuscripts. They never found what they were looking for. HB inherited their research from his father and continued looking for..." V paused and took a deep breath.

"Looking for what, V?" Kenneth asked, leaning forward in the chair.

"They were on a secret expedition to explore odd phenomena connected to archaeological discoveries in Peru. HB was put in charge of a group of highly qualified scientists."

"Kenneth asked what they were looking for, Mom."

"They were looking for… extraterrestrials." V barely whispered the last word. "And I think HB—"

"—You mean, like space aliens?" Daniel was practically bouncing out of his chair with excitement. "So, David was right."

"Right about what?" Kenneth asked.

"About R.A.T.S, that educational game he was helping Grandpa test," Daniel said. "He thought the game was training the players to defend Earth from an alien attack."

"By the way, where is David?" V asked.

While the others were talking, Rachel had walked over to the window, drawn by faint sounds in the courtyard, like the tinkling of high keys on a piano or the quivering strings of a harp. The courtyard was lit with the same shimmering light she remembered seeing on that San Francisco night more than two decades ago. She twisted the glowing ring on her finger. Her head stopped throbbing and she heard a voice calling her name.

Rachel, listen to the spheres. It's time.

She touched her Spher@. As David's recording played in her head, she closed her eyes.

Remember what you told me a long time ago? If we look back and find no way out, and then look ahead and still find no way out, we must start to look up. Well, I looked up tonight and saw this bright light. I am going toward it now.

Then she whispered a prayer to the Blessed One to protect her son and turned to explain to her bewildered family what she'd always known would happen one day. "David is on the plane with HB."

***

During the remaining hour of their flight to D.C., HB explained to David the development of the underground space station near Las Vegas.

"You'll be proud to know your father helped design the spaceships that will carry our defensive forces to the Starlight Moon Station. From there, the R.A.T.S will operate drones to locate any incoming attacks and defeat them with our highest-powered weapons."

"Did my father know all about these plans, too?"

HB smiled at David. "Kenneth didn't have top security clearance, so I couldn't tell him the real purpose of the vehicles he was designing. But he knew a space force had been created decades earlier, so I guess he was satisfied with my vague explanation that his work was a major contribution to the planet's safety."

"I thought the Moon Station was just a fancy travel destination." David shook his head in disbelief.

"That's exactly what we wanted people to think."

"You and Grandma V visited there so often, I should have figured it was more than just a vacation spot. Hold on, how much does Grandma V know about R.A.T.S?"

"She knows I designed the game to educate kids and that you helped me test it. And she knows what happened to me in Machu Picchu. V's a smart woman. I'm sure she put two and two together. I knew I could trust her to keep my abduction a secret. But, before I left, I told her to explain everything to your parents before the whole world learns about our plans."

David's heart sank as he realized his parents might not have gotten his message before V told them where he and HB were headed. He hated the idea of his mother thinking he'd departed without leaving any kind of goodbye. Just then, his Spher@ signaled an incoming call from Rachel. Prepared to be chastised, he slowly pressed the device in his ear and was pleasantly surprised to hear her sounding resigned and calm.

"David, are you all right?" she asked.

"Yes, Mom… I'm sorry if I scared you and Dad. But when I realized what was really happening, I knew I had to join Grandpa HB."

"I know; I understand. Did you take your ring with you?"

"Yes, I asked Sonic to bring it to me while you were busy getting the house ready for lockdown."

"Good. And is it glowing now?"

"Yes, very brightly. So is grandpa's," David said, grateful to acknowledge the special bond he'd always felt with his mother and now knew he also shared with HB.

"Keep it on your finger at all times. Don't worry, not everyone can see it glow. But whenever it does, you'll know you've chosen the right path. We'll be waiting for you to return home as soon as you can. G-d bless you. Remember, your father and I love you! Now, I need to talk to HB alone."

"Mom wants to talk with you," David said. He changed his Spher@ to music mode to give his grandfather privacy and stared out the window as the plane coasted over the Potomac River, descending toward Washington National Airport. At one end of the National Mall, the obelisk of the Washington Monument pierced the sky like a giant white arrow and at the other end, he glimpsed the domed Capitol Building. He remembered stories his grandfather had told him about the many laws and promises that had been crafted, and sometimes broken, inside that hallowed building. When the arched portico of the White House came into view in the near distance, he felt a sudden rush of hope. If HB could convince the president to unite the Earth's people, they'd be able to stop the destruction they'd brought down on themselves and maybe have a chance to heal from all the hate and violence that had sickened humanity and polluted their homes for so long.

HB tapped him on the shoulder and David silenced the music. "Yes, of course. He'll be with me the entire time. Don't worry. I won't let him out of my sight," HB said and gave David a thumb's up. "Give V a kiss for me and tell her I love her. Keep watching the news for that announcement I described. Love you all."

Just then the co-pilot announced they were moments from landing. HB leaned forward and clapped David on the shoulder. "Soon we'll meet Sarah Hoffmann, the president, and my friend John Singer, who's head of Homeland Security. They were both with me in Peru. John never believed my reports about Machu Picchu. But I hope, now that he's seen many more like mine, he'll have changed his mind and will help me persuade Sarah, I mean, Madame President, about what we need to do."

That his grandfather explained everything to him in great detail made David feel both honored and a little scared at the responsibility he'd undertaken.

"Anyway, stay alert, major," HB continued. "I'll need every ounce of your attention from now on."

"Sir, yes, sir," David replied with his best salute and brightest smile, feeling more and more like a real Earth warrior with every passing minute.

Chapter 11

Washington, D.C.
Arriving D.C., Same Day

The plane had barely landed on American soil when the co-pilot emerged from the cockpit to open the cabin door. As David followed his grandfather out of the plane, he saw two officers dressed in full military regalia salute HB. Below them, on the tarmac, a long, black limousine awaited, its windows darkened out for security. Four government officials—two women and two men—stood around the vehicle, dressed in long, unbuttoned black coats over black pants and crisply starched white shirts with ties. David assumed they were part of some secret service detail like the ones he'd seen depicted in spy movies.

"Good afternoon, general," one of the officials said.

"Good afternoon," HB answered and got into the limousine with his grandson.

His grandfather laid out some papers from his briefcase on a foldout desk and began to make notes while David, dumbfounded, watched the empty streets of Washington whizz by. The air was thick with smoke. Broken glass and other debris littered the roads and sidewalks. It looked as if the city had suffered some immense upheaval, worse than any riot or civil disturbance might have caused in the past. Ambulances rushed past their vehicle, sirens blaring, lights flashing. Nothing seemed normal. But then, David wondered, what was normal supposed to look like when the planet itself had convulsed, screaming for help?

They reached the White House, which somehow managed to still look grand and stately amidst all the chaos. The entrance gates slowly opened. When the limousine parked near a side entrance, a Marine officer in a dress blue uniform wearing pristine white gloves opened the door and stiffened his arm into a salute.

"General Williams, please accompany me," he said.

David followed his grandfather up a set of stairs into a wide hall, around a corner, and through a set of automated doors that opened and closed with a slight upward tilt of the officer's capped head. When they reached a smaller room off to the right, the Marine handed HB a uniform.

"And who is this young man, general?"

"My grandson, who is also my assistant. He goes wherever I go."

"But gener—"

"Wherever I go," HB repeated, giving the young Marine a stern look.

"Of course, sir," the Marine said and pointed HB in the direction of a private changing area. "I'll return to escort you to the Oval Office in fifteen minutes."

HB took the uniform into the changing area and emerged in a jacket glistening with more medals than David had ever seen.

"I wish I had something better to wear than this silly food service uniform," David said, pointing to the emblem on the disguise he'd been given to hide his identity from security. He felt a little embarrassed by his attire considering the grandeur of his surroundings.

"Soon, David, you'll have your uniform. But always remember, it's not the uniform that makes the man, it's the man who makes the uniform."

"Or woman," David said.

"I stand corrected, major. Yes, man or woman, whoever is equal to the task."

The Marine returned to guide them to the meeting room, where his grandfather was scheduled to brief the president. A rush of people filled the halls of the White House, racing in every direction at once. David walked behind HB, brushing his hair back with his hands and tucking his shirt tightly into his pants. When they reached the door to the Oval Office, the Marine knocked, entered, and announced HB's arrival.

The president was seated behind her desk, hunkered over a ream of papers. She signaled to the Marine to leave and stood as HB saluted her.

"Madame President," he said, and stepped back, hiding David momentarily from her view.

"General," she said, returning the formality before her voice changed to a friendlier cadence. "I'm grateful you've arrived so quickly, HB. Grateful and relieved."

"I hope my plan can offer much more than relief, Sarah."

"I do, too," the president said. "But I remain worried. I've read your reports. They've deeply troubled me. Time seems to be running out."

David cleared his throat and stepped out from behind his grandfather's giant frame.

"And who is this handsome young man?" Sarah asked.

"You remember my grandson, David, don't you?"

Sarah came from behind her desk. She was a stately woman, almost as tall as his grandfather. "I didn't recognize you, David; you've grown so much since we met." She turned toward HB. "That was only a few years before the election, but it seems like a lifetime ago."

HB nodded. "I imagine this office costs anyone who holds it several lifetimes before they leave."

David saw a brief shadow of sadness pass across the president's face. It faded almost before it had fully arrived and for some reason, that bittersweet expression made him aware of how much her daughter resembled her. Except for a more heavily furrowed brow, worry lines deeply etched around her green eyes, and gray hair crowding Sarah's temples, Becky was the spitting image of her mother. It took a few seconds for David to compose himself enough to dry his sweaty palm on his pants and shake her outstretched hand. "Madame President, it's an honor to meet you," he said, feeling color rising in his cheeks.

"I've briefed David on the security reports I've been monitoring," HB said. "He also knows about Machu Picchu."

Sarah nodded and gestured toward a pair of couches in the room's center. David took a seat next to his grandfather and Sarah sat across from them, gathering her thoughts before she spoke again.

"For several days now, we've been receiving signals from an extraterrestrial spaceship that's been slowly approaching our planet. As you know, I've ordered the U.S Air Force and Navy drone pilots to prepare for an attack and put the Army Special Forces and Navy Seals on standby alert."

"I'm aware of those orders," HB said.

"I've also put out an urgent call to our NATO allies to prepare the alliance for action. But we're fighting on several fronts at once. Trying to calm the civilian population, in the face of numerous simultaneous disasters, has already overwhelmed the local authorities. Many states have mobilized the National Guard. The Army Corps of Engineers is working with FEMA on rescue operations in the flooded areas. But we simply don't have enough personnel to keep up with the level of evacuations necessary to save lives. We're doing everything we can but it's not enough." Sarah closed her eyes for a second and took a deep breath. "And once we announce we're facing an imminent extraterrestrial attack, you know what will happen. We'll be faced with the choice of whether to use military force to control civilian chaos that is likely to be worse than anything we've ever seen."

"Do you have any idea how close the invaders are?" HB asked.

"An hour ago, we received data indicating that they've entered our solar system. I ordered the activation of the advanced space defense system, but to no avail. They're undeterred."

"How large a force are we talking about?" HB asked.

"That's the worst of it. Their ships defy anything we've ever come close to developing. It's like fighting some unknowable, invincible giant. We can't destroy them." Sarah crossed her arms and sighed. "And I'm afraid we can't stop them." She reached for a stack of papers piled on the table in front of her. "Here are the latest reports."

HB took the papers from her and started to page through them. David glanced over his grandfather's shoulder and saw the names of several prominent coastal cities, including Tokyo, Shanghai, Lagos, Mumbai, Charleston, New Orleans, and Los Angeles, where once rising sea levels had been feared, but which were now experiencing disastrous levels of depletion of their surrounding waters.

"Just like Aruba," he whispered, pointing to the list.

"Yes, David," HB said in a hushed voice. "We're all in this together. Now, we must convince everyone else to see what we see." He turned his attention back to Sarah. "I suggest you arrange a press conference, invite representatives from all nations, so we can explain to everyone what's happening on a global level."

"I anticipated that suggestion and have already asked my press secretary to prepare the briefing room for a holographic conference call with our allies."

"No, Sarah. Not only our allies. With everyone."

Sarah's eyes widened in shock. "Are you suggesting we invite countries we aren't on speaking terms to an international diplomacy meeting? If I did that, my cabinet might try to invoke the twenty-fifth amendment!" She stood up from the couch and walked swiftly back to sit behind her desk. "I sent for you not to advise me on diplomacy but hoping you'd provide insight into the behavior of these otherworldly beings who are bringing us to the brink of destruction. According to your reports from Machu Picchu, you're the only one who knows anything verifiable about them."

David wanted to ask what the twenty-fifth amendment was, but from Sarah's cool response to his grandfather's suggestion, he figured it had something to do with her losing power, so he said nothing.

"That's what I'm trying to do, Sarah. The behavior of those beings who abducted me taught me an important lesson. They're more evolved and powerful on every level than we are. But they're not the ones attacking us now. They'd never intend to harm."

"How can you be so sure?" She waved her hand and news from every corner of the Earth flashed across a GraphoScreen©, filling the walls of the Oval Office with images of one disaster after another. "Have they contacted you again?"

HB shook his head. "I've tried communicating with them telepathically, as I'd done before. But they don't respond. And I think I know why. They've watched what's happened on our planet. They've seen how we've been destroying ourselves, Sarah, and now that we've displayed the full scope of our selfishness and greed by failing to protect our home, our planet, they know others have come to finish the task we began. In the end, this is all our own fault."

"And what are your precious, peaceful aliens doing now?" Sarah asked angrily. "Watching the show and cheering?"

David could no longer contain himself. "No, they're sending us a message by not interfering."

"Really? And what message is that?"

She'd spoken in such a cutting tone of voice; it made David flinch. He took a few breaths and then sat up as straight as he possibly could and looked directly at the president. "It's pretty simple, really. But hard to grasp at the same time."

"Stop talking in riddles, young man. This is no time for games," Sarah shouted.

David hesitated to say anything more. But then he remembered something his mother had taught him: The Creator gives us success when we concern ourselves with the interests of others and are generous toward others. He drew enough strength from that reminder to overcome his fear and speak truth to power. "If we treat everyone on this planet who doesn't look like us, or believe what we believe, or like what we like, as if they're our enemies, pretty soon, we won't have any friends or even any family at all. The Earth is our home; it's everyone's home. We can only really protect this planet if we join together. No

157

one else can save us but ourselves. Like we do in the game."

"That's fine for a game, David. But this is the real world and in the real world I have an obligation to protect this country first and foremost." Sarah crossed her arms as if to signal the conversation was over.

Emboldened, David continued anyway. "But the game's taught us how to stop the attack."

"Us?" Sarah looked at him quizzically. "You mean the U.S.?"

"No, I mean us teenagers, all around the world."

"Teenagers? You can't be serious."

"Well, actually Sarah," HB interrupted, "I've spent years developing the game David's talking about to prepare for exactly the moment we find ourselves in now. It's called R.A.T.S and has trained an entire army of young soldiers."

"I don't believe what I'm hearing," Sarah sputtered, shifting her eyes back and forth between David and HB.

"It's not at all unbelievable. After all, the youth will inherit the world as we leave it. They understand that better than we do. That's why they've been challenging us adults for decades to wake up and listen. But so many of us didn't want to hear what they had to say. We believed we were the experts. And look where we are now. Besides, teenagers are a courageous, powerful force. They're still able to change their minds about the world and see it anew, as something better. If all the teenagers around the world unite, regardless of their country, social class, race, gender, or creed, we'll have a chance to survive."

"Are you out of your mind?" Sarah protested. "How can we fight with an army of children? You're suggesting we put their lives at stake. I'm surprised you had the audacity to present me with this solution. These teenagers have a future."

"What future do we have if the Earth is destroyed?" David asked. "We've got nothing left to lose."

A knock on the door interrupted their conversation.

"Excuse me, Madame President, but your daughter, Becky, needs to see you. I told her you were in a national security briefing, but she says it's urgent," the assistant said.

"Perhaps suspending this conversation for a few minutes will clear all our heads. Do you mind waiting outside while I speak with my daughter?" Sarah stood and gestured toward the door.

"I think Becky wants to talk to us together," David said.

Sarah looked at him as if he'd just uttered gibberish. "And what makes you say that? I suppose you think you can read her mind."

"As a matter of fact, I can. We've been communicating telepathically for several years."

Sarah dropped back into her seat as Becky entered the room.

"It's true, Mom. David, I, and a handful of the more advanced R.A.T.S players send messages through our minds to each other all the time. We've become great friends with people all over the world. Even Sabrina plays sometimes, though she hasn't reached my level. And of course, not David's, he's a major now. Mom, everything he told you about the game is true. It's taught us to work together as a team in small squads. We've accomplished amazing things; we've even come up with strategies to fix the Earth's problems that the greatest scientists hadn't yet imagined were possible. We've had incredible results."

"Both my daughters have been playing this game and I knew nothing about it?" Sarah sounded as if she was talking to herself. "What other surprises are in store for the leader of the free world, I wonder?" she asked, looking to HB for an explanation.

HB took a piece of paper out of his briefcase. "I've prepared the R.A.T.S players for this day, Sarah," he said, handing the paper to her.

"What am I looking at, HB?"

"It's a map of the underground base NASA built under my team's direction in the Mojave Desert, outside Las Vegas. It's called Elias I.E."

"Why did I not know about this before?"

"At the proper time, we were prepared to inform you about the project. We thought everything out before building this underground base, and agreed to use it only if we had no option. We just didn't think we'd need it so soon. I programmed R.A.T.S to replicate scenarios exactly like the one we're in now. The game's controls mirror the controls in the spacecrafts built to take youth to the Moon Station Space Center. Luckily, these teenagers have become insanely accomplished strategists. We kept adapting the game, adding glitches to make it practically impossible to beat. That's how we trained them, measuring their abilities and rewarding their achievements. I guarantee you they know what they're doing and will have everything they need to defend us from this attack."

"And you imagine, HB, that parents will allow their children to do this? I certainly won't."

"Mom... I don't think you understand... We're not afraid... The world needs us." Becky looked to David for support, which gave him an idea. He touched his Spher@ and called his mother while Sarah continued to protest.

"Don't even think about it. You and your sister are the president's daughters; it's out of the question!"

"But you've always taught us to live our lives with integrity. Look at the world now." She gestured again toward the screens filled with horrifying images. "If we don't fight, everything will be destroyed. Please, Mom, without your permission, Sabrina and I can't go. But is the world going to trust a plan if the president won't let her own daughters fight? What kind of leader would that make you?"

Sarah's Spher@ buzzed in her ear. "Rachel, I can't talk now, I'm in the middle... Oh, you know... Yes, yes, he explained that to me...Yes, David's here...I know they're confident, but it's youthful naivety...Oh, I didn't know you gave him your blessing. I suppose I should have realized he wouldn't have come without it... Yes, I am proud of them... I understand, yes... Thank you, Rachel."

She ended the call and looked at her daughter. "I realize Rachel has agreed to allow David to go. But—."

"—Mom, I need you to trust me. Please, give us your blessing," Becky pleaded.

Sarah hesitated a few moments longer and then stood and walked toward her daughter, pulling her into an embrace. Then she held her at arm's length and, with the melancholy smile of a woman about to send her own children into the gaping maw of the unknown, gave her consent. "All right, let's show the world what you're all capable of," she said.

Chapter 12

Together Forever
New Delhi, Same day

Deepak had been on his way to Akshardham, the largest Hindu temple in New Delhi, when David called the assembly of all senior R.A.T.S officers to announce their impending mission. So, he'd messaged David telepathically to say he couldn't attend. Today was a special day, so special he'd have to miss the assembly. For months, he'd planned to meet his beloved Alisha near the temple before the ceremony. It was his only chance to catch her attention without raising his family's suspicion. And with all the horrors he'd witnessed erupting around the world, he suspected the opportunity to meet with her again would soon disappear. When David explained, they'd soon be called to action, he wasn't surprised.

"You have my commitment to whatever plan you determine is necessary," he told David.

"Good. I'm promoting you to Captain. Tutla will call you with more details as soon as I know them."

"I'll be ready when needed," Deepak said and continued toward the temple.

As he approached the temple plaza, his Spher@ rang. It was Tutla.

"We're supposed to travel to Las Vegas, where an underground launch station has been prepared. A special musical signal will summon us to the staging area," Tutla explained.

Deepak gasped at the thought of journeying to a city that was the antithesis of everything he cherished in life. "Las Vegas? That degraded place is filled with sin and waste. It's the last place I'd imagine locating an Earth defense station."

"And that's probably why it's the best place to put it," Tutla laughed.

After their conversation ended, Deepak sat down on the temple steps with a heavy heart, trying to sort out the array of conflicting emotions troubling his thoughts. At nineteen, he was the oldest of the R.A.T.S players, often acting like an honorary big brother to the younger ones, who sometimes got so caught up in the technologically dazzling aspects of the game they lost sight of its more serious dimensions. He was committed to sharing the wisdom of his years with the team and working with them to defend the Earth. But he was also eager to take on other adult responsibilities outside the game like marriage and family.

In the last months, he'd become more determined than ever to marry Alisha, despite the obstacles that stood in their way. They'd met a year ago in the marketplace quite by accident. His mother had sent him there to buy ginger and cumin seeds for the special samosas she wanted to prepare for his birthday feast. Ordinarily, the robot maid would have fetched the spices, but it was out for maintenance. His mother gave her the day off and asked Deepak to get them.

He made his way to the market slowly, slightly disgruntled at having to run such an errand on his birthday. Then, as he rounded the corner to reach the row of spice merchants, he caught sight of a lovely young woman seated at one of the stalls. She wore a simple mustard-colored sari with a matching veil that struggled to prevent her jet-black hair from falling in curly tendrils around her slender shoulders. He watched her arrange coconut shells filled with cardamom and cumin seeds, interweaving the shells with twisted stalks of ginger and skeins of garlic, as if her hands were partnered with those savory objects in an elaborate Kathak dance. He wondered what story she'd created with those gestures and moved closer to discover. She'd constructed a labyrinth in the center of her cloth-covered table. She glanced up at him and quickly looked down, as if embarrassed to see someone of his high caste among the raucous crowd pushing and shoving its way toward the best bargains, littering the already filthy streets with paper and other carelessly discarded debris.

"That's quite a beautiful spiral display," Deepak said. "I hate to disturb it but I'm in need of some of those." He pointed toward the cumin.

Without looking up, she poured a portion from the shell into a small paper sack and placed it near the edge of the table.

"And a stalk of ginger, please," he added, hoping she'd raise her eyes to meet his. Again, she kept her head bowed, placing a long, gnarled root next to the paper parcel.

He thought perhaps if he stood still, saying nothing for a few moments, the silence would provoke her to look at him. She remained still, her patience rousing his curiosity even further. Then he hit on a bold plan.

"Today is my birthday," he announced.

She nodded, pushed the packet toward him, brought her hand to her heart in a gesture of honor and slowly raised her eyes to meet his. Although the corners of her mouth curved upward into a faint smile, Deepak could read a hint of sadness in her expression. He reached into his jacket for his coin purse, but she shook her head to reject payment.

"To honor your day," she said. "May you be blessed with many more."

Deepak had always respected and honored his family's traditions. Yet, like many Indian youth, he failed to see the point in mapping the boundaries of friendship or love by the arbitrary coordinates of caste into which every person in India was born. In fact, he considered such restrictions inhumane. And so, he returned to the market stall, week after week, until his affectionate persistence and dignified manner persuaded Alisha that his love for her was sincere and his will was firm and unbreakable.

Now, sitting on the temple steps, Deepak felt as if he was being torn apart by warring feelings. Anguish at having to leave Alisha behind, not knowing whether he'd even return from the risky mission he was about to undertake with his fellow R.A.T.S, was matched by a growing excitement as he imagined defeating whatever destructive forces were aiming to ruin the planet. A Kshatriya warrior would never run away from a battle. But a man as in love as he was with Alisha wouldn't shy from sanctifying that love before heading into the unknown. He decided they must exchange marriage vows before he departed.

In the near distance, he could see his parents approaching the temple. Soon, he knew, Alisha would arrive with hers. To have even a chance at realizing his plan he needed his mother's support. Since she already understood and supported his devotion to R.A.T.S, he resolved to confide in her about his desire to marry. He felt certain she'd be able to convince his father of how strongly he felt in his soul, not only to duty but also to love.

He stood to greet his father and mother.

"You arrived early, Deepak," his father, Sanjay, said, looking at his watch.

"To enjoy a few moments of quiet before the crowds fill the temple," Deepak said. "Mother, can I speak with you a minute?" he asked.

Indira took her son's hand. "Of course," she said.

"There's no time for chatting, or you'll be late for the ceremony," Sanjay said as an expression of irritation overtook his face like a sudden storm.

Indira turned toward her husband and gave him a look more penetrating and persuasive than a thousand words, indicating she intended to talk to her son now, regardless of the time. Sanjay threw up his hands and walked alone up the temple steps.

It was beginning to rain. His mother gestured toward a sheltered bench and sat down next to her son. "What's troubling you, Deepak?" she asked.

Deepak took a deep breath and explained the game's real purpose to Indira, describing the mission he'd been called to serve.

"I understand now why you must leave tomorrow. Don't be afraid, my love. You've been well prepared for this day. I am proud of your bravery, as I'm sure your father will be."

Deepak shook his head. "Mother, you don't understand. I'm not afraid of fighting or dying. My heart is anguished with a different worry."

"What do you mean, Deepak?" she asked with such a puzzled expression that he touched her arm, hoping to relieve her concern.

"Mom, I've pledged my heart to someone. We love each other and respect each other's dreams so deeply, it's as if I've found a part of me, I never even knew had been missing."

Indira's face burst into an expression of joy as bright as the marigold shawl around her shoulders. "This is news to warm a mother's heart." Then, as suddenly as her face had brightened, a dull look of apprehension overshadowed it, making Deepak realize she knew there was more to the story to tell. "Who is she, Deepak?"

"Her name is Alisha Gupta. She comes from a different family than ours."

Indira rose from the seat and walked a few paces away. The rain had stopped and the leaves of the trees in the nearby Banyan grove glistened like the tears Deepak imagined were now streaking his mother's face. But when she returned to sit next to him again some moments later, he was surprised to see her face was dry, and sensed that she had somehow resolved to defeat any obstacles put in the way of his happiness.

"Listen well to what I'm going to tell you and obey me." She touched his shoulder affectionately. "Many years ago, I was forced to carry out my parents' dreams. My own was destroyed. Out of an odd mixture of fear and respect, I threw away my true love and married your father. Although, in time, I grew to love him in my own way, I was wounded by the loss. I don't want you to make the same mistake. You've always been an excellent son and a boy of great character. You deserve to be happy, and Alisha does too. Go, Deepak, and find Alisha and her parents. Ask them for her hand in marriage today. And if they refuse, then run away. You have my blessing, my beloved son. Go now before your father returns to call us."

Deepak was shocked, as much by his mother's story as by her willingness to bless his betrothal. "Mom, he's going to be very angry."

"Leave your father to me," she said, untying the beige antelope bag she always carried with her and opening it. "Son, this was the only thing I inherited from my parents, and I carry it with me wherever I go." She handed him an antique pocket watch. "This belonged to my grandfather. Keep it with you always as a token of my love."

Deepak turned the watch over. The back was inscribed. "*Ek saath hamesha ke lie,* together forever," he whispered, choking back his own tears.

"I will always be with you, Deepak. The hours of one's life go by too quickly to waste. Now, run, my son; run like the wind."

Deepak embraced his mother and disappeared to look for Alisha.

He found her standing with her parents and sister on the temple steps. He wanted to shout her name, tell her the amazing news, but hesitated. It would do no good to act as if everything were already settled.

Before he could formulate a plan, her eyes met his and she ran toward him, as if unconcerned with her parents' reaction.

"Deepak, Deepak," she cried, falling into his embrace. "You won't believe it; my parents said they'd give us their blessing if your parents agreed. What did your parents say?"

"My mother blessed us with her love and support," Deepak said.

"And your father?" Alisha asked, holding her breath. "Does he approve

"He will after my mother explains everything to him. But there's something else you need to know. I've been called on a mission. I must leave soon."

After Deepak explained what Tutla had told him, Alisha reached up to hold his face in her hands and pulled him into a kiss. "My love, then we have no time to lose. We must marry at once."

"But what if I don't return? You'd be left alone and-"

"*Hush*, beloved! You'll return to me before I'll even have time to miss you," she said with a laugh that made him pick her up and twirl her around, as if neither of them had a care in the world, as if even death's possibility wasn't strong enough to delay love's fulfillment.

Deepak put her down again to discover Mr. and Mrs. Gupta standing nearby. He turned to face them. "Since the moment I met your daughter, I've loved her. I promise to love and respect her all the days of my life. I humbly ask for your daughter's hand in marriage."

Alisha's father put his hand on Deepak's shoulder. "Nothing would make us happier!"

"There's no time to delay, Father," Alisha said. "Deepak must leave soon on an important journey. We must marry today." As she explained to her parents Deepak's role in the planet's defense, their expressions changed from astonishment to admiration, as much for their daughter's courage as for Deepak's.

"Whoever lacks purpose in life, starves their soul of nourishment. You have been called to a sacred task—to save Mother Earth from destruction," Mr. Gupta said and turned to his wife. "As soon as the ceremony has ended, we must return to our village and prepare for our daughter's wedding, which we will host this afternoon. I'm sure everyone in our family will help. After all, we've seen the Earth's suffering. We know nothing can heal it fully except love."

Mrs. Gupta nodded and entered the temple with her husband, followed by Alisha, while Deepak went home to gather his things and left again before his parents returned from the temple, uncertain he'd see them at the ceremony.

In the modest house where Alisha lived, everyone busied themselves preparing bouquets of flowers and displays filled with fruits and nuts for the wedding feast and lighting candles and incense, transforming the humble residence as if by magic into a beautiful setting. Other relatives and friends helped the bride decorate her simple dress with borrowed jewels and paint her hands with henna tattoos.

Alone in another room, Deepak dressed in a long, fitted, burgundy shirt and loose, tan-colored leggings—wedding clothes he'd borrowed from Alisha's older, married brother. By now, his parents should have appeared. Since he'd received no news of their arrival, he assumed they weren't coming.

His parents' absence on this auspicious day felt almost unbearable. He touched the antique watch he'd pinned to the embroidered shirt's pocket, silently thanking his mother for her strength and devotion, and his father for teaching him to have integrity, even if it meant defying tradition. A current of sadness disrupted the flow of happiness that had been coursing through him like a wild river as he recalled the loving words inscribed on the watch. He knelt in the room for a few moments, praying to

Vishnu, the sustainer of the universe and God of compassion.

"May my mother's wisdom persuade my father to bless this day and the journey on which I will soon embark," he murmured. Then he rose, pushing a feathered turban onto his head, and left the dressing room to walk toward the patio.

A few feet before reaching the wedding tent, he was stopped in his tracks by the sight of his father dressed in his finest attire waiting to greet him.

"Father, I am honored by your presence," Deepak said in a trembling voice. "Honored and grateful."

"As you might imagine, I was shocked when your mother told me you intended to marry, even without my permission."

"Father, I apologize for—"

Sanjay raised his hand. "No need. Your wise mother erased my anger with her eloquence."

Deepak gave his father a mystified look.

"Her marriage is a sign of mutual love and respect between families. Marry her, she said, with all your heart, and you will remind everyone that harmony is still possible in our divided, fragile world. I have come to bless your wedding, my son."

Overjoyed, Deepak bowed deeply to his father.

His father embraced him. "Let us go now to offer a prayer to Ganesh, remover of obstacles, and join your mother on the *mandap* to await your beautiful bride," Sanjay said. Then he escorted Deepak to the marriage altar under the tent, where Indira was already seated, smiling.

That night, the young lovers slept together in a candlelit room and caressed each other with kisses and embraces until dawn's light appeared like a gentle, golden angel creeping into the room. Deepak rose from the marriage bed, kissed Alisha gently on her still-sleeping eyes, and began the long journey to whatever future lay ahead of him in Las Vegas and beyond.

Chapter 13

While HB continued briefing Sarah in preparation for the world leaders' meeting, Becky gave David a tour of the White House.

"I never realized how huge this place is!" David exclaimed, marveling at the polished marble walls, the floors covered in plush, burgundy carpeting, and the huge chandeliers dangling like gigantic, illuminated jellyfish along the wide corridors and hallways of the West Wing.

"There are hundred and thirty-two rooms, thirty-five bathrooms, and six different levels in the President's House," Becky said, sounding very much like a professional guide. "Would you like to see where the First Family resides?"

"That'd be awesome," David said. He stopped for a second to admire a bust of Abraham Lincoln. The statue was carved out of green marble and displayed on a pedestal in a far corner of the room they'd wandered into. "He looks really sad and worried, like the future he'd dreamed about hadn't turned out the way he'd hoped it would after all."

"The great task remains before us, the living," Becky said in a low, somber voice.

"What?" David looked at her quizzically.

"It's a line from the Gettysburg Address, the speech Lincoln gave on the site of the bloodiest battle of our civil war. We had to memorize it in high school. I remember thinking it was a pretty dumb assignment until I realized it was exactly the right thing to get us young people to do—imprint the message deep in our brain cells about why we should dedicate ourselves to a cause until everyone is free and equal. I guess that's why I like the game so much. It makes me feel like I'm doing my part to keep hope for a better world alive."

David felt his heart swell with so much affection for Becky he couldn't resist giving her a hug. He thought it took courage to stand up to her mother like she did. Courage and commitment to the same principles he believed in—compassion and helping those in need and loving your neighbor as much as yourself. If they hadn't been standing in a part of the White House filled with people, he might have kissed her right then, and might have confessed that he felt like they were becoming more than just friends.

"C'mon," Becky said, breaking the spell, "let's take the elevator up to our private quarters."

Half an hour later, they'd finished touring the family's living quarters and were about to head back downstairs to the briefing room, when David decided to share something he'd been thinking about ever since the president had agreed to include all states and territories across the globe in the emergency meeting she was calling. He touched Becky's arm. She stopped walking and turned to face him. He cleared his throat.

"After your mother proposes the defense plan, I want to be the one to explain R.A.T.S and introduce the youth teams to the world's leaders." David waited for Becky's reaction. From the confused look on her face, he figured she didn't think it was a good idea. "Or do you think it's not my place?"

"Have you been reading my mind without telling me?" she asked.

"Of course not," he said, shaking his head for emphasis.

"Because I was going to suggest that same thing to my mother," Becky said. "And also say that I want to be the one to introduce you to the assembly. After all, each of us played a part in convincing her about R.A.T.S." She crossed her arms, her green eyes flashing with confidence.

The urge to kiss her bubbled up inside David again. He glanced quickly over her shoulder and saw no one in sight. So, he uncrossed her arms, pulled her closer, and grazed her lips with a gentle kiss. Her soft lips tasted like summer cherries.

She rested her head on his shoulder for a few seconds and then whispered into his ear. "I've been hoping you'd do that for some time now."

"Me too," David admitted, holding her at arm's length and smiling. "I just had to find the courage."

Becky laughed so hard that tears came to her eyes.

"What's so funny?" David asked.

"You're the bravest person I know. You're ready to confront space aliens but kissing a girl makes you nervous."

David reddened with embarrassment. "Okay, so you've discovered my Achilles' heel, but you better keep it to yourself." He poked her gently on the shoulder with a mock-serious expression on his face.

"Your secret's safe with me, major." She pointed to an antique clock in the hallway. "Anyway, we better get going or my mother will send the Secret Service to find us."

"Give me five minutes," David said. "I must alert the R.A.T.S to what's about to happen. Where's the nearest room where I can have privacy?"

"There's an office down the hall. I'll show you."

Becky led him into a small room a few steps down the corridor. He opened a Spher@, touched his chip-finger to a button on the screen, and accessed the game. He didn't have time to wait for everyone to appear, so he messaged Tutla, intending to ask him to put out the word. After a few seconds, when Tutla didn't show up, he called him telepathically.

"Tutla, where are you?"

"You'll never believe it, David. All the tribes of the surrounding region met us at the Canyon rim to escort me to the desert when needed. We can arrive in Las Vegas in three days."

David was perplexed. "I didn't think Las Vegas was that far from your reservation."

"We follow the ways of the ancestors when we head into battle. We would be traveling on horseback."

David imagined how excited his friend must be to be honored by such multi-tribal support. It gave him hope that the rest of the nations of the world might also set aside their petty disagreements and unite around a common goal. "Tutla, I'm heading into the meeting now. If all goes well, the President of the United States will announce our mission within the next hour or so. Inform the R.A.T.S to stay tuned to the news."

"Yes, sir!" Tutla said. "Ready to meet you in Las Vegas."

"I sure hope so," David replied.

David changed out of his food service uniform into a clean white shirt and blue pants the Secret Service had given him to use before he and Becky joined HB, Sarah, John Singer, and the head of Homeland Security in the briefing room. The meeting of all the world's leaders was about to begin. Sarah agreed to have HB provide an overview of the origin of the threats facing the world. Then, David would introduce the R.A.T.S mission, followed by Sarah's appeal for diplomatic unity. She hadn't wanted Becky to be showcased at the meeting, fearing someone could use her participation to sabotage the project somehow. Although Becky had been disappointed, she'd conceded that her mother had a point.

As they were seating themselves around the meeting table, John turned to HB. "From all the verified reports we've received in recent years, yours is the only one that explains what's happening today. I'm sorry for all the damage I caused you in the past with my doubts about your research. When we went to Machu Picchu, I was young and very ambitious. I thought it would ruin my reputation to be associated with UFO reports. I apologize. I was wrong."

"Apology accepted," HB said and shook John's hand. "Now let's get to work."

Screens filling every wall displayed images of cataclysmic disasters wreaking havoc across the globe. No corner of the Earth had been left untouched by fires or mudslides or earthquakes or floods, devastating evidence of the consequences wrought by the long decades humans had spent willfully ignoring science. In the grip of fear and selfishness, a greedy scramble for money had overtaken more and more people's lives, spreading hatred between neighbors and even within families and polluting the planet's atmosphere with the poisonous fumes from hostility and lies. Now, alien invaders' steady depletion of all the Earth's waters had multiplied all that human-made wreckage into something nightmarish in proportion. Seeing the scope of damage made David tremble with worry. He steadied himself. Better not dwell on the horror film playing before his eyes. That would only invite fear to materialize in the room like some sinister, invading snake, swallowing the possibility of action in its snapping jaws. He resolved to confront the reality of catastrophe with the blunt instrument of hope.

Within moments, more than a hundred holograms of all the world's leaders appeared in the conference room. They were seated at their desks, eager to hear the president's report. Not only were all the countries of the NATO alliance present, but also representatives from China, North and South Korea, the Arab nations, Israel, the entire African continent, India, all of South and Central America, a host of smaller states and territories, and even Vatican City.

Becky looked at David, astounded by the size of the assembly. "This is amazing. I didn't think they'd all turn up."

"I wasn't sure either, but I'm glad I pushed for it," David said.

Hundreds of tiny lights lit up in front of the world leaders' desks as John introduced Sarah. "Ladies and gentlemen, world leaders, the President of the United States, Sarah Esther Hoffman!"

Wearing a serious expression on her face, Sarah walked up to a podium. "Assembled leaders, we are grateful for your attendance today in this hour of Earth's greatest need. We have reached a critical moment, unlike anything we've confronted before, where we must decide the future of the planet. No part of the Earth remains untouched by damage, no safe haven exists to hide from global destruction." She gestured toward the graphic images around the walls. "Yet, I believe that what we have witnessed so far is minor compared to what lies ahead." The room filled with a low murmur of shocked voices. "I have invited General HB Williams to present the findings of a research project he's directed for several decades and ask for your patience as he explains his unsettling report. General," she said, inviting HB to the podium.

"Good evening. As I'm sure you're all aware, our planet is in chaos. Around the world, both the military and local security forces have exhausted themselves trying to control the catastrophic situations we face—extreme climate changes in the last twenty-four hours, rising levels of panic, outbreaks of civil unrest, and incidents of unspeakable violence around the globe. We're under enormous pressure to overcome whatever differences have divided us in the past, if we are to have even the chance of survival." HB paused and reached into a folder he'd carried with him in the room, taking out some papers. "For more than two decades, the U.S. Air Force conducted an immense research project into extraterrestrial life. The summary reports of those investigations were sent to you electronically."

"Just a minute," the President of China interrupted. "We've read your reports. I, for one, found them ridiculous. Alien abductions. That gave me a good laugh."

"I wasn't convinced either," the North Korean President chimed in. "The idea of an alien threat sounded like typical U.S. propaganda designed to persuade us into abandoning our own defense systems, which, in our case, are the most sophisticated in the world."

"With all due respect to my Chinese and North Korean colleagues, we've been able to verify those reports independently," Rosana Kelter, the President of Germany interjected. "In fact, we've tracked the spaceships heading toward us. My question is, General HB, are they the same ones you had contact with years ago?"

"That's an absurd question," the Chinese president sputtered. "It assumes that he *was* abducted."

"I understand abduction sounds implausible. However, I assure you, I spent a year with beings of immense intelligence and dignity, although when I was brought back, only thirty days had passed here on Earth," HB said.

"General, please, could you explain more specifically what happened during that time?" the Prime Minister of Norway asked. "We, too, have had verification of alien sightings, as have our Chinese neighbors, though they prefer to deny it." She smiled at the Chinese president, who dismissed her with a wave of his hand.

The briefing room fell silent as HB recounted his surreal experience on the aliens' planet, explaining how the energetic beings of light he'd met were not hostile forces but were beacons of peace, who had welcomed him. "We finally had proof that extraterrestrials existed," he concluded. "And to answer the President of Germany's earlier question about whether these are the beings attacking us now, I'm certain they're not. They treated me with extraordinary kindness and respect."

The Turkish president shook his fist in anger. "How can you be so sure? For that matter, how can *we* be so sure you're not tempting us into an elaborate trap? Perhaps you struck a deal with those precious aliens of yours and are trying now to lull the rest of us to sleep with some mumbo-jumbo about world peace while you secretly carry out a plot with them to dominate the world."

"If anyone struck a secret deal with the aliens, it's more likely it was the Chinese," the Prime Minister of the Netherlands countered.

As a few of the more conspiracy-minded leaders nodded assent, David squirmed in his seat. He nudged his grandfather, who had paused to scribble something on a piece of paper. HB offered him a wink of reassurance and passed the note to David. "One must be strict with oneself and tolerant with others," the note read. David nodded and smiled to himself.

HB continued to address the critics and doubters. "The idea of bringing us together isn't mumbo-jumbo. And to prove that we have no intention of tricking you, I've been authorized to reveal the location of the secret planetary defense system we established in case of an attack by a more malevolent force." He called up a map of the base on a screen visible to everyone. "This fortified base is located in the Mojave Desert, close to Las Vegas. Using reverse-engineered technology from crashed extraterrestrial space crafts, we've equipped it with advanced space machines capable of interplanetary surveillance and flight that would have taken us hundreds of years to develop."

"Then what's the plan, general?" Kunihiro Myamoto, the Japanese premier, asked.

"We plan to assemble an immense defensive force to launch a counterattack against the aliens stealing the Earth's resources."

Confusion murmured through the crowd.

"What army are you referring to? You've already acknowledged that every nation's military personnel have been overwhelmed by the chaos in their regions," Annie Heilberg from South Africa pointed out. "In my own region, our forces have been battling an outbreak of diseases from areas polluted with toxic waste, and levels of drought beyond anything the continent has experienced before. It's become impossible to provide food and safe drinking water to most of the sub-Saharan populations."

"Here, too, disease and starvation are overtaxing our resources. And now, even the waters of the sacred Ganges have shrunk to a sickly trickle," the Prime Minister of India added.

HB raised his hands to halt the discussion. "I understand all your concerns. That's why, with a game that's been in development for more than twenty years, we've trained one of the most talented and qualified armies ever imagined. A planetary-wide army, made up of millions of soldiers. You may have heard of the game, R.A.T.S, but not know its real purpose. With scenarios very much like the one we're facing right now, depicting massive interstellar warfare, we've created a highly qualified army of teen warriors, excelling in skills, tactics, and intelligence. They are our only chance of survival."

All the world leaders looked at HB with a sense of disbelief.

"You must be out of your mind," shouted another leader. "Our youth are our future. Those of us who have experienced the devastation of the twentieth century's worst crimes against humanity would never tolerate casting the future generation to the lions."

"I have to underscore the Israeli prime minister's point," Mr. Kunihiro said, nodding to the previous speaker. "After Hiroshima, I, too, would never be willing to sacrifice our nation's future leaders to this folly."

One after another, the world's leaders rose to speak their dissent, until HB gestured to David. "I would like to introduce my grandson, Major David, one of the game's most accomplished warriors. What he has to say should set all your doubts aside."

David gathered together every ounce of fortitude stored in his heart and walked to the podium. He looked out at the sea of disgruntled holographic faces staring at him from every corner of the vast, embattled world. Then, he looked over at Becky, whose bright smile of encouragement fortified his will. Besides her loving support, he felt the power of meditation and prayer renew his courage and give him the strength to begin to speak.

"Many have gone through dark times before these and been wounded by things that should never have been allowed to happen. But we, who are young, have gone through our own dark times in these recent years. The spread of disease, the violent rupture of the Earth, the loss of many species of animals and plants, the outbreak of so much corruption and hostility have made us feel more and more isolated, as if the world were disappearing and we were alone, cut off from each other, living in a bubble." David called up various images to amplify his points. From around the world, records of the decades of youth calling for action appeared on the surrounding screens. "But when we discovered the game, R.A.T.S, we found a way to reconnect and began to feel as if we were the generation that would change division into cooperation.

"We learned R.A.T.S was inspired by an old folk tale some of you will recognize—the story of the Pied Piper of Hamelin, who promised to help a smalltown suffering from a rat infestation. The terrorized citizens of the city accepted his offer to help and promised him a reward. He played a mysterious tune and led the rats out of the city to drown in the river. When the people refused to pay him for his services, he returned to the town and lured the children of Hamelin with his eerie music, and they were never seen again."

"You're making our point," one of the leaders opposed to the plan said with a smirk. "We don't want to sacrifice our youth to a doomed cause!"

"I know that folktale has a dark ending. But R.A.T.S players see it differently. To us teens, the Pied Piper's haunting music represents our call to rid evil from our lives by defending ourselves against these extraterrestrials trying to annihilate us.

"Twenty years ago, Marcia Sisla addressed the world. She said 'The planet cries out in agony, its forests ablaze and seas swallowing lands. The future watches us, silent and severe; change now or face the abyss.' The world refused to listen. But the youth of today are united behind this mission. Neither religion, nor money, nor country, nor sex, nor race can divide us. Through the R.A.T.S game, we have become 'Guardians of the World.' In every nation, state, territory, on every continent on this once-beautiful planet, a team leader has been prepared to answer the call to action. We are ready for the ultimate test."

David looked around the room. No one said a word. Finally, the President of Angola stood. "The words just spoken were exactly what needed to be said. To hear a boy in the White House with the consent of the President of the United States announce the plan to save the world must mean we truly have reached the moment when the world is about to end. We cannot afford to waste a moment deliberating this action." Then, like the cresting of a wave against a beach, the assembly erupted in applause. After allowing David a few moments of recognition for the power of his speech, Sarah stood to quiet the assembly.

"The time has come for a decision. Let me begin by announcing that the United States of America fully supports this plan."

One by one, the world's leaders indicated their unanimous consent.

When the voting ended, Sarah made an announcement. "Tonight, we will inform the entire planet about what we have learned here about the impending apocalypse and about what we must sacrifice to achieve victory. We will activate a Planetary Emergency Alert System on every communication device available to broadcast this message: "The Day of Judgment has arrived. Our planet stands on the threshold of destruction from an imminent, extraterrestrial attack. The only way forward is to unite across our differences and defend our planet with our strongest, most dedicated, and most courageous forces. All teens ranked in the video game R.A.T.S are immediately called to service. You are the only hope of survival. G-d protect us all."

David's Spher@ rang in his ear, announcing his promotion to Commander of R.A.T.S. He switched his device to a private R.A.T.S channel, sending the mystical vibrations of the tune HB had received from those wondrous beings of light into the ears of every R.A.T.S player in every corner of the globe. The time had come to leave their homes and make their way to Las Vegas.

***

Hearing the sounds signaling the R.A.T.S mobilization, Roy and Butch danced a jig of celebration.

"Guess we best be heading to the city of sin, my friend." Roy clapped Butch on the back.

"Couldn't ask for a sweeter spot for revenge than that big flashy billboard of a town. Let's show them who's the real boss of this here planet!" Butch said, high-fiving his partner in crime.

Chapter 14

The Blessings
Dubai and Nepal, Israel, New York, and Various
Locations, Same Day

In a far corner of the luxurious, two-story house floating below the waters of the Persian Gulf, where Omar lived with his family in Dubai, his computer played a passionate, rousing song. He recognized the signal. It was time to join his friends and prepare to defend the Earth. He walked over to a thick window that filled the semi-circular wall of his room across from his bed and watched a school of giant tang fish swim past, their bright blue, yellow-tailed bodies swaying together in the azure waters. So far, the waters around Dubai hadn't experienced the mysterious forces that had been draining the sea around Aruba. As he thought about how this underwater paradise and all its inhabitants would disappear if the R.A.T.S weren't successful at their mission, a sense of dread crept into his body, making it hard to breathe. But what troubled him even more than the possibility of failure was having to deliver the news to his father that he, Omar Abdallah, son of Fauze Abdallah, a highly respected, immensely wealthy businessman and prominent member of the Muslim community, was going to war to defend the Earth. He shuddered at the thought of explaining to his father about the game he'd become an expert in, a game his father had forbidden him to play. He expected his father would be furious when he told him he'd been trained to become a warrior in a youth army.

Then he remembered what Namkhai had said. *Our parents raised us with the values that bring us together to defend this beautiful planet.* Perhaps, Omar thought, he would find the inspiration and strength to approach his own father by talking with his young friend. He looked at the digital numbers on the wall behind his bed. There were only a few hours before he was supposed to board a plane commissioned by the government to send volunteers from the Gulf region to Las Vegas. He called Namkhai on his Spher@.

"Hey, how's it going, dude?" Omar tried to sound calm, but his insides were doing somersaults. "Are you ready for the big adventure?"

"Yes. I just returned from praying at the Potala Palace with the oldest monks. They sent me off with prayers and garlands of flowers," Namkhai said.

"Everything's cool with your mom and dad, then?" Omar asked, almost afraid to hear Namkhai's answer.

"Yes. They told me they have seen the world's pain. They said the Earth is suffering because, for too long now, its people have known the price of everything but the value of nothing. They embraced me and gave me their blessing. And your father, what did he say?"

Omar swallowed hard. "That's the thing... I haven't told him yet. I need your help."

"I had a feeling that's why you called. Then, let us meditate together for a few moments to bring peace into your soul and love into your heart," Namkhai suggested.

"Okay, if you think it'll help," Omar said.

"Your thoughts are like a thousand chattering monkeys disturbing your soul's aim. Close your eyes, rest your hands on your knees. Take a deep cleansing breath in and out slowly, slowly. Allow your mind to still… Imagine a candle burning in a dark corner of your room… Bring all your attention to that light… It is a shimmering beacon of peace, growing brighter and brighter…"

As he listened to Namkhai's soothing words, Omar felt the heavy burden of worry drift away. "Thanks, Namkhai," he said. "You may be young but you sure are wise."

Omar found his father in the living room on the floor above. He was in an agitated state, walking in circles and shaking his fist at the images projected on the GraphoScreen©. "Son, I've just learned that another horror has been added to the earthquakes we suffered last week and the many other catastrophes occurring around the world: We face an alien attack. We must go to the mosque and ask Allah to restore order and peace to our planet. Many young people from our community will join others from around the world. They've been trained to fight these foes trying to destroy us. We will pray for all who are involved in this project. Call Mr. Jamal and tell him to have the helicopter ready." His father stopped pacing and turned toward him. "Why are you still standing there? Haven't you heard what I said? Call Mr. Jamal at once."

Omar took a deep breath, stood tall, and looked directly at his father. "Dad, I have something to tell you. You know that game you told me not to play anymore? Well, it's called R.A.T.S and—" Before he could finish his sentence, his father had crossed the floor and grabbed him by the shoulders.

"—Have you disobeyed me? Have you been wasting your time with that ridiculous distraction instead of studying?"

"I *have* been studying, Dad… But, yes, I've also been playing the game. And, Dad, believe it or not, I'm so good at the game I've been promoted to lieutenant and been called up to lead a team into battle."

Mr. Abdallah's face reddened in anger. Omar knew his father would never raise a hand to him, but he could feel his father's rage coursing through his fingers like white heat as he gripped Omar's shoulders even more tightly. "I don't believe what you're telling me. Have you no respect? How dare you disregard my rules?"

Omar began to shake. In his head, he recited a mantra Namkhai taught him to regain his composure as he tried to explain why he'd kept playing the game. "Father, I meant no disrespect. But you've always taught me that my actions and words must bring good into the world to counter all the damage done by ignorance, ill will, and harmful words. R.A.T.S players believe in and practice these things; that's why we're prepared to battle against those attacking us now."

His father loosened his grip and held Omar at arm's length, giving him a stern look. "You are my eldest, Omar. I need you to understand your role in this family. With the terrible things we've seen happening across the globe, it's important for us to remain together as a family, safe in the home I've worked so hard to build. Your siblings need you during this time of crisis, as do I. If your mother were alive, she'd certainly oppose your leaving."

Omar flinched at the mention of his mother. How he wished she were with him now. "I don't think so, Dad. Even if she'd worry about whether I'd survive the battle, she'd understand why I needed to leave. Besides, each one of us R.A.T.S is someone's son or daughter; most of us have siblings. Mom would understand that I've been called to save the future not only for our own families but for everyone's."

Tears swelled in Mr. Abdullah's eyes. "Your mother was a woman as wholesome and beautiful in soul as she was in body. When you speak with such conviction in your voice and passion in your eyes, you remind me so much of her I feel the pain of her loss all over again. Perhaps that's why I want to keep you close, especially now." He embraced his son and then clasped Omar's hands tightly in his own. "*Allahu Akbar*! You must go, my son. I won't oppose you a moment longer. You have my blessing! Your mother would recite words more beautiful than mine, but I lack her poetry. So, I will simply say, I bless you, my son. My prayers and all the community's prayers will be with you."

Omar hugged his father again, feeling as if he were floating on a cloud. "Thank you, Dad. I disobeyed you by playing the game, but I would never have gone on the mission without your blessing."

"Omar, you may have broken my rule, but you obeyed a higher calling. Now, tell me, what do you need?"

"I must be at the airport in less than two hours. We've received word that planes are waiting to take us to the launch station. Perhaps Mr. Jamal can take me."

"No, son, I will take you. Now, hurry and get ready. I must tell your brothers we're about to send off Omar Abdallah, the great warrior of our family!"

Omar was so excited when his father left him at the airport, he wanted to tell Namkhai about how much he'd helped him. But before he called his young friend to thank him, another thought crossed Omar's mind—maybe some of the others were facing opposition from their families and could use his support. Rather than celebrate his own good fortune with Namkhai, he decided to check in on Chava and the New York gals, Mariana and Juliana. Thinking those New Yorkers had enough moxie not to be stopped once they decided to do something, he sent a telepathic message to Chava in Israel first.

"Hey girl, are you all packed and ready to bounce?" he asked, sounding like his usual, carefree self once again.

"Not yet," Chava said. "My brother, Reuven, heard the news announcement and decided he wanted to go too. He's in his room packing a bag. So now I have to figure out how to stop him from doing something stupid before I can explain anything to my parents."

"Is he good at the game? How old is he?" Omar asked.

"Almost thirteen," Chava said. "He's never played; he's only watched me."

"Well, girl, that settles it," Omar said. "He's too young and not qualified."

"But he's stubborn. And he's really good with computers. He says he'll mess everything up for me with my parents if I don't take him with me."

Omar thought for a moment. His younger brother, Rashid, was the same age as Chava's and just as stubborn. He told Chava how Rashid had thrown a fit when he heard Omar was going to space to defend the Earth, and learned he was too young to go with him. He wailed, insisting Omar should stay home too. His father finally calmed him, explaining that there were moments for everyone, and now was Omar's moment to defend that planet. "Perhaps you know someone besides your father who could give that lesson to Reuven," Omar said.

Chava paused for a few moments. Omar could almost hear the synapses in her brain firing with ideas. "OMG, Omar. I've got it. Our rabbi! He's been preparing Reuven for his Bar Mitzvah; he'll know what to do about my brother and my parents. Thanks, Omar. You're a lifesaver."

"I'm just paying it forward, my sister, Chava," he said and told her about his conversation with Namkhai. "Let me know how it goes."

"Okay. Bye, Omar."

"Bye, Chava."

A few hours later, Omar's plane was about to take off from the Dubai airport, loaded with youth—not only hundreds of Muslims, but also teenagers from the large community of expatriate groups of Hindus, Christians, Buddhists, and Sikhs who lived and worked in the emirate. Omar was seated next to a Christian boy named Phillipo, who told him his parents had worked as cooks in the restaurant of one of its most luxurious hotels, until the building had been damaged by fires that broke out after the earthquake. "When they saw all the destruction, and learned I was an expert R.A.T.S player called to serve in this mission, they told me how proud they were of my courage. My mother even gave me this to wear." He pointed to a silver cross dangling on a long chain around his neck. "It belonged to her grandmother. She said it would protect me from harm."

Omar smiled and nodded. He knew his mother would have given him something special to carry with him, had she still been alive. But what he carried with him now was just as powerful a protection, even if it had no material quality—his father's love, understanding, and blessing.

The plane gathered speed as it headed down the runway and began to climb into the clouds. Omar looked out the window and gasped at the sight of the damage the city had sustained from the wicked storms that had swept through the region like furious witches. The tall spires of once graceful skyscrapers were bent and distorted into ugly shapes. Everywhere, debris littered the modern landscape, turning the modern city into a dump. Then, as the plane ascended higher, the city took on the shape of an enormous palm tree and, higher still, transformed again into some thin, many-armed creature, its outstretched arms reaching across the sea, as if begging for mercy from the heavens. Omar remembered what his father had once told him. He'd said "to know Allah was to know love". Sitting in that cabin filled with young people so very different and yet so very like him, Omar understood then exactly what his father had meant. Everywhere, in everything, one could feel the energy of the Creator.

Chava's voice broke into his consciousness just then. "Omar, you won't believe where I am." She sounded excited. "I'm on an El Al jet heading for New York. Mariana and Juliana are meeting me at the airport. We're going to fly to Vegas together."

"I guess your rabbi put your brother in his place."

"Something like that." Chava laughed. "I got Reuven to go with me to Rabbi Noach's house. Reuven insisted on taking his backpack. He thought it would show the rabbi how prepared he was. Okay, I said. But I made him promise he'd follow the rabbi's advice, no matter what.

"We snuck out while our parents were busy preparing for Shabbat. The rabbi's house is near ours. When we got there, Rabbi Noach was in a hurry to get to the Kotel, the Wailing Wall, to pray with everyone for peace. But he never denies anyone who comes to his door in need. And boy, was I in need. So, he invited us in.

"I told him everything—that Reuven wasn't experienced in the game and that I was afraid of my parents finding out about my role in R.A.T.S before I had a chance to explain—and I asked for his advice. He sat down behind his desk. He had such a worried look on his face, I thought for a second he was going to call my parents. But he didn't. Instead, he asked Reuven if he'd gotten the call to the mission, like I had. When my brother said no, rabbi got up, walked over to him and put his hand on my brother's shoulder. What he did next was so amazing it almost made me cry.

"He told Reuven it was not possible to love G-d if you don't know him. Then he asked him if he believed there was a time for everything. Reuven nodded. 'And do you know where that idea comes from, Reuven?' My brother shook his head, saying no, he didn't. 'Well then,' the rabbi said, 'I will read something special to you now and you must listen carefully. These words are the counsel of a very wise man, King Solomon.' Then he read to my brother:

Everything has an appointed season, and there is a time for every matter under the heaven.

A time to give birth and a time to die; a time to plant and a time to uproot that which is planted.

A time to kill and a time to heal; a time to break and a time to build.

A time to weep and a time to laugh; a time of wailing and a time of dancing.

A time to cast stones and a time to gather stones; a time to embrace and a time to refrain from embracing.

A time to seek and a time to lose; a time to keep and a time to cast away.

A time to rend and a time to sew; a time to be silent and a time to speak.

A time to love and a time to hate, a time for war and a time for peace.

"Rabbi explained that since Reuven hadn't been called to this mission, it must be for a reason. 'There must be a greater calling for you here, a wonderful purpose G-d has for your life, the reason why you came into this world. To honor and obey that calling is far better than to sacrifice yourself without reason. Think with your mind, not with your heart because the heart can mislead. Be patient and wait for the right time to act. Then, you will receive blessings!' he said.

"He told my brother to hug me and go home, because our parents would be worried and needed him. He invited Reuven to go with him to the Kotel later that day, saying that the work of praying is just as arduous as fighting. Then he turned to me and said 'Don't forget to say your kabbalistic prayers and meditations, Chava. They might save your life! And tell David we are praying for him. Now, go; I'll explain everything to your parents.'"

Omar was happy for Chava. But he couldn't help thinking something was missing from the story she'd told him. "Did you just leave, I mean, without getting permission from your parents?"

"Of course not!" Chava replied. "I felt so excited by the rabbi's support, I ran home to tell them myself. And you know what, Omar? I had nothing to worry about after all. I don't know how, but they knew everything about R.A.T.S. They even knew I'd been promoted to lead a team."

"That's awesome," Omar said. "Are they telepathic, or what?"

Chava giggled. "No. I guess sometimes we don't know our parents as well as we think we do."

Omar continued checking in with friends around the world. Hearing heartwarming stories from everyone about how families, and even whole neighborhoods, were uniting to support the teenagers' bravery filled him with joy. He imagined threads from all of these stories weaving themselves into a pattern of stars like a bright constellation of hope shimmering in the night sky.

Chapter 15

A Time for Everything
Aruba, Same day

A time to cast stones and a time to gather stones; a time to embrace and a time to refrain from embracing. A time to seek and a time to lose; a time to keep and a time to cast away. – Ecclesiastes

Yes, Rachel thought, there was a time for everything and the time had come for her to continue along the pathway she'd glimpsed hours earlier, unfurling before her like a long, silver ribbon of light pulling her toward the stars. She'd been called to release her son, David, from her embrace to help the wounded world heal. She'd been called to help her friend, Sarah, do the same with her daughters. As she closed the book of prayers, she'd been reading, she looked at the ring glowing brightly on her finger and wondered what else she'd be called to do along the way.

Outside her study window, she saw the waters in the fountain glistening in the light of the crescent moon and realized it was well past dinnertime. In the chaos of the day, they'd forgotten to eat. The body must remain healthy for the mind to be made strong with principle, she thought, and was about to tell Sonic to prepare the dining table for a meal when she noticed a small group of people gathered near the entryway to the courtyard. Wondering who they could be, she opened the glass door of her study that led to the front porch and walked across the courtyard to greet them, immediately recognizing the man standing at the front of the group. It was her good friend, Yftach, who was the director of an Aruban relief center for refugees.

"Rachel, I'm sorry to bother you, but I have an urgent request," he said in a low voice. "Thousands remain stranded at the airport. We've filled all the island's hotel rooms, but many are still without shelter and the situation is worsening by the hour. Fights have broken out as people scramble for a safe space to wait out the disaster. Many stores have been looted. I thought perhaps you might have room for this family for a few days until flights resume and they can get home to Argentina?" Yftach stood aside to introduce the family to her. "This is Diogo and Antonia Fernandez and their daughters, Vitoria, Rosa Maria, and Zeze."

"*Con mucho gusto.*" Rachel extended her hand to the parents whose faces lit up when she spoke to them in their native Spanish. The children were trying their best to appear brave but Rachel could tell by the way they lowered their eyes and fidgeted with their clothes how frightened they were. The oldest girl, Vitoria, was wearing a prosthetic device on the lower half of her right leg. She was a lovely girl, probably a year or so younger than David. Rachel wondered how she'd lost the leg but didn't want to embarrass the girl by asking. The girl looked up for a moment and smiled slightly, then quickly looked away again. "Let me talk with Kenneth. I'll be right back."

Rachel found Kenneth in the kitchen, preparing food and discussing something animatedly with Daniel. "Dushi," she said, using a term of endearment to catch his attention, "I need to talk with you right away."

"What is it, *Amor*?" He put down the knife he'd been using to chop vegetables for a salad and waited for Rachel to explain.

"There's a family at our gate in need of shelter for a few days. Yftach brought them here. They're from Argentina and have been stranded, since all flights have now been canceled. We have plenty of room here and enough food. I'd like to invite them to stay in our guesthouse and join us for dinner tonight. They look exhausted and hungry."

Kenneth smiled at her with an expression of surprise mixed with relief. "When we give to others, we receive. Isn't that what we always say, Dushi? I believe their being here will be a much-needed blessing."

Rachel turned her head to the side and gave her husband a quizzical look. He was a generous man, but he seemed especially eager to welcome the guests. "I'm happy to hear you agree with me, Kenneth, but what makes you say having them here will be a much-needed blessing?" She suspected she understood his reason.

Kenneth glanced at Daniel. "Are you going to explain, or should I?"

"Explain what?" Rachel turned to Daniel. Her eyes widened as she noticed his backpack hung over the chair in the corner. Yes, it was as she'd thought. Without hesitation, she called her son to her. "Daniel, come here, my love." She opened her arms to hug her eldest son, holding him close for a moment. "I understand. There's no way you can remain behind while David is risking his life to defend the Earth. You must go to help your brother. Your father and I will give you our blessing." She signaled for Kenneth to join her and together they embraced Daniel. "May you both return to us safely," she said. "Now, please go tell our guests we have more than enough room for them while I talk with your father."

After Daniel had left the room, Kenneth opened his mouth to speak but Rachel raised her hand and shook her head. "You don't have to say anything, Dushi. I already know what you must do, too. HB explained everything to me when we spoke before he landed in Washington. He told me your designs were used to develop the spacecrafts that will take the teens to the moon station. No matter how much you want to encourage the youth to take on leadership roles, I can't imagine you'd be able to live with yourself if you didn't use all your skills as an engineer to make sure the entire mission went off safely. You'll be heading to Las Vegas, along with Daniel, to assist in the control station."

Kenneth smiled and pulled Rachel closer to him. "I've been tormented with worry since David left, not only about him, but about you. I should have known you'd understand that I needed to go, too. You're a brave woman, my love."

She caressed her husband's face, as if she were trying to memorize every nook and cranny with the tips of her fingers, not knowing when she'd see him again. "My faith and our love give me all the courage I need to make it through whatever lies ahead. Plus, V will help me take care of everything until you all return."

"Until who returns from where?" V asked as she entered the kitchen carrying a bunch of flowers.

"Daniel and Kenneth will be traveling to Las Vegas to meet HB, as I'm sure you already know," Rachel said, arching her eyebrows as if daring her mother to deny it. "Or are you going to pretend HB hasn't called to fill you in on every detail since he left?"

V gave Rachel an impish smile and nodded. "Yes, HB told me all about Las Vegas. And, of course, I'll be here to help you, Rachel," she said. "Sonic, please get a vase from the cabinet in the dining room."

"Of course, V," Sonic answered immediately. "I'll arrange the flowers and put them on the table for dinner for our guests to enjoy."

"What guests?" V asked Rachel, looking surprised.

"A family from Argentina will be staying with us until the airport can open again. There were no more hotel rooms available on the island, so I agreed to house them here."

"It'll be good for both of us, Rachel, to be doing something for others," V said, hugging Rachel.

Just then, Daniel rushed back into the kitchen, bubbling with excitement. "You won't believe who I just met. Vitoria Fernandez! She's one of the most famous R.A.T.S players in South America."

"How do you know that? You don't even play that game," Rachel said.

"I got interested after watching David play a couple of times. Anyway, I recognized her from seeing a scenario she created to protect the Amazon rainforest from being cleared by cattle farmers. Boy, is she clever! She had everyone on her team climb trees and refuse to come down until the farmers agreed not to chain saw any more of the forest."

Rachel was stunned. "How could a girl with a prosthetic leg climb trees?"

Daniel laughed. "I forgot you don't know much about the game. The avatars climbed the trees, Mom. Anyway, Vitoria wants to go to Las Vegas with us. While I was showing them around the guesthouse, she took me aside and told me she's afraid to explain to her parents that she's an officer in R.A.T.S. I said you'd be able to convince them to let her go."

Rachel hesitated to agree. It was one thing to persuade her dear friend Sarah to let her daughters fight in the battles ahead and another altogether to interfere with a family decision involving someone she'd only just met. "I don't think I'd feel comfortable doing that."

"Please, Mom," Daniel begged. "If you're worried about her physical strength, you shouldn't. She's participated in the Paralympics for years. She's amazing! And she can operate a drone better than anyone I know. David thinks she's one of the best. Anyway, you wouldn't have to say anything. Your example will persuade them. When the Fernandez's learn that you and Dad gave both me and David permission to leave, I bet they'll agree to the plan right away."

"I can suggest she remain at Space Control Center with me in Las Vegas," Kenneth said, looking to Rachel for support. "Some of the other teens will also stay there, the ones most skilled in strategy who we need to assist with planning. It sounds like Vitoria fits into that category."

Rachel thought it over for a few seconds. "If that's enough to convince them, fine. But I don't think we should pressure them more than that. They've already suffered a terrible ordeal and are far from home. They need to decide for themselves what to do as a family, as we would want to do if we were in their shoes," Rachel said. "Let's finish preparing dinner. It's the last meal we'll all share together for some time, and I want it to be very special." She told Sonic to set the table for five more people and went to check on her guests.

She found the Fernandez family in the main room of the guesthouse, seated around the table talking quietly. The father rose to greet her with an outstretched hand as Rachel entered. "*Señora*, we cannot thank you enough for offering us these rooms. If there is any way we can repay you, please do not hesitate to ask."

"It's no trouble at all. We're happy to share what we have. It will be good to have your company after my son and husband depart." As soon as the words were out of her mouth, Rachel realized that some other power, some unseen force, had driven her to speak. She smiled to herself. Words that come from the heart can penetrate the heart, she thought.

Mr. Fernandez shook his head in disbelief. "I don't understand. Where could they possibly be going? Everyone has been ordered to shelter in place."

"We'll explain everything after dinner. Please come to the house; you are welcome as if you were family." She glanced over at Vitoria, who stood, smiling as brightly as the crescent moon.

* * *

"What an extraordinary meal!" Antonia Fernandez exclaimed as she handed her plate to Sonic, who was clearing the table. "What do you call that meat dish we shared? I've never had anything so delicious."

"It's called *picanha*, a traditional steak recipe that's been in our family for nearly a century. I'm glad you enjoyed it," Rachel said. "Our son, David, refuses to eat meat of any kind. I understand his objections, but at a time like this, I feel it's important to honor family customs. Sharing traditional foods is one way for us all to remain connected to family ties whenever we must be separated from our loved ones, as we are from David now."

Antonia wrinkled her brow. "Your son, David, has left home in all this chaos as well? I don't understand how you wouldn't want your children to remain at home during such a frightening time as this. Even though we're far from home, at least my family is all together," she said, reaching for her eldest daughter's hand.

Vitoria stiffened at her mother's touch and cast a pleading glance in Rachel's direction.

213

"Of course, any parent would want their children to stay home and as far away from danger as possible. But sometimes we're called upon to make sacrifices that we think we could never bear to do, until we realize that refusing to do so might cause unimaginable harm. This harm can befall not only those we hold closest but also those we call strangers, people—even other species—everything we're connected to, whether by blood or simply because we share this planet that together we call home." Rachel looked directly into Antonia's eyes. "That's why we gave our son, David, our blessing to leave. And soon his brother, Daniel, and my husband, Kenneth, will also leave to assist the teen army assembling in Las Vegas to battle against the forces threatening the Earth with annihilation." She paused and nodded to Vitoria. If the girl had the strength of character Rachel imagined she would have to possess in order to battle the challenges she'd faced, she'd rise to this occasion as well.

Without hesitation, Vitoria took the cue. "And I've been summoned to go with them, Mami and Papi." She stood up from the table and tapped her Spher@, opening the game with the special R.A.T.S code all officers carried. As it appeared on the living room GraphoScreen©, she quickly touched the edge of the screen with her finger. Her avatar was dressed in full R.A.T.S uniform. "I'm a trained officer in the R.A.T.S army, ready to report for duty, with your permission."

A parade of emotions marched across Antonia's face, fear jostling with pride, worry careening against hope, until they finally settled into peaceful coexistence. An expression of calm came into her eyes and a smile slowly curled up the corners of her mouth. "I did everything I could to protect you as a child, Vitoria. Only now, when I see you standing before me, so strong and beautiful and courageous, do I realize how much that debilitating illness taught you about love and bravery. I will not hold you back, dear daughter." She turned to look at her husband, whose eyes were already welling with tears. "Nor will your father."

"She'll be most useful to the mission working beside me on the base in Las Vegas. I'll keep an eye on her." Kenneth said.

Reassured their daughter would be safe from harm, Vitoria's parents enveloped her in their arms and whispered a prayer.

Daniel squeezed his mother's hand. "Thanks, Mom," he said in a low voice. "I knew you'd help."

***

A few hours later, the special plane HB had sent to fly Kenneth and Daniel to Las Vegas was ready for takeoff. Vitoria had joined them and was reviewing different strategies with Daniel on her computer screen.

"There will be plenty of time for planning in Las Vegas. Get some sleep," Kenneth advised. "You'll need all your energy for the complicated mission ahead of you."

Someone else heard those words—a boy who usually hated loud noise, who preferred the company of computers to close human contact, who was a wizard with maps and numbers.

David and Daniel's neighbor, Tyler, had snuck onto the plane.

Chapter 16

Welcome R.A.T.S

Mweep, mweep, mweep... The distinctive blare of an alarm sounded across the globe, alerting the Earth's citizens to the news of the cascading crisis threatening the planet's future and catapulting all of its species toward extinction.

"Alert. Alert. Alert. This is a message from the Planetary Emergency System. Extraterrestrial spacecrafts have breached our planet's atmosphere and threatened to deplete our precious resources. The world's leaders have united their nations behind a plan to initiate an emergency counter-attack. All teenagers ranked in the video game R.A.T.S are instructed to report to their designated stations for immediate deployment.

"The system is making an urgent appeal to our brave warriors' families. There is no time to hesitate. Encourage and support what your children have been called to do. Together, they will fight for us and save our home. Entrust our future to their skillful hands. G-d bless this planet!"

Finally united, humanity confronted the adversity its own troublesome deeds and words had wrought. This destruction was now amplified by the damage hostile aliens, hurtling toward them at rocket speed, had created by robbing the Earth of her tremendous gifts.

As the crescent moon journeyed along its elliptical path around the endangered planet, lines of difference and division that once sparked mortal conflict were erased. From the farthest reaches of the Chinese steppes to the icy crags of Antarctica, across the Amazon and the Sahara, on tiny islands in the Pacific and Indian Oceans and on the great island continent of Australia, along the Indonesian shoreline and its inland regions, throughout the vast expanse of India, and across Japan, and all across North and South America, summoned by the sounds of a flutist playing an inspiring tune, youths of all backgrounds left their familiar surroundings to gather at their stations. Whether they came from humble or wealthy backgrounds, whether they lived in mansions or refugee camps, no matter their gender, race, class, or physical abilities, years of R.A.T.S training had prepared them for the mission they'd been summoned to undertake. They were ready to fight for their planet.

Parents, grandparents, guardians, and friends begged G-d to protect and bless their children before releasing them for the journey ahead. Prayers from these households swirled like doves to the heavens, joining those of other believers who'd gathered together in mosques, churches, synagogues, and temples to honor and bless the voyagers heading to space.

To recognize the unity binding everyone across religious boundaries, the Pope celebrated a special ecumenical mass at the Vatican. Even agnostics and atheists whispered pleas to whatever forces they imagined had the power to reward victory to the children battling to save the planet from destruction.

Each nation had ordered airline companies to arrange passage on jumbo jets for every teenager fighting in the war. Namkhai boarded a plane at Tribhuvan International Airport in Nepal. Soon, he thought, R.A.T.S warriors from all over the world would come face to face for the first time in Las Vegas, binding them forever as if they were family. He reached into his saffron robe and touched the strand of wooden beads his parents had given him before he departed, grateful to have this token to remind him of home. Another boy took the seat next to him, removed a micro-hub from his backpack, and quickly launched the R.A.T.S game on the computer screen he'd projected in front of him by touching his chip-finger to the hub. From the expensive clothes he wore and the fancy equipment he carried, Namkhai figured the boy was probably from a foreign family visiting Nepal as tourists.

"Guess you can never get enough practice," Namkhai said, extending his hand to introduce himself. "I'm Lieutenant Namkhai. What rank have you reached?"

The boy was so engrossed in the game he didn't respond. He kept moving his avatar from scene to scene at lightning speed.

"Have you been playing long?" Namkhai asked, trying a different approach.

Still, the boy said nothing. Perhaps he's just shy, Namkhai thought. Then he noticed the boy wore an old-fashioned, leather-banded mechanical watch on his left wrist. "Was that a gift from your parents?" he asked.

"Huh?" the boy mumbled without taking his eyes off the screen.

"That's an unusual watch you've got," Namkhai said.

As if suddenly aware that the voice he'd heard speaking had come from a living being and not from an avatar on his screen, the boy turned his head toward Namkhai and frowned at him.

"I didn't mean to interrupt, but I noticed your watch and wondered if someone in your family gave it to you for good luck. I'm Namkhai, by the way. What's your name?" Namkhai offered his hand again.

The boy looked at Namkhai's hand and without shaking it, turned back to his game. "Richard. And this piece of junk belonged to my grandfather." He flicked the watch with the tip of his finger as if it were an annoyance he wanted to be rid of. "I never see the old guy much. Too busy with R.A.T.S. My mother made me wear it. She's a sucker for the sentimental." He removed the watch and put it in his pocket. "And to answer your other question, I'm a lieutenant like you. But I'm working on something now to get me promoted before we reach Las Vegas and I'd rather not be disturbed."

"Of course," Namkhai said. "I did not mean to break your concentration." Although he was curious about what

Richard thought would win him a quick promotion, Namkhai was reluctant to ask. He'd expected all R.A.T.S players to be friendly, curious to meet their eco-defense partners, not barricaded inside the game as this boy seemed to be. Could it be that even the R.A.T.S community wasn't immune to the negative energy circulating around the world like the plague? No. To worry about evil penetrating the team was to open the door to chaos. He pushed the disturbing thought out of his mind as quickly as it had poked itself in and calmed himself with a mantra. *To sow love is to receive love*, he intoned to himself and soon fell into a peaceful sleep.

Back in Washington, D.C., David was preparing a speech he wanted to deliver in Las Vegas when Becky called him on his Spher@. "Hey, David, when you get a second, can you come to my room?"

"What's the matter?" David asked.

"My sister, Sabrina, is being a real pain. She's packing like we're going to a celebration at the Kennedy Center. I told her we don't need any fancy outfits in outer space, but she says the president's daughters have to look the part."

David rolled his eyes and sighed. "I'm not sure how much I can help with that problem."

"I've got an idea! What if you show her the R.A.T.S uniforms? That'll change her mind. But please don't tell her it was my design, or she'll be jealous."

"Sure thing," David said, grateful he and Daniel weren't caught up in that kind of sibling rivalry. Of course, like all brothers, they'd had their disagreements. They certainly had different tastes in just about everything. But jealousy never reared its ugly green face or stopped them from appreciating each other's distinctive interests and talents.

David finished his notes, grabbed his backpack, and walked down the hallway to Becky's room. As he was about to knock on the door, Sabrina came storming out, trailing an overstuffed duffel bag behind her.

"Hey, Sabrina, got a minute?" David asked.

Sabrina stopped and turned toward him, crossing her arms in a huff. "I suppose my sister called you. She thinks we should just blend in with the rest of the team. But I said Mom would want us to keep a dignified appearance, even in space. We're the president's daughters, after all!"

"Well, Sabrina, it turns out you're both right," David said.

Sabrina laughed. "Don't be ridiculous. One of us has to be wrong. And this time, for sure, it's Becky. She's ignoring White House protocol."

Becky poked her head out just in time to hear her sister's accusation. "David, will you explain to my sister that when we're in space, we'll all follow R.A.T.S protocol?"

"That's correct," David said. "And that's why you're both right. Sabrina, we won't dress like we do in the game; we'll all have the same uniforms, except for the insignias of rank. Our uniforms will give us a dignified appearance."

"Uniforms," Sabrina shrieked. "Like military camouflage? Yuck! I refuse to be caught in anything so, so boring."

"Ah, but these aren't boring uniforms," David said, touching his Spher@ to bring up a display. "They were created for us by a famous fashion designer. Let me show you." A hologram of Sabrina dressed as a R.A.T.S warrior appeared. She was wearing a form-fitting uniform made of shiny white material that glistened like newly fallen snow. A waist-length jacket emblazoned with the R.A.T.S insignia—a triangle with a ring in each corner and with the four letters, R.A.T.S, in the middle—was cinched at the waist with a rippled white sash that accentuated her hourglass shape. She removed the jacket revealing a sleek white shirt underneath it with gold epaulets and semi-circles of gold braided embroidery swirling around the shoulders and front toward the waist. Sleek unisex pants were made from the same fabric as the jacket. Her long legs were encased in tall boots made from what looked like golden leather but had been specially manufactured in an indestructible, climate-controlled substance David called Zzyyxx.

"Wow! That's an amazing costume. Looks like a cross between Vera Wang and Elie Saab. Who's the designer?" Sabrina asked.

"R.A.T.S arranged a contest in which designs were submitted anonymously to give everyone an equal chance of creating a uniform both girls and boys would wear with pride and dignity," David said, not revealing that Becky had been the winner.

"Well, this is better than any uniform I've ever seen. I guess I'll repack my bag." Sabrina turned to leave and then hesitated. "Wait a minute. Where are these outfits now? I want to make sure mine fits me as well as it fit my avatar."

"They're in Las Vegas." David raised his chipped finger and wiggled it. "And our dimensions have been stored in our chip finger. HB told me they're updated whenever we sign into the game. They'll fit perfectly."

Sabrina suddenly turned away from the door and dashed down the hall.

"Where are you going?" Becky called after her.

"I haven't touched my finger to the screen since I ate lunch," Sabrina said. "I don't want mine to not fit right."

Becky shook her head and raised her eyes to the ceiling. "My sister is so predictable."

David laughed and tussled her hair. "And that's why your plan worked like a charm," he said, kissing her on the cheek.

Located about five miles outside downtown Las Vegas, Harry Reid International Airport had been bustling with excitement for more than a week as jet after jet touched down on the tarmac, parked at one of the dozens of gates, and unloaded hundreds of teenagers. By the time the crescent moon had waxed more than half full, their numbers had swollen to nearly one hundred thousand filling the hotels of Las Vegas that had been emptied of tourists to house the young warriors instead.

Chava arrived in the evening from New York with Mariana and Juliana. As they walked through the terminal, they were stunned by the spectacle that greeted them. Balloons floating high above them in the ceiling spelled out WELCOME R.A.T.S in every color of the rainbow while holograms of internationally famous musical artists from all around the globe lined the walls.

"Oh my G-d," Mariana screamed. "Dios Mio! That looks like a famous pop star. I remember mommy playing her music whenever Papi worked the night shift. She'd sing along with the chorus and start doing salsa, dancing, and laughing with him all around the apartment."

Mariana mimicked her mother's dance moves, recalling how joyful those nights were. "Papi always left for work with a big smile on his face."

She grabbed Juliana and Chava, and the three girls began to dance, swirling together in a circle of laughter and joy. "Let's celebrate and dance all night, showing everyone our spirit and pride." They sang, their voices merging in harmony.

Someone tapped Mariana on the shoulder, and she stopped, still giggling, and turned around to find a handsome, dark-haired young man in a flowing white kaftan smiling at them.

"Hey, *chicas*, don't stop. That was wicked beautiful," he said.

As soon as he spoke, Mariana recognized him. "Omar! You made it!"

"With Namkhai's help. Have you seen him yet?" Omar asked.

"No. But I'm sure it will take him a little longer to get here from Katmandu. We'll meet up with him at the hotel," Chava said.

"Which hotel are you staying at, Omar?" Juliana asked. "We're at the Bellagio."

"Cool! I'm at the Bellagio, too," Omar said.

Juliana pinched Chava's arm.

"Ouch!" Chava rubbed her arm, making her backpack slide off her shoulder. She blushed and turned away in embarrassment.

"What's the matter? Is your bag too heavy?" Omar reached out to help her.

"I'm fine," Chava said, jerking her backpack onto her shoulder again. "Just a little muscle spasm." She squinted at Juliana as if to tell her to back off.

The group of four friends exited the terminal and quickly located the large hover bus labeled "Bellagio" waiting to take them to the luxurious Las Vegas resort. Juliana and Mariana grabbed the first row of seats near the front, motioning Chava and Omar to sit next to them. The teenagers stared out of the bus's curved glass windows, amazed by the scene unfolding like an endless multimedia show along the famous Las Vegas strip.

Multicolored flashing lights illuminated the wide avenue as the bus sped silently past tall glass and steel hotel towers. On every corner along the way, another famous band serenaded the teens with popular songs, filling the air with the rhythms of rap and reggae and hip-hop and funk and electronic music until it seemed as if an entire universe of sound had created new harmonics to welcome the teens.

"I thought New York was the city that never sleeps," Mariana said. "I've never seen so many sparkling lights or heard anything so magical as this, not even in Times Square on New Year's Eve."

"Wow!" Juliana shouted. "Look at that!" She pointed to a message glistening across the night sky.

WELCOME R.A.T.S! WE FIGHT TO HAVE A FUTURE.

The hover bus zoomed along, as holographic images of R.A.T.S arriving from every corner of the Earth appeared along the avenue. Juxtaposed with these were images of their families and friends who'd gathered in town squares and villages to encourage the young warriors to stay brave. Chava gasped when she saw one of her parents standing with her brother outside their Jerusalem home carrying a banner decorated with Hebrew writing.

"What does it say?" Omar asked.

"It says '*To our brave daughter, Chava. We believe in you and your friends. Together, you will bring peace to our planet.*'"

Omar touched her hand gently. "Chava, I'm happy and proud to serve on your team."

Chava beamed a bright smile at him. "I'm happy too, Omar," she said and squeezed his hand.

Outside the Bellagio, an enormous globe of the planet twirled atop a revolving tower. As the four friends bounded off the bus, they were halted by the troubling scenes depicted on the globe's surface, like a time-release video of the Earth's decimation by drought, fire, human conflict, and alien invasion. They stood for a moment of silence.

"And that's why we're here," Juliana said, giving the R.A.T.S split-fingered salute. "We're here to make the Earth *tiene la cara bonita*—have a beautiful face again."

They entered the hotel to find robots scurrying across the marble lobby floor, snatching backpacks and directing all the arriving teenagers to a food hall filled with meals provided by big global companies.

"All food and beverages were generously donated by various companies from around the world," a loudspeaker announced as they walked into the hall. "Please enjoy these healthy, vegetarian meals. Inspired by the teenagers of R.A.T.S, the companies have pledged all future profits to planetary repair."

"Well, I guess we can eat that food without a guilty conscience, Mariana," Juliana said, tickling her sister.

"I suppose," Mariana said. "But I pledge to make sure they keep their promise."

After they'd eaten, the robots escorted them to their rooms. Omar was happy to learn he'd be sharing a room with Namkhai.

The young Buddhist arrived a few hours later, exhausted from his long journey, but eager to share news with his friend.

"I met David downstairs in the lobby. He told me tomorrow the President of the United States will appear with all the world's leaders to address the assembled R.A.T.S!" Namkhai was hardly able to contain his excitement. "And guess what? David's been promoted to Commander."

"Praise Allah," Omar said. "With David leading us, we're certain to be victorious!"

"*Heh, heh, heh!* That's what you think. You're sure in for a big surprise, partner." Roy removed the special listening device he'd used to eavesdrop on their conversation. When he'd seen the robot leading Namkhai to his room, he'd made sure to request the one next door for him and Butch. "We got us a couple hundred sitting ducks in this pond. How about we get us some shut-eye before we go shooting' fish in a barrel tonight?"

"You got me confused, Roy. Is it ducks or fish we're hunting'?" Butch asked.

"Never you mind. Just remember to say your prayers."

"Sure thing, Roy. Whatever you say."

***

David expected to share a room with Deepak and Tutla, but neither one had arrived yet, so he asked the robot who'd helped him to his room to arrange for a hover taxi to take him to Elias I.E., the base headquarters in the Mojave. He knew he'd find HB there and wanted to help him check the equipment and review maps for R.A.T.S' upcoming flights to the moon.

As the taxi left the glitter and din of the illuminated, pulsating city farther and farther behind, David watched darkness slowly descend over the desert like a great, gray cape. The Milky Way appeared above him like a glistening pathway to heaven, making him shudder at the vastness of the universe. What a tiny speck he was on this small, spinning planet he called home. But even a tiny speck could dislodge a giant if he was as determined as David was to become a disturbance in the eye of whatever giant was causing such destruction to his beloved Earth.

The taxi deposited him in the middle of a sandy terrain populated only by thorny cacti and a few rambling tumbleweeds. It took his eyes a few seconds to adjust to the darkness. Then he saw a mound in the near distance and walked toward it. Embedded near the mound's top was a small computer panel. He punched in the code HB had given him and with a sudden whoosh of sound a large metal trap door opened to reveal a ladder. He descended to the third rung and the ladder automatically carried him deep below the desert to settle him on the floor of a cavernous room. It was filled with blinking lights and dozens of computer screens and, most surprisingly of all, the waiting arms of his father, Kenneth, and a welcoming slap on the back from his brother, Daniel.

David's eyes welled up with tears. "Dad, Daniel, what are you two doing here?"

"As I'm sure you know by now, son, I designed these ships you're about to fly to the moon. I want to make sure they bring you safely back home," Kenneth said, hugging David tighter.

"And I'm here to see what it's like to play beach tennis on the moon!" Daniel said.

Chapter 17

May G-d Protect Us and Bless Us!

"I can't believe you kept this huge underground station secret for so long," David said as HB took him on a tour of Elias I.E.

"We had to maintain heightened security, David. It would have been too risky for many people to know about it or information about the project could have leaked before we'd worked out all the bugs. Your father's been enormously helpful with the designs, although even he didn't know everything about what his designs were supporting."

"Can I see the control room now, Grandpa?" David asked.

"Sure thing. I want you to meet the lead programmer before you go back to the hotel and prepare for the opening ceremony tomorrow."

David followed HB down a narrow hallway and into another smaller room, where a gigantic GraphoScreen© filled an entire wall. Displayed on the screen was an enormous field of rocket launch pads, each one holding a glistening vehicle being readied to carry the first wave of R.A.T.S warriors to the Moon Station. He noticed what looked like a long, rectangular, electronic billboard at the foot of the field and was about to ask what it was when the programmer, who'd been checking data on a smaller computer below the big screen, whirled around in his chair.

David let out a cry of shock. "Dude, how did you get here?"

Tyler's ordinarily expressionless face erupted into a broad smile. "Your grandfather helped me. After he'd arranged for the plane to bring your father and brother here, he sent me a message and my cousin Michael took care of sneaking me on board. Couldn't let you go into space without the benefit of my excellent coding skills to guarantee your safe return, could I, Commander?" He gave David the split-fingered R.A.T.S salute. "And this is my assistant—"

"Vitoria Fernandez!" David shouted. "I watched your team save the Amazon." He turned toward his grandfather. "I suppose you're responsible for making sure she got to the base, too. She's one of our best technical advisers."

"Actually, your mother convinced my parents to let me come. They're staying with her in Aruba. Along with my sisters," Vitoria said. "I came on the plane with your father and Daniel."

David sent a telepathic message to Sonic. *Please thank my mother for getting Vitoria to the base. And tell her I'll call her tomorrow.*

Okay, David, Sonic replied. *She'll be expecting your call.*

An alert sounded in the control room. "Time to get to work. Activate countdown clock, Lieutenant Tyler," HB called to Tyler.

Tyler tapped the screen and 43:00:00 appeared on the rectangular billboard, which turned out to be a digital clock.

"Countdown clock activated, sir," Tyler replied. "T-43 hours and counting."

"Backup flight systems check," Vitoria reported.

"Loading backup software into rocket memory units and displays," Tyler said.

"Software loaded. Navigational systems activated and tested," Vitoria said.

"Complete flight deck inspections," Tyler ordered.

"All systems go," Vitoria confirmed.

David followed HB out of the room while the others continued to monitor the computers.

"In less than two days, we'll launch the advance team in four rockets for the three-day journey to the Moon Station for preliminary reconnaissance work. Once you've assessed the threat level, David, you'll determine the amount of crew you'll need to carry out the mission." HB put his hand on David's shoulder. "Go back to the hotel now, organize your lead team, and prepare to address the assembly tomorrow. Then get some rest."

David nodded.

"I'm so proud of you, David. Proud of all the R.A.T.S. The years I spent developing this game have finally come to fruition. Under your leadership, the youth of the world have shown us what real courage looks like." HB hugged him and returned to the control room to oversee Tyler and Vitoria's work.

David found his father and brother checking fuel calculations in the main room. He said goodbye to them and headed back to the Bellagio. When he got to his room, Tutla still hadn't arrived, but Deepak was waiting for him. Still dressed in his wedding garments, he was slumped in a chair by the window, holding something tightly in his hand.

"Why do you look so sad, Deepak?" David asked.

Deepak let out a deep sigh. "Do you remember how I couldn't attend the assembly when you announced the mission to all R.A.T.S?"

"Of course," David said, pulling up a chair next to Deepak. "You told me it was a special day and you had to go to the temple."

"I didn't tell you why, though. I was meeting someone there. Someone very dear to me. My beloved, Alisha." Tears trembled on the edge of his eyelids. "We were married two days ago. And now she will have to face whatever happens in the world without me." Deepak hung his head and quietly sobbed.

David was stunned by the news. As the eldest on the team, Deepak had been the one David relied on most to keep the rest of the R.A.T.S focused on the game's purpose. Although he knew about crushes between some of the players—including his own feelings for Becky—it had never occurred to him that Deepak's maturity meant he might be ready to take on the responsibility of having a family of his own.

"You should have told me, Deepak. I would have understood why you couldn't join the expedition," David said.

"No, David. I had to come. Although I feel the pain of separation from Alisha, the promise I made to wed my life with hers would be meaningless if I didn't keep the pledge I made to defend the Earth. The wise ones taught that we come into the world not only to satisfy our personal needs but to subdue evil and make good triumph." He opened his hand and handed the watch he'd been holding to David.

David took it and turned it over to find an inscription on the back. "What does this say?"

"Together forever. My mother gave it to me to remind me of the power of love."

David nodded, feeling the weight of the ring on his finger. "I understand, Deepak." He stood up and touched his friend gently on the shoulder. "We should get some rest now."

Deepak agreed and went to his room.

After David showered, he set his Spher@ alarm and took a nap. Two hours later, feeling refreshed, he sketched the organization of the advance team on his computer and sent a telepathic message to Becky, who was staying with her mother and sister in the presidential suite.

"Can you meet me in the lobby in ten minutes?" he asked, watching the ring on his finger start to glow.

"Sure," Becky said. "Anything wrong, David?"

"No. I just want to share something with you." The ring became brighter.

"Okay," she said. "I'll be right there."

They settled into two chairs in a quiet corner of the lobby and David opened his computer. "My grandfather explained the mission to me. He asked me to select an advanced team who'll be launched in four rockets to the Moon Station. So, I've decided Omar and Namkhai, Deepak and Chava, Mariana and Juliana, and Tutla, you, and I will be the rocket leaders. The leaders will choose a group of ten support personnel to assist in each rocket."

"What about Sabrina? She'll throw a fit when she finds out she isn't a leader," Becky said.

"She's not experienced enough. Besides, I promised your mother—"

"When did you talk to my mother?" Becky's eyes widened in surprise.

"Before we left D.C. She knows Sabrina has other talents and asked me to make sure she didn't go on the first flight."

Becky sighed. "My mother's wise. But I'm the one who'll have to shoulder the consequences her wisdom will bring out in Sabrina. It won't be pretty."

David took her hand. "We're a team now, Becky. We'll shoulder the consequences together. We need Sabrina to stay back at the base."

Becky snapped the fingers of her other hand. "I know what we can do. Put her in charge of wardrobe and gadgets; that will make her happy."

"Brilliant! I'll promote her to lead maintenance officer at Elias I.E."

"Hey, look at that!" Becky pointed to David's ring. "It's throbbing with light."

David smiled to himself, remembering his mother telling him that whenever the ring glowed, he'd know he was on the right path. "It does that sometimes," he said. "It helps keep me focused." Since Becky had seen it flashing with light, David knew she was destined to be on the path with him. "Just like you do, Becky," he said, squeezing her hand.

Becky's idea worked like a charm. Sabrina was thrilled with her new assignment and headed to the base immediately to make sure everyone's uniforms would be properly distributed to the changing rooms.

After he returned to his room, David sent messages to the other team leaders. "Please send your selections for support personnel to me for review," his message said. "I'll send the approved list to Captain Sabrina and Lieutenant Tyler at Elias I.E."

Everyone confirmed, including Tutla, who assured him he'd arrive in time for the opening ceremony.

T-40 hours.

David was completing his review of those crew members selected by the rocket leaders for the first R.A.T.S expedition to space. He recognized the names of the most accomplished R.A.T.S players on the lists. The few unfamiliar names led him to question the leader who'd suggested them. He messaged Namkhai first.

"Who's this Richard, you've added to your support personnel?" David asked.

"I met him on the plane from Nepal. He's not the easiest guy to talk to, but he's a wiz with computers," Namkhai said.

"I trust your judgment, Namkhai," David said and messaged Mariana next to ask about a youth named Butch.

"Juliana and I met him in one of the scenarios. He's funny and a little weird, but he follows orders perfectly," Mariana explained. "He's got a cousin named Roy who catches on fast, too. Roy wants to work at the base."

"Okay, I'll approve those assignments," David said.

"Thanks, David. We'll have a stellar team," Mariana said. "See you tomorrow at the ceremony."

It was nearly midnight when he finished sending the names of R.A.T.S Space Team I to Sabrina and Tyler. Outside, the flashing neon lights made Las Vegas bright as day. Before he climbed into bed, he pushed a button on the wall and the windows of his room darkened instantaneously. He soon fell into a deep, untroubled sleep.

T-30 hours.

David waited in the wings as HB appeared on the grand stage outside the Bellagio and on GraphoScreens© all around the city.

"Youth of the world, we're grateful to you and your families for the extraordinary courage you've shown by coming to the Earth's defense. Without your dedication and support, the future of our planet would remain bleak. It is my honor to present the President of the United States, Sarah Esther Hoffman, joined by all the leaders of our planet at this crucial moment in humanity's history."

As Sarah walked to the stage, holograms began to flicker and take shape all around her until images of every world leader came into focus. The entire army of R.A.T.S gasped at the sight and then filled the air with round after round of thunderous applause.

Sarah raised her hand to quiet the audience and began her speech.

"Good morning and welcome, youthful defenders of our beloved planet. Each one of you has answered the Earth's cry for help. Whether you've traveled from near or far, you've each left behind family and friends to come to Earth's defense. You will battle alien forces whose powers we do not yet fully understand, forces wreaking extraordinary damage, only adding to the destruction we ourselves brought to our doorsteps, whether through thoughtless words or harmful deeds.

"For centuries, we've fought among ourselves. But now, you've given us hope. You've shown the world how we are one, a common humanity sharing this Earth we call home. Union will bring us victory. So, raise your heads, fill your hearts and souls with love and courage to defend this planet.

"In the name of all the world leaders, thank you. May G-d protect us and bless us."

Suddenly the ground began to shake, and a low rumbling noise grew louder and louder. From the desert in the near distance, immense clouds of dust swirled in the air like funnels of energy, drawing closer and closer until the sounds of whoops and cries became recognizable, announcing the arrival of the indigenous people of the region.

"It's Tutla!" David cried, pulling Becky onto the stage just in time to see the spectacular sight of the assembled tribes arriving on horseback, led by Tutla's father, Chief of the Havasupai. "I knew he'd make it."

Tutla's father dismounted and approached the stage. Sarah gestured for him to join her at the podium.

"As you are custodians of the land on which we stand, we ask for your blessing," she said.

"The Earth is our mother and we have come to protect her," the chief said. "May the Creator of all things enable victory over those who threaten her survival."

The crowd burst into applause. Sarah quieted them again and called David to the podium. "Commander David will take charge of this mission. I leave you in his capable hands," she said and walked off the stage with HB.

David took a moment to adjust the podium to his height. Then he cleared his throat and began to address the assembly.

"R.A.T.S, we've been called to defend our planet from alien invaders and repair the harm from centuries of discord and disregard for the gift of life. I'm honored and humbled to serve as your commander. The courage you've shown the world by your willingness to leave behind loved ones and dedicate yourselves to Earth's future is an inspiration. The knowledge we've developed through the game will win that future, not only for humanity but for all species with whom we share this planet we call home. Tomorrow, I will lead an advanced team to the Moon

Station for the first phase of our mission. Each of you has received instructions through your Spher@s about your role in the mission. Some of you will serve as astronauts; others will staff base operations at Elias I.E. But whatever you've been called to do, remember to perform your task with dedication, dignity, and faith. Let us bow our heads now in a moment of silence."

A hush came over the assembly. Moments later, David issued a command.

"All platoons report to the uniform distribution center. At T-11 hours and counting, be prepared to carry out assigned duties. We are one!"

Then he turned toward the president, who was standing next to HB in the wings. "President Hoffmann, world leaders, thank you for entrusting us with this task. We won't let you down."

Raising their arms in the R.A.T.S salute, the youth began to chant in unison. "We won't let you down, we won't let you down. We are one, we are one!"

We Are One

Anthem of the Revolutionary Army of Teens

The anthem created for these young people began to play, reaching every corner where they were, and in a fraction of a second, it echoed through every part of the world. A small spark ignited a blazing fire.

[Verse 1]

The world is changing, the time is now
No more silence, we take a vow
Rise together, stand up tall
We won't break, we won't fall

[Chorus]

We are one, we are strong
Through the storm, we march on
Hearts ignited, shining bright
Together we will win this fight

[Verse 2]

Truth is calling, hear the sound
Hope is rising from the ground
Side by side, hand in hand
This is our time, we take a stand

[Final Chorus]

We
God's our strength, He leads us all
Through the trials, through the night

His love shines, His truth is light

[Chorus]
We are one, we are strong
With His love, we march on
Faith unshaken, hearts set free
By His grace, we will see

[Verse 2]
Hope is rising, hear His call
With His power, we won't fall
Side by side, hand in hand
We will follow His great plan

[Final Chorus]
We are one, we are strong
With His love, we march on
No more fear, no more night
God's our hope, our guiding light.

As the final note soared into the air like a prayer carried by the wind, silence fell—not the kind of silence that speaks of emptiness, but the sacred pause that follows something holy. For a moment, time itself seemed to kneel. The hearts of thousands beat as one. Across continents, languages, and beliefs, a single truth echoed: they were no longer alone. They were no longer afraid. They were one.

As the crowd dispersed, David noticed a base security officer present himself to HB. They pulled together in a huddle and then quickly headed for the exit. "Carry on, David," HB called over his shoulder.

Tutla was waiting for David outside the Bellagio. "Your father seems very proud of you, Tutla," David said as they rode the elevator to their room.

"He told me he's honored to be the father of such a brave warrior," Tutla said with a smile.

Deepak was already waiting for them in the room. "Where's this uniform center you mentioned, David?" he asked.

"There's one in every hotel. I'll show you." David messaged the other members of R.A.T.S Space Team I and led them to a ballroom on the top floor. Along the walls were changing rooms labeled with each of their names.

"Bro, this is so cool," Omar said, entering his cubicle and exchanging his kaftan for an exquisitely tailored white uniform with gold epaulets. "Mine fits perfectly," he said.

Chava emerged from her room and twirled. "These side panels make me feel like I could fly."

"They make you look like an angel," Omar said.

Blushing, Chava smiled at him. "And you look like a prince."

One after the other, they exited their rooms, admiring how dignified they appeared.

"I feel like a real officer," Namkhai said.

"But you already were one," David said. "Like my grandfather says, it's not the uniform that makes the officer, but the officer who makes the uniform."

David's Spher@ rang in his ear. "Commander David here," he answered.

"David, I need you to report to base immediately. We have an urgent situation here."

Not wanting to alarm the others, he told them to return to their hotel rooms to await further orders. Outside the hotel, a hover vehicle was already waiting to speed him toward Elias I.E. He found HB and Sarah in heated discussion in the strategy room.

"We've been contacted by the extraterrestrials. They want to talk to a world leader," HB told him. "Sarah has informed the rest of the world leaders. We expect them to appear any minute."

"What do you think they want?" David asked, trying to stay calm.

"We don't know," HB said.

"Whatever they have to say, the world will be listening together," Sarah added.

Once the holograms of all the world leaders had assembled, Sarah opened the multi-modal communication line.

A sharp sound pulsed into the room. Soon the sound transformed into a fuzzy image that sharpened and reformed itself into a gigantic, grotesque shape, like some immense, rough beast. Its entire surface was covered in stones and sharp-angled, black metallic scales oozing some sort of thick substance, as if an ancient, long-buried body had emerged from a tar pit, dragging the dregs of centuries of pollution along with it.

An orifice opened and the creature began to speak in a deep, almost human voice.

"Greetings, Planet Earth. My name is Grutan. I come from the planet Daktaryon in a faraway galaxy. Our planet has slowly been drying out for lack of water. Now, we have come for yours. You have a simple choice to make— give us your water or we will destroy you!"

The room erupted in outrage. One leader after the other protested.

"This is madness," one shouted.

"We will never sacrifice our precious resources to aliens," another cried out.

"Then you have chosen destruction," Grutan said. "A crueler destruction than you could ever imagine."

"You make a mockery of choice," Sarah said. "Without water, life on Earth is impossible."

Grutan's cruel laughter filled the air. "Then you should have guarded such a precious resource more carefully. We have already begun to seize it from you, and you've been unable to stop us."

"We're prepared to stop you now," Sarah said, rising from her chair as all the world leaders stood in solidarity behind her.

"Then this means war!" Grutan shouted. "Our superior technologies will easily defeat the witless youth army you've assembled."

The room shook with the vibrations his booming voice caused. David steadied himself and rose to address the menacing figure.

"You are the foolish one, Grutan. Your technology is no match for the determination of R.A.T.S to defend the future of this planet in unity and faith. Let the battle begin!"

T-11 hours and counting.

David's image appeared on the GraphoScreen© in every hotel in Las Vegas.

"Fellow R.A.T.S, we are united in strength against an alien enemy threatening to deprive our planet of the fountain of life. We are one in uniform and spirit, capable in mind and heart of winning this war. Form your squads, as we've been trained. We've got this!"

As the soulful sound of the flutist's melody floated across the desert, the R.A.T.S made their way to their stations.

T-3 hours and counting

David, Becky, and Tutla—the pilots of SpaceCraft *Alpha*—led their crew toward the vehicle's launch pad, followed by Omar and Namkhai, Deepak and Chava, and finally, Mariana and Juliana, who positioned themselves on the launch pads of each of the other rockets. After giving the R.A.T.S salute to each of his team leaders, David entered and climbed into the cockpit with Becky to begin air-to-ground checks.

"Mission Control, this is Commander David."

"Read you loud and clear, Commander," Tyler said.

"Commencing pre-flight," Becky said.

"Roger that," David replied.

"Crew hatch secured and sealed, Commander," Tutla reported.

"Fuel levels confirmed," Vitoria reported from Mission Control.

For the next two and a half hours the crews of each of the spaceships prepared their vehicles for departure.

"Onboard and backup computers set to launch," David reported at T-20 minutes and counting.

Ten minutes later, Mission Control conducted the final go/no-go checks.

"Advice activate flight recording devices," HB said.

"Roger, activated," David said.

After five more minutes, the rocket boosters roared to life.

David looked at Becky and she nodded, locking the visor on her helmet. Then he whispered a final prayer as the countdown continued.

"T-10 seconds and counting… Five, four, three, two, one."

At liftoff, a blinding light and billows of smoke signaled the departure of the four rockets of R.A.T.S Space Team I for the moon while everyone else on Earth held their breath and prayed.

***

"May Hashem protect you and bring you home safely, my son," Rachel whispered as she stood in front of the living room GraphoScreen© and watched the rocket carrying her son and his crew lift off into the broad, blue Nevada sky.

Chapter 18

Elias I.E., Roger That!
T-2 Days to Moon Landing

"Alpha, this is Elias I.E. Thrust is Go, all engines. You're looking good," Tyler said.

"Roger, you're loud and clear, Elias I.E. Visual is Go, today," David said.

"This is Elias I.E. Roger, Out," Tyler said.

David monitored the controls as the rocket thrust itself higher and higher, traveling at a velocity of more than 25,000 miles per hour. Pressure slowly built on his whole body, until he felt as if he weighed three times more than usual. His cheeks were pulled toward his ears, his teeth chattered, he was glued in place for nine long minutes. Then Vitoria's voice came over the intercom.

"Alpha, this is Elias I.E. You are confirmed. Go for orbit."

"Roger, staging, and ignition," David said.

"Ignition confirmed, Alpha. Thrust is go. Good luck and G-d bless," Vitoria said.

"Thank you very much," David said as a cheer went off in the cabin.

SpaceCraft *Alpha* escaped the gravitational pull of the planet, slowed, and entered an elliptical orbit hundreds of miles above the Earth.

David checked the controls again. "All systems Go, Elias I.E."

"This is Elias I.E., Alpha. You've reached Zero-G."

"Prepare to remove launch gear," David announced to his team, taking off his helmet. He released his safety harness and, still tethered by a cord to the captain's chair, floated weightlessly toward a portal to catch a glimpse of Earth below him. Everywhere there were signs of the wounds the planet had sustained from cataclysmic hurricanes, fires, earthquakes, and war brought on by centuries of human neglect and needless conflict. Now, where the ocean had begun to recede along the coastlines of North and South America, he could also see visible evidence of Grutan's plan to steal water, the planet's lifeblood. Yet somehow, despite these scars, Earth remained a beautiful orb, spinning in the silent depths of space like an azure jewel glistening in the glint of the sun's beams, illuminating the darkness, beckoning her brave warriors to return home and rebuild.

"I've never seen anything so breathtaking," Becky exclaimed as she floated next to David to look out the portal. "Why would anyone want to harm something so extraordinary, so alive?"

"I've been wondering that myself. In the game, we've learned how to repair damage. But what causes us to harm in the first place?" David asked.

"I guess it's because someone wants what someone else has," Becky said.

"Okay, but where does that kind of want come from?" David asked.

"Well, some people have a lot and some have nothing, so maybe it comes from need. Like hungry people need to be fed," Becky said.

"Then shouldn't the folks who have more be willing to share with the needy?" David asked.

Becky gave him a look of disbelief. "You're not saying we should share with this Grutan, are you?"

David shook his head. "No. He doesn't want to share. He wants to take it all. But I've been trying to figure out why." David looked at the shimmering Earth.

"Maybe he wants to hurt us because he's afraid," Becky said.

"Of what?" David asked. "He's shown us how powerful he is by taking the water."

Becky turned to David. "Maybe he's afraid of being alone; afraid of not being loved or valued."

"Well, he sure isn't doing a very good job of trying to win anyone's sympathy," David said.

"Maybe he's forgotten how to." Becky grew quiet for a second. "Sometimes I get scared of being alone, David. Don't you?"

David hesitated before replying. "I used to. I guess everyone does sometimes. But I'm not afraid anymore. Because I realize, even when I'm alone, I still have memories and dreams to keep me connected to people and places I love."

"I guess that's why my mother gave me this before we left." Becky pulled out a locket from underneath her shirt. A small gray-green stone was embedded on its surface and inside was a picture of her family. "She found the stone on a research trip to Machu Picchu a long time ago. She said the stone would remind me never to stop searching for the truth and the picture would help me remember that home is a place in your heart."

He pulled her closer and put his arm around her shoulder as they stared at the receding planet in silence for a few moments longer until a message came over the intercom.

"Alpha, this is Mission Control. HB has a special report, over," Tyler said.

"Ready, over" David replied.

On the big screen, David saw the President of the United States with HB waiting for him with a mysterious grin on his face.

"David," HB said, "I have a surprise for you."

Suddenly, from behind the President emerged the first humanoid in the history of humanity: Phoenix. David's eyes widened in amazement. Phoenix was a tall and strong figure, with wise gray-blue eyes and a peaceful countenance.

Phoenix introduced himself, "Hi, David, I am Phoenix, and I will help you on your mission."

David was stunned. "What can a humanoid do to help me save the world?" he asked skeptically.

HB took a moment and a deep breath and explained everything to David and why this decision needed to be approved.

"Trust me, David," HB replied, "Phoenix is unlike anything you've ever seen. He has been specially designed and trained to assist you in this mission."

David trusted in HB's words and realized that Phoenix was more than just a machine; he was a loyal ally and friend. With Phoenix by his side, David felt invincible, he knew that Phoenix was his secret weapon. He trusted Phoenix with his life and knew that together they could save the world.

David looked at HB and said, "Thank you, Grandpa, for everything you've done for me. I could not have done this without you."

HB replied, "Of course, David. You are not just the Commander to me; you are my grandson. I will always be here for you, no matter what. You have made me so proud, and I know that you will continue to do great things."

David was overcome with emotion, realizing the depth of his grandfather's love and support. He knew that no matter where his mission took him, his grandfather would always be there to encourage him and provide a listening ear. With renewed strength and determination, David vowed to make his grandfather proud and to continue fighting for the safety and well-being of humanity.

Later on, after eating their packet meals, the crew climbed into their hammocks and fell asleep, leaving Tutla on watch. In the middle of the night, he called David's Spher@ from the communication room.

"David, I think we've got visitors," Tutla said. "I just spotted something approaching us. I can't make out what it is, but whatever it is, it's not one of ours."

"Activate defense shields," David ordered.

"Roger. Activated."

He released himself from his hammock, floated back to the ship's controls, and opened the external monitors. A shimmering, shape-shifting light hovered nearby. It looked strangely familiar. The luminous object pulsated a few seconds and then disappeared.

"Never mind, David. I adjusted the transparency on my portal. Must have been the sun's reflection on the glass." Tutla laughed. "Guess I'm not used to seeing the sunshine at night!"

"Roger that," David said. But when he looked out his portal again, the object had reappeared. He watched it expand into the shape of a star and then vanish as the ring on his finger glimmered and dimmed. "Nothing to worry about, Tutla," David said. "Deactivate shields."

"Roger. Shields deactivated."

After confirming with the other rocket ships' captains that everyone was on course, David returned to his hammock and slept peacefully for several more hours.

T-1 day to Moon landing.

"Butch, do you read me?" Roy asked from a secret channel he'd established at Elias I.E.

"Loud as a cowbell," Butch whispered.

"Well, what exactly are you doing up there?" Roy sounded annoyed.

"Same as everyone else here. Flying to the moon in this big metal basket. Kinda nice being here in space, Roy. Everyone's real friendly," Butch said, staring out his portal on SpaceCraft *Beta* as the sun glinted across the Earth. "And I got a real good view. Earth looks about as big and beaten as a Houston basketball at the end of a game."

"Well, you ain't there to make friends. You got a job to do, partner. And it doesn't involve no sightseeing, you hear?"

"Yes siree, Bob... I mean Roger, er Roy. Whatever. I got us set for the big roundup on that giant cheese ball in the sky."

"You better not mess up, or you know what'll happen."

"Don't you worry about me none. I do what I'm told. Gotta get me some shut-eye before the landing. Oops, I mean, attempted landing. Heh, heh, heh. Over and out now."

T-3 hours to Moon Landing

"Space Team I, this is Elias I.E. We expect maneuver to landing altitude to begin at 9 plus 20 plus 00. Complete at 9 plus 30 plus 20," Tyler said.

"Roger. Time to begin maneuver is 9 plus 20 plus 20. Complete at 9 plus 30 plus 20," Butch said.

"Roger. That's an error, Space Delta. Time to begin maneuver should be 9:20:00. Confirm," Tyler said.

There was a long pause.

"Space Delta, this is Elias I.E. Over," Tyler said.

No Answer.

"Space Delta, this is Elias I.E. Over," Tyler repeated.

Another pause.

"Space Delta—"

"—Read you loud and clear, Elias I.E.," Mariana said. "Had to take control from First Airman Butch and switch channels. He fainted. Repeat time to maneuver. Over."

"Roger. Expect maneuver to landing altitude to begin at 9 plus 20 plus 00. Complete at 9 plus 30 plus 20," Tyler said. "Glad to hear your voice, Captain Mariana."

"Roger. Time to begin maneuver is 9 plus 20 plus 00. Complete at 9 plus 30 plus 20. Over," Mariana said.

"Affirmative. Safe landing, Space Delta. Out," Tyler said.

"Roger," Mariana said.

"Well, I'll be hog-tied," Roy said to himself after listening to the communication on the secret channel. "Either that boy chickened out or he's a scaredy-cat. No matter. I got me a Plan B. Ain't nothing gonna stop me from getting that reward I been promised by that hunk of oozing Daktaryon metal."

T-30 minutes to moon landing.

"I can see the stars, now," Becky shouted. "There's Ursa Minor. And look, David, look. There's the Big Dipper. They seem so close, almost like I could touch them."

David took a quick glance out the portal and turned back to monitor the commands from Elias I.E. and prepare for the final descent.

"Space Alpha, this is Elias I.E. You are Go-to powered descent," Tyler said.

"Roger," David said. As he completed the yaw maneuver, rotating to descend, the moon fell away from view and the dark sky, dappled with dazzling stars, appeared in his window, stunning him with the sight of the vastness and beauty of the universe. Among the millions and millions of stars, the sun was but one, and the Earth was an even smaller blip in the celestial panorama above him. *Small, yes, but still a home worth protecting*, he thought to himself. "Throttle down."

"Roger. Still. Go," Tyler said. "You're the news of the day, David. People have gathered around the world to watch this landing. But, hey, no pressure," Tyler teased.

"If I can take the pressure of escaping Earth's atmosphere, I can take the pressure of a little public attention."

"A little? Try ten billion pairs of eyes watching. But who's counting," Tyler said.

A little while later, David received data about the distance to the moon's surface on his monitor. One thousand feet to landing. As he slowly guided the spacecraft closer to the base, he could see the force of the rocket's engines scattering dust across the moon's western plane. When it cleared, the Moon Station came into view. He adjusted the altitude of the spacecraft to control descent and looked up at the sky once more. Becky was right. The stars seemed so close he wanted to touch them. In less than three minutes, the rocket was on the ground.

"Space Alpha landed," David said. The crew erupted in loud whoops of joy.

"Roger. We copy that." Tyler let out a deep sigh of relief. "Thanks. We're monitoring the others. They're a couple of hours behind you. All still go."

"Roger. Out." David beamed the R.A.T.S salute through the rocket's camera to every communication station around the world. Then he sent a special signal to Rachel's GraphoScreen© in Aruba, knowing she'd smile at the sight of his glowing ring. After shutting off all systems, he ordered his crew to prepare for disembarkation.

The moon was arid and pocked with craters, but the Moon Station was an oasis of delight. Water trickled down the stone walls of the long entranceway. Lush, fragrant flowers—bougainvillea and jasmine and plumeria—cascaded from high planters to the floor. The flutist's music was playing over the intercom as David and Becky entered the lobby with their team and then stopped suddenly, shocked at the sight of the President of the United States standing with several others, waiting to welcome them.

"Mom, how did you—" Becky stammered.

"—Holograms. We've had a secret channel operational for some time now, in case of emergencies like this," Sarah said. "As a sign of our solidarity, I invited all the presidents to join me in welcoming you to the moon. Dear presidents, I am proud to introduce you to Commander David, leader of the R.A.T.S," Sarah said. "And this is my daughter, Captain Becky, co-pilot of Space Alpha."

The world leaders had assembled to witness this important moment for humanity and to extend an invitation for all nations to participate in this historic event. Before they had known David as a boy, but now he stood before them as a commander. "It's an honor to meet you both. President Hoffmann allowed us to meet Phoenix, the first humanoid in the world, who will arrive at the moon station soon to help our children."

"We are grateful for the support," David said.

The leaders expressed their gratitude for the support, and Becky bid farewell to her mother before joining David in watching the world leaders disappear into a flurry of light particles. It was an epic moment, and they all knew that the fate of the world rested on their shoulders.

Over the next hour, the three other rockets of Space Team I, Space Beta, Space Gamma, and Space Delta arrived without incident and headed for the Moon Station. David was waiting in the lobby to greet them. He'd already changed into his moon clothes—a sleek, white, atmosphere-regulated jumpsuit with gold braiding edging the shoulders and cuffs. Days earlier, Sabrina had transmitted the room and costuming assignments to the robot who staffed the registration desk. She made sure to instruct him to escort David to the best room and allow time for him to shower and relax before he welcomed his team.

"Wow, you sure got your glamour on, dude," Omar said as David extended his hand in welcome. "I guess I gotta turn my swag on to keep up with you."

David smiled. "Welcome to Starlight Moon Station, Omar. No need for—swag. Everyone has the same outfits, in space or on the moon."

"I was just kidding, bro. I know the drill." He clapped David on the shoulder and walked over with Namkhai to register.

"We made it!" Mariana said, high-fiving David.

"Almost without a glitch," Juliana added.

David noticed Mariana shot Juliana a worrying look. "Did something go wrong?" he asked.

"Not really," Mariana said. "Just a little miscommunication with Butch that I cleared up pronto."

"What kind of miscommunication?" David asked.

Mariana took a deep breath. "Butch fainted. He's all right now, though."

"Yeah, I'm right as rain," Butch said, coming up behind Mariana. "Probably a little anti-hydrated is all."

"Check in with the doctor at Medical Bay I. If she certifies you're healthy, you can stay on. If not, you'll be in quarantine for a while," David said.

Butch headed to the health facility without saying another word.

Deepak and Chava entered next with their team. David was pleased to see Deepak seemed more upbeat than he'd been before the launch. "Feeling better?" he asked.

"Yes, being so close to the stars renewed me," Deepak said.

"I helped cheer him up, too," Daniel said, stepping out from behind Deepak, where he'd been hiding. "Turns out it's easier to teach beach tennis without gravity."

David couldn't believe his eyes. "What are you doing here, Daniel? Your name wasn't on the manifest for Space Gamma."

"Did you think Mom would let you go into battle without your big brother to make sure you get home safely?" Daniel asked and pulled David into a tight hug. "She told HB to make sure I got on the flight."

After everyone had their room assignments, David instructed them to rest. "We'll regroup in the drone station at eight a.m. to review the battle plan."

David headed back to the guest rooms, stopping at Becky's door to say good night. He knocked gently. When she didn't answer he figured she was already sleeping and went down the hall to his own room.

The room was semi-circular in shape, and except for the floor and back wall where the bed was, the curved walls and ceiling were made of glass. David lay down on the bed. Instead of pictures of the stars appearing overhead on a canopy, like in his room at home in Aruba, he stared up at a dazzling spectacle—the constellations themselves, shimmering above him, with Vega conspicuous among them. It was impossible to look up at the millions of stars and not believe there were other beings besides earthlings and the Daktaryons alive in the universe. His thoughts were interrupted by a knock on his door. He got up and opened it to find his brother standing there.

"Can I come in?" Daniel asked.

"It's late," David said. But when he saw a look of disappointment fall across Daniel's face, he relented. "Sure, come in."

They walked over to a floating couch and sat looking at the stars in silence for a few seconds, before Daniel spoke. "I didn't exactly tell you the truth before, David."

"About what? David asked.

"It wasn't Mom who got HB to put me on the rocket ship. Not exactly, anyway," Daniel picked at the braiding on the cuff of his moon suit. "After you disappeared and got on the plane with HB, I was excited, hearing about the aliens. I'd always thought that game you played was a waste of time. But it wasn't. It taught you and all the other players some really important lessons, like why it's important to treat everyone the way you want to be treated, and to share what you have with others." He looked up at his brother and smiled. "Turns out, I was the one wasting time, thinking only about girls and fancy cars."

David hugged his brother and Daniel continued.

"Anyway, later that night, I went to find Mom in her study to tell her I needed to go to Las Vegas and join R.A.T.S. When I got there, she was reading that book she's always studying and asked me to sit down, so I did. She finished making some notes and looked up at me and said,

'Daniel, you and your brother are both gifts in our life. As precious as you both are to this family, I believe it's important for you boys to be together, helping one another. Go, be with your brother.'

"I was kind of shocked at first. I had a whole speech prepared about how I understood now what the really important things in life were. But I didn't have to say a thing. It was like she already knew what I wanted to do. So here I am, bro, eager to help and feeling so blessed to have a brother like you."

Although David's eyes filled with tears, he was smiling. "We're both blessed. I couldn't ask for a better brother than you," he said, hugging his brother again.

"Thanks, bro. You really are special," Daniel said, letting out a big sigh.

They sat together for a moment longer, staring at the stars. Then Daniel cleared his throat. "There's something I still don't understand, though."

"What's that?" David asked.

"Why are those fools stealing our water?"

"Because it's the surest way to make life on Earth impossible. Water is life. Even our own bodies are made mostly of water," David said.

Daniel started to laugh. "Maybe that's why I like hanging out at the beach so much." He stood up and gave David the R.A.T.S salute. "Lieutenant Daniel, reporting for duty," he said, smiling.

David laughed. "Right now, your duty is to rest."

"Aye, aye, sir."

After Daniel left, David verified that all the other rockets launched from Elias I.E. had arrived safely and went to sleep, falling into a dream.

He was standing in a splendid, aromatic garden lit by the sun's golden rays. In the sky above, birds flew, spinning and twirling as if in slow motion, while on the ground below, every species of animal rested together peacefully, even a lion beside a lamb. At one end of the garden, pure, crystalline waterfalls cascaded. In the garden's center, stood a magnificent tree with an illuminated white top and a transparent trunk inside which golden sap flowed. On the tree's branches, fruit sparkled like brilliant diamonds and from its center, four calm rivers flowed toward the four corners of the Earth. David felt a cool wind caress his face and envelop his body. To admire all the beauty, he sat down in a nest of birds, where to his surprise, he felt very comfortable and fell asleep. When he awoke in the garden, his body was cloaked in a robe embroidered with threads of gold, silver and bronze and edged with precious rubies, sapphires and emeralds. He looked at the design on the robe and the pictures on it began to move, illustrating the story of humanity through the ages. When the tale reached the current era, David was upset by what he saw.

Moments later, he awoke from the dream and looked down at the ring glowing on his finger, where a new leaf was sprouting on a branch etched into its design. Deep in his heart, he understood instantly: *I must change the course of humanity's story.*

Chapter 19

The Past Will Find You

David had awakened two hours before he was due to meet his team in the control room to brief the battle plans. He donned his moon suit and oxygen helmet, made his way to the lobby, and went outside, hoping to catch a glimpse of Earth.

Although it was morning, the stars sparkled as if it were night. *Of course*, David thought, *the moon has no atmosphere so the stars are always visible.* He adjusted his helmet to reduce the sun's glare and Earth appeared before him like a gigantic, darkened ball, so much larger than the moon appeared from Earth. Because they'd launched when the moon was visibly full from Earth, the planet wasn't basking in sunlight from David's viewpoint on the moon, but he could still make out its outline. Here and there across its surface, lights from urban centers flickered like dying candles. He raised his arm and traced the Earth's circumference with his finger. Then he spread his hand wide as if he wanted to grab the planet, pull it from the universe, and hide it away for safekeeping until whatever dangers now threatening it had disappeared. His grandfather's words came back to him then: *We are not robots or puppets. With our G-d-given free will, we must defend ourselves.* Yes, and with that G-d-given free will, he could choose between right and wrong, and what Grutan was doing was wrong. They'd gone to the moon not to hide or escape but to face this menacing force and together defend their home from the Daktaryon invasion.

Back in his room, he opened his GraphoScreen© to study data from Mission Control about the scope of the alien attack and was stunned to learn the size of Grutan's force. Besides the fleet of spaceships siphoning water from Earth, a battalion of enormous spacecraft, each one larger than anything known to Earth scientists, was barreling at warp speed toward the moon. David swiped the screen to display another table indicating the strength of R.A.T.S' defensive arsenal. At his team's disposal were hundreds of drones in moon silos, armed with fusion bombs. Besides these, they could deploy other weapons stored on the scores of satellites the United States, China, Russia and India had launched into space to threaten each other during periods of intense international conflict. The rapid approval of an international defense treaty among those nations had put all of those supplies under his command too.

"Elias I.E., this is Commander David. Over."

"Read you loud and clear, Commander. Over," Vitoria said.

"I estimate time to incoming attack as T-5 hours," David said.

"Confirm, Commander. T-5 hours," Vitoria said.

"Roger," David said. "How's everything down there? Over."

"Fine here at Elias I.E., but..." Vitoria hesitated. "Grutan's forces are siphoning off the Colorado River. At the rate their going, the entire western United States will be without drinking water in less than three weeks. Tens of millions of people will die."

David was so horrified he couldn't speak.

"Commander, do you copy?" Vitoria's voice cracked with emotion.

"Roger, Mission Control. Copy. R.A.T.S won't let that happen. You have my word. Over."

"Roger, we're all counting on you, Commander. Over and out."

As David signed off, he thought about the many scenarios they'd faced in the game. They'd defeated numerous attacks, and wounded or killed hundreds of enemies. But it had only been a game. Now, the battle ahead of them was real and the hardest thing for him to face was the fact that he might have to commit violence on another living being, even to the point of causing death. *A time to love and a time to hate; a time for war and a time for peace.* However necessary this fight might be, war was a tremendous burden they'd all have to bear. With a heavy heart, he made final preparations for the briefing.

The eight leaders of Space Team I, along with their many assistants, including Daniel, Richard, and Butch, followed Commander David in silence along the long corridor of the underground tunnel that separated their luxurious living quarters designated especially for the highest-ranked officers among them in the east wing from the west wing, where the control room was located three levels below ground. Around the room, dozens of computers whirred and beeped with information. Behind the bank of monitors, an immense GraphoScreen© covered the entire wall. It displayed every light blip or energy flux detected by orbiting satellites and then converted anything identified as an incoming missile or weapon to calculations of real-time to destination, enabling the drones to be readied for a counter-attack.

"Wow, how cool!" Omar exclaimed, heading toward the computer station labeled with his name. "This place is an exact replica of the control room in the game."

"Except for the view." Namkhai pointed to the GraphoScreen©. "What are those pulsating lights?"

"Most of them are signals from another star or planet within fifty million miles of us. But this cluster here," David circled a group of flashing lights with a laser beam, "is the Daktaryon fleet approaching."

"They're thirty minutes from the moon's orbital path," Mariana said as calmly as she could, sitting down at the computer station assigned to her.

Juliana, sitting next to her and reading her screen said, "And it looks like there are—"

"—a dozen spaceships heading right for us," David said. "We haven't received an exact reading yet, but each of those ships is bigger than our four rockets combined."

"Actually, they each weigh 5.2 million kilograms and are two hundred and eighty meters long," Richard said, projecting his calculations onto the GraphoScreen©.

"I told you he was a wiz with computers," Namkhai said, winking at David.

"Thanks, Richard. Becky, calculate defensive shield dimensions to accommodate and transmit to Deepak."

"Roger." Becky swiped her screen. "Calculated and transmitted," she said.

"Shield ready to activate, Commander," Deepak said.

"Activate now, Deepak," David ordered.

"Roger," Deepak said. "Shield activated."

"Energy flux in quadrant four," Daniel reported.

"Deepak, amplify shield to 0.8532," David said.

"Roger, shield amplified," Deepak said.

"Tutla, unlock drone silos three through nine," David said.

"D-3 through 9 unlocked and ready for launch," Tutla reported.

"Launch and hold steady, Tutla," David said.

"Copy that. D-3 through 9 launched and holding," Tutla said.

"Chava, ready backup drones in silos ten through fourteen."

"Roger," Chava said. "D-10 through 14, ready for backup."

As the first seven drones zoomed into position a mile above the moon's surface, armed and ready for attack, the R.A.T.S warriors watched the flashing lights on the GraphoScreen© grow brighter and brighter until a battalion of black metallic, shape-shifting spaceships appeared in the moon's orbital path and hovered in formation behind the largest vehicle. Each ship looked like it was made from a seamless array of interlocking metal balls, some of which seemed to expand and contract like lungs. The pattern of ships looked like some gigantic, hydra-headed beast, ready to strike.

"What are they doing?" Omar asked, his voice a little shaky.

"Waiting to see if we'll fire first," David answered.

"I'm picking up an energy spike again, David," Daniel called out. "Some kind of radiation I can't identify."

"Amplify shield to max capacity, Deepak," David said. "Tutla, verify drones holding steady."

"Roger, shield to max," Deepak said.

"Confirm D-4 through 9 steady. Detect missile hatch malfunction on D-3." Tutla's eyes widened with worry. "The hatch is open, David."

"Execute weapon release function override, Tutla. We'll use D-3 as a decoy, if necessary," David said. "Chava, stealth launch D-10 and 11."

"Roger. D-3 missile deactivated," Tutla said, looking relieved that David had figured out a backup plan so quickly.

"Roger," Chava acknowledged. "D-10 and 11 launched and hiding in plain sight."

"David, sensors detecting enemy missile above quadrant 4, sector 315, approaching fast," Becky shouted.

"Lieutenants, to your battle stations. Richard, monitor the shield. Butch, open the communication channel. Daniel, eyes glued to those energy indicators," David ordered.

"Roger, Commander," each one answered in unison while the others remained attentive at their assigned stations.

"Becky, Tutla, Deepak maneuver D-4, 5, and 6 into triangle position. Mariana, Juliana, Chava, Omar, Namkhai, position 7 through 11 in U-formation. Do you copy?"

"Roger, Commander."

While David sent D-3 into an erratic, spiraling dance to distract the incoming missile from its course, each of the others took control of one drone and steadied them for attack.

"The decoy maneuver's working, commander!" Richard shouted. "Missile diverted, following D-3 off course."

David increased the speed of the drone, spinning it out of orbit with the missile chasing behind until it collided with the drone and exploded in a giant fireball.

"Missile destroyed, shield intact," Richard reported as the room erupted in applause, a celebration immediately eclipsed by the sound of an alarm.

Red alert, red alert, red alert.

"Activate all weapons. Prepare for full battle," David said, watching Grutan's group of battle ships spread out across the sky. "Drone Teams II and III, report to operations on the double," he announced on the Moon Station intercom.

"Getting some weirdo signal on the comm channel," Butch said.

"Convert to multi-modal," David said.

"Roger." Butch adjusted the frequency. A hazy image appeared on the GraphoScreen© and soon morphed into the unmistakable stone and metal shape of Grutan. "Well,

I'll be… that there makes a hornet look cuddly. What in the world is that thing?" he asked with a disgusted look on his face.

David took control of the channel. "Grutan, we are prepared for your attack."

Grutan laughed. "You may have been able to trick a heat-seeking missile with that clever maneuver, but you will never defeat the full force of a Daktaryon attack. Save yourself and surrender now. Your planet is doomed."

"We will not be bullied. Surrendering is out of the question. If you wish to avoid doing harming our people and yours, let's negotiate a cease-fire and find a peaceful settlement to this dispute."

"What a fool you are! You're fighting a lost battle. Your people have sacrificed life on Earth by the mistakes they've already made. Neither you nor we have time left to negotiate," Grutan said.

"Please, I wish to understand why you think there isn't time. Compromise must be possible," David said, trying hard not to appear weak or defensive.

"Then I will grant your wish by telling you a story," Grutan said. "Many millennia ago, my ancestors were like you: earthlings, masters of the planet. And, like you, they were ambitious and possessed a high level of astrological and technological knowledge."

While Grutan was speaking, David signaled to Butch to open the communication channel to Elias I.E., so HB and the others could listen, too.

Grutan continued. "Our ancestors conquered territories across the Earth. They built and sustained a great empire. Then, disaster struck, depleting their resources, and they were forced to abandon the planet. In their wisdom, the leaders selected a few special ones to accompany them on a voyage to establish a new colony in space. On the journey, they fell into a wormhole in space and, as chance would have it, exited near a planet close enough to Earth's atmosphere to allow them to breathe. Over time, their bodies mutated to adjust to the new environment, transforming us into the appearance we have today."

David looked confused. "If you've found a new home and have adjusted to it, why do you need to steal from Earth now?" he asked.

"Because all life depends on water and on planet Daktaryon, we haven't enough left to survive," Grutan said.

"So, you squandered your resources and now you want to steal ours," David said.

Grutan emitted a loud, piercing noise, like the sound of a dentist's drill amplified a hundred times more than normal. David tried not to cringe, but it was so loud he and everyone else in the room had to cover their ears. A few moments later, Grutan's voice returned to normal range, and he continued his angry speech.

"How dare you judge us! When your planet is on the verge of collapse from your own foolish behavior, yet you still have plenty of water. You call it stealing, but we are merely salvaging from the wreckage of a greedy people what my people need to live."

David suddenly hit on a plan. "Grutan, compromise *is* possible! In Aruba, where I come from, we lack a reliable source of fresh water and have learned how to convert the sea into drinkable water. If we work together, we can create enough of that precious resource to share."

"You're a trickster and a liar! You'll pretend to collaborate but will betray us if we agree to lay down arms, just as my ancestors were once betrayed by a promise of cooperation from the Shalticons, who refused to help in the end," Grutan said.

"If you sign a treaty with us, I promise we would honor it," David said.

At once, holograms of Presidents Sarah and HB appeared behind David. "Commander David speaks the truth," Sarah said. "All Earth's nations have united to support the proposed treaty."

"The history of Earth's treaties is littered with violations and nullifications," Grutan said, raising a fist in defiance. "Time has run out. Surrender, or prepare to die!"

"The past does not predict the future. We've offered peace and you've responded with hostility. We won't capitulate to your evil enterprise," David said.

"It appears the time for war has arrived!" Grutan shouted.

As Grutan's image disappeared from the screen, HB said:

"Phoenix and his spacecraft are only a few moments away from the Moon Station. He's traveling in our most advanced rocket, equipped with the most sophisticated weapons, and is ready to join any battle that might be taking place."

"We need him desperately!" David exclaimed. "But Grutan will destroy anything that comes near the moon from Earth."

HB shook his head. "Our rockets are undetectable. Grutan will never see him coming." He smiled at Sarah. "David, if you hadn't given that inspiring speech to unite us all, we might have used these weapons against each other instead of deploying them to defeat this alien that poses a threat of extinction to all living beings on Earth".

As the holograms of the presidents and HB began to dissolve, David felt a sense of gratitude toward Sarah for her inspiring leadership, and toward HB for his unwavering support. David looked around the room at each member of his team and then back at the GraphoScreen© to watch Grutan's forces take up their battle positions. He raised his hand and gave the R.A.T.S salute. "Ready on my command."

The room full of R.A.T.S responded in unison. "Aye, aye, sir."

**

Back on base, Roy had heard every word of David's plan. "Don't you worry, none, Grutan. Butch might prove he ain't worth spit, but I got your back, partner. This ain't my first rodeo," he muttered to himself, preparing to send a message to the alien leader on a secret communication channel.

Except Roy's channel wasn't as secret as he believed it was. The ever-vigilant communication specialist, Tyler, had his suspicions about Roy as soon as he arrived at Elias I.E., so he'd attached one of his special tracking markers to Roy's computer codes. The data he'd amassed on Roy confirmed what he'd guessed from the start—Roy was trying to subvert the R.A.T.S mission.

"Not on my watch," Tyler thought as he scrambled Roy's message to Grutan. "You may think you're clever, but you're not the sharpest tool in the shed. I'll let you play this game of yours a little while longer and then, when your guard is down, I'll expose you for the nasty traitor you really are!"

Chapter 20

Time for War

"Energy surge in quadrants 4, 5, and 6," Daniel called out. "Detecting incoming missiles."

"Fire weapons from D-4 through D-6!" David ordered.

Becky, Deepak, and Tutla swiped their screens, launching a barrage of independently targeted fusion bombs from the underbelly of each drone. Streaks of light scattered in multiple directions across the sky, as if some immense spider had spun a gigantic, illuminated web in space to trap and devour anything that wandered into its elaborate design. Within seconds, the entire GraphoScreen© turned a blindingly bright white as the first bombs hit their target.

"Target A neutralized. Missile destroyed," Tutla announced, and the room erupted into wild applause.

Moments later, there was another massive explosion in space, and then another and another, sending waves of sound back toward the moon so forcefully that the control room shook with their impact.

"Richard, I need an updated report on the shield's functioning," David said as calmly as possible.

"Shield intact," Richard reported. "But there's some kind of dust covering one of the external monitors."

"I can't get an accurate reading on whether my weapons hit the other targets," Becky shouted in a voice shrill with worry. "Wait a minute, the monitor's cleared now." She exhaled deeply.

"I was able to scrub it," Richard said.

"Thanks, Richard," Becky said, sounding relieved. "Confirm Targets B and C neutralized. Two missiles destroyed."

Before they could celebrate, Deepak interrupted. "Drone 6 intercepted and incapacitated before strike."

"No worries, Deepak," Tutla said. "We've launched enough other weapons to take up the slack."

"I'm not so sure about that, bro," Omar said, pointing to the GraphoScreen©. The display was no longer white. Instead, it showed that the array of ships in Grutan's fleet had expanded in size in the few moments since the first incoming missile attack. What had first appeared as a hydra-headed beast suddenly morphed into a gargantuan monstrosity, blocking out whole constellations of stars.

"Sure, looks like we got us a big hole in our fence," Butch said.

David's Spher@ buzzed, and he answered immediately. "Great, thanks for the update. You know what to do," he said.

Without missing a beat, David called out new orders. "Mariana, Juliana, Chava, Omar, switch drones from U-formation to right-angled V-formation and maneuver to right and left flank of the enemy's forces. Namkhai, move yours center and hold steady."

"Aye, aye, sir," all five pilots acknowledged.

"David, I've calculated the force of all those weapons. I don't think the shield can withstand that powerful explosion," Richard said.

"I realize that. I'm not planning to fire all at once. We're going to tempt Grutan with a few sacrificial lambs to distract him," David said.

"Are you crazy? You're going to let Grutan wipe out those drones?" Daniel asked, looking at his brother in disbelief.

David nodded. "Phoenix just called me to say his aircraft is approaching Grutan's rear guard. He won't see them coming and he'll be too excited about bringing down the drones to think clearly," David said. "I've ordered Phoenix to strike as soon as I give the signal."

"Ready in V-formation on the right flank," Mariana and Juliana called out in unison.

"Ready on the left," Chava and Omar said together.

"At center and steady, Commander," Namkhai said.

"Prepare to deactivate weapons and begin decoy maneuvers."

"Hold on, David. I'm getting some wild readings on the energy indicators," Daniel suddenly shouted. "We're being hit with some kind of huge force field!"

"Operationalize emergency intake coils at highest voltage capacity to initiate counter electromagnetic force," David ordered.

Daniel manipulated his controls and a loud whirring noise filled the room.

"CEM ineffective, David," Richard shouted as an alarm buzzed and blue lights flashed across his screen. "Whoa! We're getting false-color imagery transmitted from the satellite positioned above quadrant six. Never seen anything like this before. Extreme ultraviolet rays. Hotter than a million Celsius. Some shield panels above the east wing of the moon station are warping."

"Identify source, Daniel," David said.

"Appears to be coming from a device at the center of Grutan's fleet," Daniel reported. "Some kind of UVC generator."

"Becky, activate artificial ozone layer," he said.

"On it, David," Becky said. "Layer activated."

David magnified the image of Grutan's fleet on the GraphoScreen© to zoom in on the emitting source and circled it on the screen with a laser light.

"Namkhai, roll drone underneath that emitting device, activate weapons, and prepare to fire."

Namkhai manipulated the drone into position and opened the weapons' hatch.

But before David could give the command to fire, an enemy rocket exploded the drone, sending a large ball of fire and metal cascading through space. Ash and shards of shimmering metal fell on the moon station dome-like slow-moving droplets of silver-flecked, black rain.

Seconds later, another louder alarm sounded, jolting everyone to high alert.

"David, some east wing shield panels have melted," Richard shouted as loud as he could above the din. "Fire on level one!"

"Activate secondary shield," David said. He switched his screen to display the interior view of level one and was relieved to see the emergency robot team had performed as expected, evacuating personnel, securing the fire doors in all corridors, and extinguishing the blaze before executing repairs to the primary shield. "Fire's suppressed," he reported to everyone's relief. "Shield repaired."

"Enemy action on the right flank," Mariana called out. "I've got heat seeking heading toward D-7 and D-8."

Chava echoed Mariana's observation. "Missiles fired on D-9. No reading on D-10 or 11. Wait a minute... All drones now under attack. How'd they find 10 and 11? I had those still in stealth mode."

"I took them out of stealth mode when David ordered the drone reformation," Juliana said with a sheepish expression on her face.

Mariana turned toward her sister with an angry look. "You did what?"

"You did the right thing, Juliana. I'd forgotten those drones were stealth," David said. "Good thing you made them visible, or my tactic wouldn't have worked."

Juliana let out a sigh and relaxed. Mariana whispered a quick apology to her before calling out the seconds to missile impact. "T-5 seconds and counting."

"Hold steady on course at 0.597, deactivate, and prepare for hit," David said.

"Aye, sir." Mariana manipulated the drone's controls. "Steady on course."

"Chava, steady on course at 4.866, deactivate and prepare," David said.

"Steady on 4.866 and holding," Chava replied.

Two seconds later, five gigantic balls of fiery light erupted in space, once again raining debris down on the moon's surface, this time far afield from the station's location. The explosion sent the statoscopes on Elias I.E. spinning so wildly, HB sent an emergency message to David's Spher@.

"No worries, Grandpa," David said. "I made the tactical decision to allow Grutan to destroy some drones. I want him to think he's winning so he'll let his guard down. Phoenix is moments away. I've got drone reinforcements ready to deploy."

David ended the call and asked Becky to relieve Daniel on the energy monitors. "Daniel, I need you to compile data from the international defense satellite monitors and report coordinates and weapons' capacities."

Right after Becky and Daniel moved to their new stations, David's Spher@ rang again. David activated his telecom communication line to make Phoenix visible and audible to everyone. As he came into focus, the R.A.T.S cheered.

"Hi, Commander David," Phoenix said with a wide smile on his face. "I have the enemy's rear guard in my sights and await your signal."

"Lock on target and prepare to fire, Phoenix," David said.

"Loaded and locked," Phoenix said.

All of a sudden, Butch jumped out of his seat, pointing to a fuzzy image forming on the GraphoScreen©. "Gosh darn it, David. That metal-plated, stony-pocked monster's buzzing' on the comm line, again."

"Hold steady, Phoenix. We've been contacted again."

Phoenix acknowledged with a thumbs' up and kept his communication channel open, while David turned his attention to Grutan, whose image came into focus.

The grotesque alien was seated at a command post on the dimly lit bridge of his massive spaceship, surrounded by several Daktaryon officers. "We've destroyed everything you've sent our way while you wasted your precious resources blowing up dummy missiles we'd fired," Grutan said. "I warned you our forces would overwhelm you. Are you ready to surrender now?"

"Surrender is unthinkable. But my offer to collaborate still stands," David said, hoping to keep Grutan distracted in conversation as long as possible.

Grutan shook his head. "I don't negotiate with tricksters."

"Grutan, I promise whatever happened to your ancestors won't happen again," David said. "Let us help each other survive."

"My people's survival is my only concern," Grutan replied in an angry voice. "Your people have doomed themselves."

Becky noticed a sudden surge on the energy monitors and telepathically communicated the news to David.

Grutan's ships are closing in on us. They're within range to destroy everything.

"You leave me no choice, but one," David said. Slowly, without taking his attention away from Grutan, David brought his hand to his heart, giving the signal for Phoenix to launch.

"Strike authorized," Phoenix communicated to his weapons' team. "Release all weapons from holds. Full rear attack. Pincer movement on right and left flanks."

Within moments, the weapons hit their targets, exploding Grutan's fleet into tiny fragments of debris. The control room erupted in shouts of joy and celebration until Becky pointed to the GraphoScreen© where an enormous fireball of light was reverberating into the path of Phoenix's rocket ship and another was heading straight for the moon.

"Abandon ship, abandon ship," David yelled to Phoenix.

In his final moments, Phoenix knew that the mission had been completed. He said to himself, "This is not about me, this is for Mother Earth."

"Goodbye," Phoenix said with honor in his voice. "The rest is up to you, my friends. Stay safe and be in G-d's hands."

David's eyes welled with tears. Namkhai moved close to him, placed a hand gently on his shoulder, and whispered a prayer he'd heard his friend say many times before: "A time to weep and a time to laugh; a time of wailing and a time of dancing."

"Thank you, dear Namkhai. I know what I must do." David lifted his head high, straightened his shoulders, and took a deep breath. He turned to his team. "R.A.T.S, prepare for impact." Then he waved his hand across the GraphoScreen©, switching to emergency controls, and entered a command. An alert sounded throughout the moon station.

Attention all personnel, attention all personnel. Head to underground bunkers immediately.

At once, ceramic cylinders made of hafnium carbide descended over each R.A.T.S' station in the control room and encased all the hundreds of others who'd scrambled below ground for shelter. Then a loud noise like the sonic boom of the sound barrier being broken vibrated across the moon station, rattling sensors and everyone's nerves.

David counted to one hundred and then raised his shield before everyone else and looked around the room to find the others emerging from their ceramic cocoons, dazed and confused. The view of the moon displayed on the GraphoScreen© showed the blast had created a massive crater, but had hit far enough away from the station to spare it. Except for damage to a couple of drone silos, their base of operations was intact.

"OMG! Look!" Omar shouted. Glistening alone in the earthlight, Grutan's menacing rocket ship hovered closer than ever to the moon's surface.

"Oh, no!" Juliana shook her head. "Phoenix bombed the whole Daktaryon fleet to smithereens. How did Grutan's vessel survive?"

"He must have made some last-minute evasive maneuver," Mariana said.

"I guess y'all better keep your saddles oiled and your guns greased," Butch said. "That mean monster looks like it's ready to bite like a rattlesnake."

"What about the other R.A.T.S in the below-ground bunkers, David?" Tutla asked.

A low murmur of worry worked its way across the room until Richard spoke. "It's a policy to appoint someone in mission command to check on the crew in the other bunkers," he said calmly.

"I must stay here in the control room. Tutla, I need you to go below and confirm everyone's safe," David said.

Tutla saluted and exited to check on the rest of the crew.

"Hold on a tiny second. I'm getting a signal." Butch adjusted the frequency of the comm channel and Grutan's image came into view.

David moved to the front of the group to face the alien.

"Perhaps now that your stubbornness has caused so much damage, you'll see the wisdom of surrender," Grutan said.

David took a wide-legged stance, crossed his arms, and looked sternly at the alien. "After reducing the size of your so-called superior forces to that single, puny mothership of yours, I think the choice to surrender is yours, Grutan."

Grutan laughed. "The ships I lost were nothing compared to the forces I have in reserve," he said.

"You're bluffing," David said. "If you had that power, you'd already have called up replacements. All I see before me is one, lonely, Daktaryon vessel. Why don't you just head back to whatever galaxy you came from and leave us alone?"

"Never!" Grutan roared.

"Then you will suffer the consequences." David shook his fist at Grutan.

"You are as foolish as the rest of your people. Prepare to be annihilated," Grutan said as his image faded to static.

"What do we do now, David?" Deepak asked.

"As soon as Tutla returns with his report, we'll prepare to attack. We're going to destroy every trace of the Daktaryons," David said.

"Tutla had better hurry up. The readings I'm getting on the shield put it dangerously low for protection from another strike," Richard said. "We need to launch before Grutan hits us again."

Moments later, Tutla returned. "Everyone is safe and ready for your command, David."

David felt a wave of emotion flow through the room. He looked around the control room at each of the R.A.T.S, so worried about the future, and knew the time had come for each of them to be as courageous as possible. He remembered his mother had once said that courage was being able to do whatever was needed in the moment, even if it frightened you. With the strength he felt from his faith, and the power of love he held in his heart for every member of his team, he turned to Tutla.

"Whenever the commander is absent from the control bridge, you're the one in charge of monitoring the action, Tutla. Take over the controls and watch the GraphoScreen© while I'm gone," David said, turning on the moon station intercom. "Attention all R.A.T.S. To your battle stations. Prepare to meet the enemy face to face." Then he messaged the engineers in the rocket bays to prepare Space Alpha, Beta, Gamma, and Delta, along with thousands of rockets loaded with weapons, for immediate deployment.

Before he left the control room, David called his father and HB on Elias I.E. to explain his plan.

"I'm proud of you, son," Kenneth said. "You made the right decision to lead your team into direct battle with Grutan."

"What are you going to tell Mom?" David asked.

"Your mother will worry, of course. But I'm sure she'll understand," HB said. "This monster must be stopped."

After donning flight gear, David and Daniel raced to board Space Alpha. Chava and Deepak, Omar and Namkhai, and Mariana and Juliana and their respective teams headed for the other three ships, while more teams of R.A.T.S astronauts prepared to board theirs. Becky stayed behind to supervise Richard and Butch on the controls, rotate new groups of drone pilots into their stations under Tutla's direction, and maintain communications with the R.A.T.S fleet and Elias I.E.

"This is moon station control room, Alpha. You're cleared for departure," Becky said.

"Roger, control room. Aft thrusters ready to fire," David said. "Daniel, we're go."

"Aft thrusters fired," Daniel said, and the rocket ship lifted into space.

One after the other, as Becky directed the pilots of the other spaceships to launch toward Grutan's immense vessel, R.A.T.S warriors took to the sky until twenty-four gleaming R.A.T.S vessels encircled the Daktaryon spaceship in a gigantic, six-pointed star formation, hovering and waiting for the command to strike.

Without warning, Grutan's ship spun rapidly until a series of metallic balls in one section opened like great, gaping maws and bombarded the nearest vessel within range.

"Energy surge heading starboard, Beta," Richard called out to Chava on the comm channel.

Chava maneuvered her rocket to evade the attack and fired back, hitting the alien ship. Grutan countered with another barrage, sending Chava's rocket hurtling dangerously close to Gamma and several support rockets nearby.

"Deepak, reverse thrusters," Chava screamed.

Deepak entered the command into the engine's computers, sending the rocket rapidly backward and into a collision course with another volley of weapons Grutan had already fired. The impact threw Deepak headlong into the ship's console, knocking him out. Chava had managed to steady herself for the hit and reached over to check Deepak's flight suit's heart monitor to make sure he was still alive. The reading alarmed her.

"I've got a flight deck emergency. I need a medic here, pronto," she called on the intercom. But by the time the medic reached the cockpit, Deepak had already expired. Then another missile hit, and Beta exploded. Before any of its astronauts had even a minute to say a final prayer of mourning for their dear friend, the entire Beta crew was gone.

Silence fell in the moon station control room and on Elias I.E., as everyone realized they'd lost the first members of the R.A.T.S army to Grutan's maniacal wrath.

In Space Alpha, David was overcome with emotion. But he knew that the heat of battle was no time to mourn the loss of his close friends. He steadied himself and opened the all-ships comm channel.

"Gamma, Delta, support teams, reposition above and behind that monster and prepare to fire all weapons," David ordered. "Now!"

Mariana moved Delta quickly to the rear of Grutan's ship with six more support rockets following her, dodging a volley of lasers Grutan had fired from his port side as she approached, while Juliana lobbed a rapid-fire series of fusion bombs in the direction of the throbbing spheres, which were expanding and contracting above what looked like the ship's bridge. She made a direct hit and the alien vessel wobbled off course and into the path of the weapons Omar, aboard Gamma, was firing from the position above and then into those Daniel had released from Alpha.

"We got him, David!" Daniel cried out to his brother.

"Watch out, David," Namkhai yelled, monitoring his screen on Gamma. "Something's coming at your port side."

David had taken up the location in front of Grutan's ship. From his position in the control room on the moon, Tutla had already noticed another hatch open on the alien ship and ordered three drones into position on Space Alpha's starboard side.

"I got you covered, David, hold steady," Tutla called. "T-8 seconds to impact and counting. Pull out of position at T-3 and we'll blast that ship out of the universe with the drones' weapons."

"Roger," David said, setting his countdown marker to coordinate.

"T-5, 4… Move now," Tutla shouted.

David ordered Daniel to fire the aft thrusters and the drones hidden on Alpha's starboard side exploded an approaching missile and sent another salvo of weapons into the already damaged alien ship. With its last gasp of energy, Grutan's flying metal fortress released a final round of lasers into space, hitting several R.A.T.S rocket ships unable to move quickly enough out of the way.

The explosion made the image on the moon station GraphoScreen© turn a blinding white. When the screen cleared, the moon station team watched the battered alien vessel lurch and break apart until the last group of linked metal balls formed themselves into a capsule and rocketed away into deep space.

Roy had been watching the battle from his station on Elias I.E. "I sure, hope Grutan escaped in that little, bitty, shiny bucket, because he sure owes me a whole lotta money. And, after what I've been able to pull off, I aim to collect, one way or another."

The moon station team was about to erupt in celebration when Becky suddenly made an announcement. "I've got confirmation of status from Delta and Gamma, but I've lost communication with Alpha," she shouted in a voice filled with anguish. "Elias I.E., can you confirm Alpha's coordinates?"

"Negative," Vitoria replied from Elias I.E. "There's no incoming signal."

"Wait a minute. I'm hearing a faint bleep. It's coming from Alpha's emergency escape capsule. Let me switch channels and see what I get," Becky said.

At first, there was nothing but static on the channel. Then, Becky heard a voice.

"Moon station control, this is Alpha. Can you read me?" the voice asked.

Becky recognized it was Daniel speaking. "Read you loud and clear, Alpha," she said, trying to stay calm. "Give us an update."

"Took a big hit. Fired with everything we had. Made it into the emergency escape vehicle," Daniel said.

"Everyone okay?" Becky asked.

There was silence on the other end.

"Daniel, did everyone on Alpha make it out?" she asked.

"Everyone except David," Daniel said, his voice shaking with sobs. "He's gone!"

"What do you mean he's gone, Daniel?" Becky shrieked, unable to control the worry in her voice.

Daniel choked back tears. "He stayed back to make sure the others escaped. He didn't make it out before the ship exploded. My brother is dead!"

"No, that's not possible," Becky said, covering her mouth to stifle a cry.

Seeing how upset Becky was, Tutla took over control of the comm channel. "Daniel, maneuver the escape capsule above quadrant two and prepare for moon landing, over," he said as steadily as possible.

"Roger," Daniel said, his voice still a little shaky. "Positioning capsule for descent. Over."

While Tutla directed Alpha's landing, Becky walked to a corner of the control room to message David telepathically. *David, this is Becky. I know you're out there somewhere. Please, tell me you're safe.* She waited for him to reply, but was greeted with silence. She tried again. *David, please, let me know if you're okay.* Silence. She took a deep breath, feeling as if her heart was being ripped to shreds, and sent one last message. *Wherever you've gone, David, I want you to know I miss you, head-in-the-clouds boy. Come back to me as soon as you can.*

Chapter 21

A Moment of Silence

News of David's disappearance spread quickly throughout the moon station, darkening the R.A.T.S' celebration of their defeat of Grutan with shadows of sorrow at the loss of their brave commander along with so many other close friends. After Tutla had verified the return of all surviving warriors to the moon, he asked everyone to assemble in the complex's amphitheater to commemorate the battle and the losses they'd sustained. In a somber mood, the R.A.T.S dressed in their uniforms and carried the flags of every nation of the world into the ceremony to demonstrate the extraordinary mix of humanity who'd come together in solidarity to aid Earth's defense. Tutla acknowledged the assembly with the R.A.T.S salute and began to address them.

"Today, for the briefest of moments, we experienced the joy of triumph over our enemies. Yet the loss of Commander David and other brave friends—Deepak, Chava, Phoenix, and so many others whose names we will never forget…"

Overwhelmed with emotion, Tutla paused a moment to compose himself.

"… The loss of these friends has brought us to the edge of a deep well of sorrow. Let us honor their memory with a moment of silence."

He bowed his head. After a few moments, he continued.

"Tomorrow, we begin the journey home. Although we leave them behind, the friends we've lost will always remain in our hearts. By dedicating ourselves to the work of strengthening the bonds among all nations to repair and renew the Earth, our mother, and becoming better stewards of her gifts by being better guardians of our souls, we will continue to honor their memory and celebrate their courage."

The roomful of R.A.T.S stood in silence a little longer, their grief made more bearable in each other's company. Daniel was near the front of the group. Tutla gestured to him, inviting him to speak. He took a deep breath, exhaled, and climbed the stairs to the podium.

"Although my heart is filled with sadness today, it is also full of gratitude for the faith my brother had in me—had in all of us—to defeat Earth's enemies. I believe David would want us to continue the work we've begun." With tears streaming down his face, Daniel gave the R.A.T.S salute. "Commander David, wherever you are, we want you to know we are ready for whatever lies ahead."

Then, from somewhere in the room, came the clear, bright notes of the flutist's melody. The tune floated over them, quietly at first, until it built to a sparkling crescendo and reverberated around the room. The sounds of the song that had first summoned them to battle bounced off the amphitheater walls, filling the entire moon station and reaching beyond, into space itself, as if beseeching the heavenly spheres never to still its powerful ode to community and compassion.

Fortified by the magical music, the R.A.T.S returned to their rooms to rest and prepare for the homeward journey.

On his way back to his room, Namkhai saw Richard sitting in one of the chairs in the hallway. He noticed Richard was fiddling with something in his hand. As he got closer, he recognized it as the watch the boy had been wearing on the plane when they departed Nepal. From the streaks on his face, Namkhai could tell Richard had been crying. He sat down next to him and touched his shoulder.

"I'm just down the hall in room twenty-three, if you want to talk," Namkhai said and stood up.

Richard grabbed his hand. "Will you sit with me awhile?"

"Sure," Namkhai said and sat down again.

Richard kept turning the watch over and over in his hand. They spent a few minutes together in silence. Then Namkhai spoke.

"I see you still have that watch," he said.

Richard nodded. "I miss my grandfather," he said. "I should have spent more time with him."

"We'll be with our families again, soon," Namkhai said.

"He was sick when I left on this mission," Richard said. "I just hope it's not too late."

"No matter what time it is, Richard, it will be the right time," Namkhai said.

"I don't understand." Richard looked at him quizzically.

"It will be the right time because the journey has prepared you, as you've shown by your calm service to the team," Namkhai said.

Richard looked at him. "Thank you for your kindness," he said.

Namkhai brought his hands together and bowed his head. "I honor the kindness in you."

Becky hadn't wanted to attend the ceremony. Mariana and Juliana had tried to convince her that it was better to be together at a time like this than to sit alone in her room, staring out the window at the stars. But the stars comforted her. When she looked up at them, twinkling with light, she had the strangest feeling that David hadn't died but had simply slipped into some other dimension in space, as if a secret door had opened somewhere in the middle of the universe and could open again and release him back to this life. It wasn't possible; she knew that. But imagining he was out there, somewhere, made her feel less alone. Like David had said when they were in the rocket on the way to the moon, memories and dreams keep us connected to what we love. She touched the locket around her neck, rubbing the gray-green stone on its surface. Yes, she thought, home is that place in your heart where everything you ever loved continues to live.

On Elias I.E, the mood was somber. HB could hardly believe David had disappeared. His heart ached at the thought of never seeing his beloved grandson again. They had shared so much together it was difficult to imagine how he'd fill the void left by David's loss. Yet he knew he needed to find the strength not only to console his family about David's loss but also to bring the rest of the R.A.T.S safely home. He went to the flight strategy room to review the damage the Daktaryon forces had caused and plot a course to bring the R.A.T.S back to the base. Kenneth was there, waiting for him.

"HB, I'm so upset about David's loss I can hardly breathe. But I'm also worried about Daniel. I must get to the moon station," Kenneth said.

"Of course. I understand," HB said, touching Kenneth's shoulder. "Daniel certainly needs you to comfort him now. I'll set you up in the holograph conversion device. Follow me."

They walked down a long corridor to another room. As they entered, the young man seated in front of a computer station quickly swiped the screen to open a different display.

"Sorry to interrupt, Roy, but we need access to this station," HB said.

"No bother. I was just fixing' to go on a break," Roy said.

"Have you finished the calculations I asked you to complete?" HB asked.

"Been jumping like hot grease on a skillet with them numbers, but I ain't done yet. Don't you worry none. I'll have it for y'all after I get back in a New York minute," Roy said and left the room.

Kenneth shook his head. "I didn't understand a word he said, did you?"

HB raised his eyebrows and nodded. "I spent enough time in Texas to be able to translate. Now, let's get you to the moon. Put your hand on this biometric reader," HB said, gesturing to a rectangular, glass-covered raised platform sitting on the table in front of them.

As soon as Kenneth touched it, an image began to take shape in the room. Soon the form became his exact replica made out of particles of light. Kenneth shuddered, seeing his duplicate shimmering in the room. Every movement he made, every word he uttered, the hologram repeated.

"I had the same reaction the first time I projected a hologram of myself. You get used to it after a while," HB said, moving the controls to position the image inside a tubular compartment. "Ready to launch to the moon?" he asked.

"Ready," Kenneth said.

Moments later, his hologram was transported to Daniel's room in the residential section of the moon station, where he found Daniel resting on his bed. Kenneth cleared his throat, startling his son, who bolted upright and stared at his father, mouth agape.

"Dad! How'd you—"

"—HB helped. I needed to be with you," Kenneth said.

"I did everything I could to save him, Dad. But he refused to leave the ship until he was sure everyone else got off. By then, it was too late." Daniel buried his face in his hands and wept.

"It's okay, Daniel. You did what you needed to do to survive. And David did what he needed to do," Kenneth said.

"Dad, how are you going to explain to Mom what happened?" Daniel asked.

"Daniel, your mother loves you and knows you'd do anything to protect your brother. We'll get through this together as a family, as we always do," Kenneth said. "Now, get some rest. I love you, son."

"I love you too, Dad."

After Kenneth left, Daniel lay awake a little longer, thinking about what his father had said. It was true. David had done what he needed to do. Funny how just hearing his father say that made him feel so much better. Maybe life was the gift of time everyone was given to discover who they really were, and the battle had been David's time. And in a different way, it had been Daniel's time too.

While HB had been busy arranging Kenneth's holographic transfer, Roy sprang into action. The calculations he'd made for the planned trajectory to return the R.A.T.S to Earth were designed to sabotage the voyage, just as he'd plotted with Grutan even before the last battle had begun. He'd hoped Grutan had escaped the explosion, but not knowing for sure whether the alien had survived or not, he decided to carry out their plan anyway.

"Pretty soon, I'll be riding the gravy train in biscuit wheels," he muttered as he began entering elaborate mathematical equations into Elias I.E.'s controls in the now empty flight strategy room. He was so busy talking to himself and being excited in anticipation of his victory celebration that he didn't notice an alarm signal lighting up yellow on a panel to his left, which measured when the oxygen levels in the underground room were reaching a dangerously low level.

Tyler had been monitoring the situation in the main control room and raced down the hall to warn Roy. Although he'd been eavesdropping on Roy's communications and knew he must be up to no good, he couldn't leave him exposed to a life-threatening danger.

"What are you doing in here, Roy?" Tyler asked.

Roy jumped at the sound of the young Aruban's voice. "You oughtn't to be sneaking up behind a fella like that," he said. "Made me jump out of my boots."

"You need to get out of here right away," Tyler said, keeping one eye on the oxygen monitor and the other on Roy.

"I gotta finish what I started. Put it in the numbers like HB said to get the team home." He continued entering the data into the computer.

"C'mon Roy, the room's not safe now. Look," he said, pointing to the flashing light that had turned from yellow to red.

Roy looked at the monitor and laughed. "That thing always goes wacky 'round this time of the day. Then it settles back down. I'll be done in a second anyways."

"I'm going to get help," Tyler said.

"You do that. But I'm telling you, there ain't nothing wrong with this room. I have seen that light flashing' before and nothing ever happened," Roy said, and turned back to his task.

Tyler ran down the hall to get HB. It took almost a minute before he found him. As soon as he told HB what was happening, the general grabbed an emergency kit, put on an oxygen mask and handed one to Tyler. Together, they hurried back down the hall to the flight control room. They found Roy in a heap on the floor, gasping for air and holding a piece of paper in his hand.

"Cancel whatever commands he's entered into the controls, Tyler," HB said. He pulled another oxygen mask from the emergency kit, knelt next to the boy, and tried to put the mask on his face.

By now, Roy was beginning to turn blue and dizziness was making him panic. His arms were flailing in all directions, making it difficult for HB to keep him still enough to affix the mask to his face.

"You've got to calm down, Roy. I'm trying to help you," HB said, holding Roy's arms still with one hand.

But the boy struggled against the restraint and suddenly jerked his arms free, dislodging HB's mask. The force of the movement knocked HB off-balance and thrust him into a sharp corner of a metal desk that jutted out at the exact height of his head as he fell to the floor.

Roy lingered on the edge of consciousness for a few seconds longer. Then his eyes fluttered open long enough for him to catch sight of an abyss widening below him before his spirit fell through and into its endless depths, leaving nothing but his battered body behind.

A second later, the flashing light of the oxygen monitor stopped flashing and turned green.

Kenneth reached the flight strategy room moments later, only to find HB immobile on the floor. He raced toward him, lifting him into his arms to help him breathe more easily. He told Tyler to call security to deal with Roy's remains and then to reset the flight plan to its original trajectory to ensure safe passage for R.A.T.S to journey home, while he tended to HB.

"The medics will be here any second. Keep yourself still to slow the bleeding," he said, putting pressure on HB's head wound with his hand to stop it from gushing blood.

HB motioned for Kenneth to lean in closer. "Need to tell you something."

"Don't strain yourself, HB. You can tell me later," Kenneth said.

HB shook his head. "No time. Now." With what seemed like every ounce of strength he had left in his body, he pointed to a golden chain dangling out of his pocket. "Take it. You're…like a son to me."

Kenneth pulled the chain out and saw it held a golden key.

"Unlocks mysteries… secrets of the universe." HB's breathing became more labored. "Give to David—"

"But David's—"

"Protect with his life… humanity survives and…" HB exhaled and closed his eyes.

Kenneth felt the general go limp in his arms and wept, crying for HB, for his son, for all Earth's children, for all that had been lost.

As soon as HB passed over, he had a vision. Rachel was standing in front of her floor-to-ceiling windows observing the expansiveness of the sky when she suddenly noticed a peculiar flock of birds. The birds were ascending through the clouds in an upward spiral, encircling each other slowly and carefully. Before she could even question the strangeness of the birds, the gateway to her house intrusively swung open revealing a mystical vision.

Her body and mind were suddenly encapsulated. All she could see in this paradisiac field was an infinite blue sky filled with chandeliers hanging from the Heavens. Straight in front of her appeared a tree so beautiful, so unique, and so vibrant.

Upon closer inspection, Rachel realized that this tree was very different from the trees on Earth. Its shimmering sap resembled liquid gold, and instead of leaves, it had crystals shooting from its branches. The tree gently swayed back and forth, consciously moving its arms. From its roots, four rivers flowed in opposite directions: north, south, east, and west.

This was no ordinary tree… It was the Tree of Life.

Something caught Rachel's eye downriver of the East root. It was David sleeping in a bird's nest hung high in a tree. David was covered in an embellished gold blanket. The gold blanket resembled the tree of life's shimmering sap, and the crystals lining the blanket were made of its leaves. Below David was a lion and a lamb sleeping peacefully under the tree. This was something Rachel had never seen before.

Her heart almost stopped as she thought to herself: "Humanity's future is changing.

Chapter 22

We Are One

As one rocket ship after another touched down in the sands of the Nevada desert, thunderous applause rose from the enormous crowd assembled around Elias I.E. to welcome the returning R.A.T.S back home. Families who could afford to travel to Las Vegas at their own expense had done so. Not wanting to penalize anyone without the wealth to make the journey, the world's governments had pooled their resources to enable even the poorest to send family or friends to greet the heroes of every nation who had made Grutan's defeat possible.

After the victorious warriors had rested, they were scheduled to appear on a special stage erected near the base for the occasion, where President Sarah would be surrounded by holographs of the other world leaders to present the returning heroes with medals of honor. Tutla hoped his father had arranged for the other tribes in the region to arrive in celebratory dress to meet him and his team.

Since David's disappearance, Tutla had taken command of Space Alpha, making sure all the other rockets had safely launched from the moon before he set off for home. Becky had agreed to co-pilot. She said she was as dedicated to their mission as David had been and wanted to honor his memory by helping to bring the team safely back home.

Home. In Tutla's mind, the word conjured images of the beautiful, bright blue-green waters of Havasupai Falls, of fields bursting with tall stalks of corn, squash blossoms, and the tiny tendrils of melon vines, and the thundering sounds of the mighty horses' hooves he'd ridden with his tribe, and would hopefully soon ride again. But as he maneuvered Space Alpha across the last miles of the southwest landscape of the United States before descending to the Earth, instead of those glorious sights and sounds, he was shocked to see how much more damage had been done to the sacred lands in the week of their absence.

"What happened to the rivers and the lakes?" he asked, pointing to the parched Earth below them. "How dry and desperate the land looks!"

Becky followed his gaze. "The Daktaryons must have continued to evacuate the waters while we were gone. Thank goodness, David didn't have to see how much more destruction they caused."

Tutla winced at the mention of David. As sad as he knew Becky was, he too suffered deeply from David's loss. Their close friendship had been a source of comfort, especially in these difficult times when his tribe's existence seemed to be teetering on the edge of extinction. David understood Tutla's anger and helped him cope. Of course, the other R.A.T.S were supportive, too, especially Namkhai. Tutla had always marveled at the young

Buddhist's passion for helping others. They'd all need to find similar wellsprings of care if life on Earth was to rejuvenate.

"Alpha, this is mission control at Elias I.E.," Vitoria said. "You're go for landing, over."

"Roger that, Elias I.E., over and out," Tutla said and directed Becky to begin angling the spacecraft for the descent.

Becky expertly guided Alpha into the altitude for landing and fired the rockets for the descent. The sun shone brilliantly through the ship's portals, illuminating the dust scattered across the desert floor like a million miniature diamonds, a dazzling sight for the eyes of the war-weary members of team Alpha, the last of the R.A.T.S to make it back to Earth.

They landed safely. Tutla emerged from the rocket with Becky and the rest of Alpha's crew and was met by a crescendo of whoops and cries from the Havasupai tribe members who were ringed around the perimeter of the landing zone and mounted on horses. They wore elaborate, plumed headdresses and carried spears decorated with eagle feathers. He saw his father at the head of the group. The chief dismounted and walked toward his son with arms opened wide.

"Welcome home, Tutla. You have proved yourself a true *Supai Kachina.* You have honored the sacred covenant, as have all your companions, by helping to save Mother Earth from the Daktaryons' threat. Now it is up to us to protect all living things from any further harm we might inflict on this planet or on each other."

"Thank you, Father," Tutla said, kneeling down to honor the chief.

"Go and rest now. You must prepare for the ceremony." The chief turned and signaled to the rest of the tribe to disperse.

After they changed from their flight gear into their regular uniforms, Tutla, Becky, and the rest of the R.A.T.S who'd traveled back on Space Alpha headed to a hovercraft waiting to whisk them back to the Bellagio. Above the hotel entrance, contrails from a plane spelled *WELCOME VICTORIOUS R.A.T.S* in the cloudless sky. As they walked into the hotel lobby, hundreds of white and gold balloons tumbled down while a band played popular music.

Becky saw her mother and Sabrina standing off to one side, surrounded by Secret Service officers, and ran toward them.

"Oh, my darling one, I'm so happy you're safely home," Sarah said, pulling her daughter into an embrace.

"I'm happy too, Mom. But not as happy as I'd be if David were here, too," Becky said, collapsing into sobs she'd been holding back for days.

"I know, my love. It was horrible news for all of us to hear about David's loss, as well as the loss of HB, Chava, Deepak, and all the others."

Becky's eyes widened in disbelief. "HB is gone too? What happened to him?"

Sarah pulled back to hold Becky's face between her hands. She wiped her daughter's tears and kissed her forehead. "There was a terrible accident. HB didn't

314

survive. I've spoken with Rachel and Kenneth. There's going to be a special memorial event in Aruba. I've arranged for Air Force One to take us there. In a few days, we'll gather with the family to support them during this difficult time."

Becky rested her head on her mother's shoulder. "Thanks, Mom," she whispered. "Being together with David's family will help."

As the sun began to set over Las Vegas, the battalions of R.A.T.S warriors who had fought so valiantly in space joined the hundreds of R.A.T.S who had stayed behind to staff the controls at Elias I.E., diligently guiding the crews to the moon and back. The teams marched in formation and took their seats at the front of the audience assembled before the grand stage outside the Bellagio for the awards' ceremony, which would be simulcast across the globe for the whole world to see. Behind the R.A.T.S sat their proud families and friends. The full moon glistened in the sky above them.

Daniel had been given the honor of introducing President Sarah. As he walked to the podium, the crowd's murmur stilled to a whisper. "Fellow R.A.T.S, family and friends, thank you for your dedication and your sacrifices. It is my honor to introduce the President of the United States, Sarah Esther Hoffman, who will be joined by other world leaders on this solemn occasion."

Sarah joined Daniel at the podium, shook his hand, and indicated for him and Becky, who had been waiting in the wings, to raise the new flag of world unity. The two youths unfurled a brilliant white silken fabric adorned with the beautiful image of Earth as seen from the moon. Around the planet's image were three words written in bold golden letters—We Are One. Then Becky and Daniel attached the flag to ropes and hoisted it skyward as the crowd watched in awe. For the first time in history, one flag fluttered above the assembled nations' leaders and citizens. Holograms of all the heads of state surrounded Sarah, along with those of the leaders from the world's many religious and spiritual traditions, completing the dramatic display of world solidarity. At the sight of this spectacular celebration of victory, the audience broke out in applause. Once they were quiet, Sarah began.

"Honorable world leaders, R.A.T.S warriors, family and friends, good evening and thank you for attending this ceremony today. The occasion is bittersweet. Although victory has brought us joy, our hearts cannot help but feel the pull of sadness for all who have been lost." Sarah read the names of the departed and the crowd bowed their heads in silent prayer.

"Tonight, we honor our victorious youth warriors with medals. But the greatest honor we can give them is to commit ourselves to defend life on this planet from further damage, much of which we have caused ourselves. I have asked our spiritual leaders to bless our commitment to be Earth's stewards and protectors of all of humanity."

Together, the representatives of all religions spread their arms wide, forming an enormous semi-circle of blessing, and intoned thanks to the Creator of all things and then invited the audience to join in. "The links between us symbolize our commitment to cherish our home and live in peace together," they said in one voice. When the blessing concluded, Sarah began to call each hero to the stage.

One by one, they climbed the steps to receive the special medals Sabrina had designed for the occasion. On each warrior's shoulder, Sarah attached a gold and white ribbon holding a gold medallion etched with a triangle of interlocked arms bearing the word R.A.T.S in the middle. Night had fallen by the time she'd finished distributing the medals. She was about to dismiss the assembly when suddenly Daniel shouted as he pointed to something hovering above them in the evening sky.

"Look at that!" he said.

"Dude," Omar said, jumping to his feet. "It looks like that space capsule we saw rocketing away after Grutan's vehicle exploded."

The object moved closer, and the Secret Service sprang into action, preparing to escort Sarah off stage. A few drew their weapons, ready to fire at the first sign of any threatening movement. Then the recognizable outlines of a much-hated image came into bold relief on the GraphoScreen© and the entire assembly gasped in shock.

"Holy cow," Mariana said. "It looks like Grutan!"

"What's that slippery eel want now?" Butch asked.

Then something happened that stunned even Butch into silence for a second—the creature raised its hand in the R.A.T.S salute.

"Earthlings, I am Grutan the Eleventh, son of Grutan, who was killed in the space battle. I come in peace," he said.

"Never trust a fox in a hen house," Butch muttered.

"Let's hear him out," Namkhai said. "Anyone can change."

Becky leaned over and whispered to Daniel. "Daniel, I think you know what David would have done."

Daniel thought for a second and then stood, bounding quickly to the stage to confront the alien directly. "My brother, too, was killed in that battle," he said. "We both lost family because your father refused to cooperate so that both our species could survive."

"My father was a stubborn man," the younger Grutan said. "Stories our ancestors told made him suspicious of outsiders. But I have studied your history. Your stories, too, have been filled with suspicion and hatred, even among neighbors, although I have learned that your books of wisdom instructed you to behave otherwise."

"That's true," Daniel said. "But the youth of this world want change. We refuse to repeat the mistakes of our past."

"I have seen the destruction our attacks have wrought, and all who have suffered, and I have been humbled by it," Grutan the Eleventh said. As he spoke those words, the tar-like substance that oozed from metal plates covering his entire body began to dry up and flake off. One by one, the plates dropped away and the rough stones ringed around his head softened and smoothed into flesh, revealing a gorgeous youth with crystal clear eyes, who was beaming a bright, hopeful smile to a new world. "I am prepared to discuss the terms of a treaty.

"Wow!" Juliana said to her sister, who was staring at the transformed creature in shock. "He looks as human as any one of us."

"Underneath the surface, we're all pretty much alike," Namkhai said.

"Like my grandfather used to say, all matter is the same atoms arranged in different patterns," Richard said. "I only wish he were still alive so I could tell him I finally got what he meant today."

Sarah consulted with the world leaders to arrange a time for an interplanetary convention to discuss the terms of a treaty. After she conveyed the information to Grutan the Eleventh, the alien had something more to announce.

"Thanks to the wisdom your leader, David, shared with us, we now understand how to desalinate water and have discovered a process that separates the atoms in water into compacted, transportable gases, which is how we were able to carry away your seas. I have ordered the return of your water as a gesture of goodwill in the hopes that together we can learn how to produce enough fresh water for us all to survive."

Waves of applause and cheers filled the night sky and continued for several minutes until the crowd dispersed to their hotel rooms to rest before their flights home.

Around the world, in large cities and towns, in rural areas and remote villages, whole neighborhoods celebrated as flights that had taken their youth into battle brought them back from Elias I.E. In Jerusalem, where

Chava had lived, in New Delhi, Deepak's home, and in Aruba, the mood was more somber as family and friends gathered to pay their respects to the departed.

**

Becky looked out the window of Air Force One as it began its descent to the island and thought about how much had changed since the first time she'd visited and stayed in the guesthouse on David's family's property. Grutan the Eleventh had kept his promise and had returned the sea to its original level, but however happy she was to see the beauty of Aruba being restored, David's loss dulled that happiness tenfold.

It was early evening when a limousine delivered Sarah, Becky, and Sabrina to the gate of David's home. Sonic opened the gate and led them across the courtyard and into the living room, where everyone in the family, except Rachel, had already gathered. Kenneth and Daniel were standing with Ariel, who had returned home from Brazil, next to V near the piano, struck with grief over David's and HB's death. Max, the family's golden retriever, was asleep on a rug underneath the instrument.

Kenneth motioned Sarah and her family toward one of the couches that faced away from the window. "I'll tell Rachel you've arrived," he said and headed across the room to notify his wife that their guests had arrived.

Rachel emerged from her study carrying a large leather-bound volume. Sarah stood up and walked toward her friend to embrace her. Becky did the same and caught sight of the book's title. "*Zohar, Book 11*. What's that?" she asked Rachel.

"The Zohar is a book of great wisdom and mystical power," Rachel said. "I forgot I still had it in my hand." She returned the volume to her study and came back to her guests. "I'm grateful you were able to join us for the memorial. I know how important David was to you, Becky," she said, touching the girl gently on her cheek.

Becky noticed the ring on Rachel's hand. "David had a ring just like that," she said. "I saw it glow once like yours is now."

Rachel's eyes widened. "You did. When?"

Before she could answer, something startled Max and he began barking loudly, running back and forth in front of the sliding glass doors that led to the courtyard.

"Quiet, Max," Kenneth said.

"Look! Where is that light coming from?" V exclaimed, her finger pointing toward the sky. The beam of silvery white light shone down onto the courtyard, illuminating the stone pavers.

Without hesitation, Rachel rushed toward the doors, slid them open, and stepped outside. The others followed closely behind her, drawn to the mysterious light. As they approached the courtyard, the light had expanded, covering the entire area. Suddenly, something began to take shape within the mist.

As the mist cleared, the group was astonished to see a giant spaceship hovering above them. Its doors opened, and a long ladder emerged, attached to a platform where four tall, shimmering figures stood. One of them descended the ladder, holding what appeared to be a limp body in its arms. Rachel tried to run toward them but was held back by Kenneth.

"Let her go, Kenneth," V urged.

With Kenneth's grip released, Rachel rushed toward the figure holding her son's lifeless body. "Please, tell me, what happened?" she cried, tears streaming down her face. "Is this the end?"

As the others watched in awe, Max the dog ran toward the boy and began licking his face. The boy's hand began twitching back to life. The shimmering figures spoke in deep, sonorous voices. "No, Rachel. This is not the end. It is just the beginning."

The group stood in amazement, watching as the spaceship disappeared into the night sky. The impact of this event would change their lives forever, and they knew that their journey had only just begun.

About the Author

Claudia Daher, originally from Brazil, has flourished in Aruba's beauty for thirty-four years. More than just a dedicated wife and mother of three academically accomplished children, she's an entrepreneur, philanthropist, passionate painter, doting grandmother, and a visionary director of the family's businesses. Venturing into the literary realm, Claudia has crafted a compelling science fiction novel targeting youth, delving into topics like artificial intelligence's societal impacts, climate change, alien life, and the melding of global cultures. Her journeys and endeavors beautifully showcase the limitless potential within us all.